Healing Faith

A Horses and Hearts Inspirational Romance

Also By Pamela Gossiaux

Horses and Hearts Inspirational Romance Series

Finding Hope

Healing Faith

Saving Grace

Russo Romantic Mystery Series

Mrs. Chartwell and the Cat Burglar (A Russo Romantic Mystery: Book I)

Trusting the Cat Burglar (A Russo Romantic Mystery: Book 2)

Romancing the Cat Burglar (A Russo Romantic Mystery: Book 3)

A Cat Burglar Christmas (A Russo Romantic Mystery Novella)

Good Enough

Ordinary Girl

Why Is There a Lemon in My Fruit Salad? How to Stay Sweet When Life Turns Sour

A Kid at Heart: Becoming a Child of Our Heavenly Father

Praise for Pamela Gossiaux's Books

Finding Hope

"*Finding Hope* is a charming wonderfully told story of Hope, Love, Forgiveness, Romance and God. Anyone who has ever owned and loved a horse will relate deeply with Victoria Jones and her horse."
— William D. Curnutt,
Amazon Vine Voice, 5-stars

"Wow! This one is a keeper!"
— J. Barr,
Amazon Top 500 Reviewer, 5-stars

Mrs. Chartwell and the Cat Burglar

"A highly suspenseful, self-described romantic mystery that tugs at your heart and satis ies your intellect."
— John J. Kelly, *Detroit Free Press*, **5-stars**

"I highly recommend it! It has everything you could wish for: mystery, suspense, romance and a great adventure. I just couldn't put it down!"
— Susan Keefe, **Midwest Book Review, 5-stars**

Good Enough

"Richly meaningful while wildly entertaining, *GOOD ENOUGH* is a major new book by an exceptionally talented author"
— **San Francisco Review of Books, 5-stars**

"*GOOD ENOUGH* touches a nerve every woman faces. Are we ever going to be good enough? Gossiaux has written a funny, revenge romance that will have you cheering on the heroine, Amy, until the very end."
— **Diana Lesire Brandmeyer,**
author of CBA Best Seller *Mind of Her Own*

Ordinary Girl

"A truly gripping and heart-wrenching story!"
— **Anita Hoepner, Founder and Director of**
Sparrow Freedom Project, 5-stars

"A novel of tremendous impact."
— **Dr. Grady Harp, Amazon Top 50**
Hall of Fame Reviewer, 5-stars

"A chilling insight into one of our society's most pernicious problems."
— **Mike Ball, Executive Director of Lost Voices,**
5-stars

Healing Faith

A Horses and Hearts Inspirational Romance

INTERNATIONAL BESTSELLING AUTHOR

PAMELA GOSSIAUX

Tri-Cat Publishing

Scripture quotations are taken from The Holy Bible, New International Version, copyright 1973, 1978, 1984 by International Bible Society.

Visit the author's website at: PamelaGossiaux.com

First Printing, June 2020
Library of Congress Control Number: 2020910461

ISBN: 978-1-7348968-9-3 (paperback)
ISBN: 978-1-7348968-2-4 (eBook)

Cover Design: llewellen Designs
Formatter: Dallas Hodge, dalhodge56@gmail.com
Editor: Rachel Song, Songbird Editing
Author Photo: Vera Davis Photography

Published in the United States by Tri-Cat Publishing.
Chelsea, MI

Tri-Cat Publishing

To Kathy, and all the horses and volunteers at Michigan Abilities Center who continue to heal hearts, bodies, and minds.

"Now faith is confidence in what we hope for and assurance about what we do not see."
– Hebrews 11:1

"There is something about the outside of a horse that is good for the inside of a man."
– Sir Winston Churchill

Chapter One

Rachel Walker pulled her car into the long, winding drive of Three Hearts Ranch and headed back toward the barn and indoor riding arena. There were several cars in the dusty lot near the barn, which she knew belonged to the farm's volunteers and clients. She turned in and shut her car off. Sighing, she tried to shake off the workday fatigue. Three Hearts was her safe place. The place she came to feel whole.

Her phone vibrated, and she looked at it. It was an incoming call from her mom.

"Not *now!*" she said.

She hesitated for a moment, her finger hovering over the button. What if was something important? But it was probably just her mother calling again to tell her how disappointed she was.

Rachel sent the call to voicemail. Then she turned her phone off all together. She didn't want any disturbances while she was here.

Rachel had started volunteering at Three Hearts Ranch two years ago, a few months after her divorce. She'd needed something to do, some reason to go on with her days, and her therapist had suggested this.

Three Hearts was an equine-assisted therapy facility. Rachel had always loved horses, and here, she could use her career skills as a child psychologist to work with the kids who came for help. When she left, she felt renewed. It was incredible to see the emotional bond that was nearly always formed between rider and horse, and how the riding itself helped them heal both physically and emotionally.

She locked her car and headed for the barn, her honey-colored hair bouncing in its ponytail as she walked. She had come from work, changing into her barn clothes in the restroom before she left, and was ready to unwind after a difficult day at the clinic.

"Rachel!" It was Kim, the farm's owner. "I'm so glad you're early. I want to talk with you for a moment."

"Sure." Rachel walked over to meet her. Kim was dressed in dirty jeans and had the sleeves of her white t-shirt rolled up to reveal her farmer's tan. She was a medium-built woman, about five-foot-six, with short-cropped brown hair that had streaks of gray running through it. "I need you someplace else today. We have enough volunteers with the kids, but we have a new adult coming in that I think you'd be perfect for. I'm short on therapists. Don couldn't make it in today."

Rachel preferred to work with the children, not the adults. Kim knew this.

"Since he's new, just concentrate on getting him near a horse. Should be simple." She nodded for Rachel to follow her into the barn. "I don't think he knows anything about horses."

Rachel gave an inward sigh. Kim never *asked*. She *told*. Kim had a way of coming up with ideas and making others think they were theirs. Rachel *had* worked with adults on a few other occasions before. She preferred the kids, but she supposed it was okay to change it up for just this one day. Only, she'd miss working with Dixie, her favorite client. The ten-year old was a charmer.

As if reading her mind, Kim said, "Dixie's not coming in today. Stomach bug. So you won't miss her session."

"Um…" Rachel trotted to keep up with Kim. Kim had seen enough pain in her life to put them all to shame. Rachel had no right to complain about a session change. "Okay. What do I need to know?"

"He's a war veteran. Afghanistan. His therapist sent him here to work on anxiety. PTSD. He came by yesterday and filled out the paperwork, so he's all set on that. Just get his hands on a horse. Brushing. Rubbing. You know the drill. Teach him to tack up the horse. Maybe get him on."

Rachel nodded. "What's his name?

"Christopher." Kim stopped to put a bucket of water in the stall of Rissa, one of their therapy horses. She glanced at her watch. "He'll be here in about ten minutes." She looked at Rachel and smiled. Kim's smile could sell cars. "Thank you. You're a dear."

Before Rachel could answer her, Kim left, hurrying on to do other chores. Rachel walked over to look at the chalkboard that hung on the wall in the aisleway near the feed room. Dixie's name had a line drawn through it. Jennifer, the physical therapist, would now be using the indoor arena with two other kids during

3

that time. In the 5 p.m. session slot for the outdoor arena, the name "Chris" was written with her name beside it. He had a one-hour slot. Angel would be their horse for today.

Rachel had seen equine-assisted therapy do amazing things. They used it regularly with teens and younger kids to combat anxiety issues. She had heard it used for veterans with PTSD before, and figured it would be a good shot for Christopher, if that's what he was here for. It was a great strengthening tool for physical therapy, good for people with closed-head injuries, and even worked miracles for kids with autism. Over the two years Rachel had volunteered at Three Hearts, she was starting to believe that equine-assisted therapy could help with *most* things.

It was doing more than she did in the clinic, anyway. Watching those kids deal with such traumatic things in their lives was tough...divorce, death of parents, bullying, drugs, abuse...

She stopped her train of thought there, before it went to the teen she had let down. But it was too late. The girl's face formed in her memory. Small, thin, dark hair with curls, dark circles under her eyes. So small and curled in upon herself, like she was trying to disappear. And she had been.

If only Rachel had seen it.

Rachel was past the point where the lump formed in her throat. Now, on her good days, she could push the girl's face away, bury it deep down, and get on with her life. Maybe, if she helped just one more kid, it would make up for how she had failed that girl.

A loud whinny pulled her out of her thoughts. It was Max, the red chestnut gelding next to Angel's stall. Rachel stopped to rub his face, then walked past to Angel's stall. Usually someone would have brought her in by now to get her ready, but the stall was empty. She sighed, trying not to let this new frustration fuel the anxiety she already had from work and her mom's call. She grabbed Angel's lead rope and went outside to the pasture in the back where her horse would be. Looking out over the grassy field, she saw Angel in the far back.

"Angel!" she called. The bay mare looked up, a bite of grass hanging from her mouth. "Come here, girl!"

The horse looked at her, then put her head back down and continued to graze.

Rachel knew Christopher would be here soon. She didn't really have the time to walk out after her.

"Angel!" she called again. But this time, she dug her fingers into the front pocket of her blue jeans and pulled out a plastic baggie containing a handful of baby carrots. Angel watched her intently, then, as if they had all the time in the world, slowly started walking toward her. But so did Tommy, Bell, and Tudor.

Rachel counted her carrots. Five carrots. Four horses. Enough.

She fed the horses their treats, then rubbed Angel's neck and put her halter on. "It's your turn to work today, girl," she said. She led the mare through the gate and brought her into the barn, where she put her in cross ties.

"Hello."

She jumped at the voice and turned around, figuring it was Christopher here for his session. What she *didn't* expect to see was Chris *Adler.* The thick sand-colored hair, the same green eyes she had been attracted to in high school.

Her stomach did something funny as her mind raced back to the one night that had changed her life. The night she had lost everything.

She stood there a moment, her mouth open. Then she abruptly shut it. She hated him. Could this day get any worse?

"Chris," she said curtly.

"Rachel." His tone was softer than hers had been.

He looked different. Last time she saw him, he was leaning against the wall outside their high school after graduation, tipping back a cold one. He had said something to her then, something she'd never forget.

The two of them stared at each other for a moment and neither spoke. Then he cleared his throat. "I didn't know you worked here."

"I *volunteer* here," she corrected. She crossed her arms over her chest and frowned.

"Oh."

The cockiness she remembered was gone. In its place was a bit of uncertainty. His eyes couldn't seem to find a place to rest. They skittered between her, the horse, the brushes, and back to her. He seemed fragile somehow. Not like the over-confident guy she remembered.

"Why are *you* here?" she asked.

He met her eyes. He was still as handsome as she remembered. Tall, nearly six-foot. His sandy brown hair had a lock that fell over his green eyes. But he was better built than when he was younger. More solid. Manlier. Arm muscles strained at the sleeves of the dark blue t-shirt he was wearing. She imagined there was a six-pack under there somewhere. He obviously *lived* in the gym. She tore her eyes away from his torso and back to his face.

"I'm here for…" he jerked a thumb toward the horse. "Some lady named Kim told me to come back here. That there was a woman who would give me a…therapy session."

He shrugged, like he didn't believe that he was here. He seemed uncomfortable. Even a little embarrassed.

"Give me a minute," Rachel said. She left him standing there alone with the horse, which was against barn rules, and went to find Kim. The barn was built with the indoor arena in the middle, and two aisles on either side where the horses were kept. Kim was in the aisle on the other side of the barn. Rachel navigated around the arena to avoid interrupting the session going on. She found Kim breaking apart a hay bale for feeding.

"Kim," Rachel said. She kept her voice to a whisper. "I can't work with him."

"Who?"

"Chris. Christopher. That man you assigned me to."

"Why not?"

Rachel stalled. "Because…" She didn't want to go into the long story of their history. Of what he was like in high school. Of how he had ruined her life.

"I knew him once. Before. I don't like him."

Kim stopped working and put her gloved hands on her hips. She studied Rachel for a minute, the fine wrinkles around her eyes crinkling in thought.

"Hmm," she said after a while. "When is the last time you saw him?"

Rachel had to think. She was thirty now. She had been...eighteen.

"Twelve years ago," she said, a bit sheepishly.

Kim snorted. "People change. He needs help, and I don't have anyone else who can work with him. I thought you'd be perfect with your background in psychology. Besides, his insurance is paying for this, and we could use the money because of the vet bills last month."

"But..."

Kim held up a finger and Rachel hushed. This woman had a way with that.

"Just for today," Kim said. "Put on your professional face, and get him through the hour."

Rachel started to protest again but then thought better of it. She had met with plenty of parents she disliked in her line of work, especially after she saw what a mess some of them had made of their kids. She was professional with *them*. She could get through this too. The last thing she wanted was for Christopher Adler to think that she couldn't handle him.

"Okay," she said.

"Good. Now go. Time is money."

Kim was direct, even a bit bossy, but had the kindest heart of anyone Rachel knew. Rachel nodded and went back across the indoor arena to where Angel was tied. Chris hadn't moved toward the horse. Instead, he had taken a few steps away and was leaning against the wall, his hands in the front pockets of his jeans. He was talking quietly to the horse. He didn't see Rachel, and she hung back, just out of sight.

"I don't know how you're going to be of help," he said to Angel. His voice was kind. "I've had six doctors, art therapy, and an odd assortment of pills that were all supposed to fix me. Now they've sent me to *you?* I guess they've gotten desperate." The mare was watching him lazily, her ears pricked toward his voice.

The Chris that Rachel used to know would never have talked to an animal. He was "above" that. He had always been so full of himself.

She cleared her throat, and Chris jumped and stood up, pulling his hands out of his pockets.

"So, let's get started," Rachel said, not meeting his eyes. She picked up a brush. "Your first job is to brush the horse."

"You want me to *brush* the horse?" Chris said.

So. Still the cocky guy she remembered after all.

"It's not *work*, it's *therapy*," she said in the patient therapist voice she saved for the unruliest kids.

"I didn't mean it *that* way… I guess I thought you'd get the horse ready, and I'd ride or something."

Ignoring his words, she took the soft brush and started at the horse's shoulder, brushing down with the grain of the hair. Angel stood quietly, enjoying it. Rachel brushed one stroke, then followed it down with her other hand. Brush, rub. Brush, rub. "It's a rhythm. Plus the contact with the horse is soothing." She looked over her shoulder at him and offered the brush.

He stuffed his hands back in his pockets. "Do you even know why I'm here?"

He was clearly as uncomfortable with her as she was with him.

"Yes. Kim said for anxiety. We treat that all the time."

Chris snorted. "I saw that you guys do a lot of work with kids here. This is a little bit more than a teen with test anxiety."

Rachel rounded on him. *The nerve!* "You think that's what these kids are here for? *Test anxiety?*" It was a sore spot with her, adults downplaying what some of these kids were feeling and going through. She realized her voice was too harsh the minute she heard it.

Chris flinched from her anger and immediately backpedaled. "No. I'm sorry. Look, I know you don't like me. I don't blame you. But I'm different now."

It was Rachel's turn to snort. "A zebra doesn't change his stripes."

"Well, this one has." Chris reached for the brush. "Let me try."

Rachel handed him the brush, and he stepped closer to Angel's shoulder.

"What do I do? Just brush?"

Rachel pushed her feelings below the surface. She was good at that. She'd pretend he was just one of her teens, and she would work with him with that mindset. She reached out and took his hand. She placed it palm open on Angel's shoulder.

"Feel her," she said quietly.

Chris laughed a little. "*Feel* her? What do you mean? Like…she's soft…dusty…"

"No. Like this." Rachel pushed down on his hand with her own palm, pressing his against the horse. "Close your eyes."

"This is weird."

"Do you want to get better or not?" She heard the impatience in her voice.

He sighed, but closed his eyes. They stood there, his hand on the horse's shoulder, her hand over his. She realized then how strong and warm his hand was and how good he smelled. He wore a different aftershave than he had in high school. Fruitier. She felt her stomach flutter slightly, but she pushed that feeling down too. She couldn't let his sexiness distract her. Not again.

"Do you feel her?" she asked.

She closed her eyes too. Through his hand, she could feel the beating of the horse's heart. The pulse of life. Warmth. Strength.

She took Chris' hand and rubbed down with the horse's hair, gently. Then she lifted it up again and rubbed it back down Angel's shoulder.

"Now, do that, and on every other stroke, use the brush."

Chris did as he was told. One. Two. Three strokes, then he quit. "This is stupid. How is a stupid horse going to help me heal? I'm supposed to pet her and feel better?"

Rachel bit her tongue and held back an angry retort.

"No," she said quietly. "It's about *focus*. Focus on what you're doing. On where you are *now*. On the warmth and strength of the animal. You have anxiety, so clearly you are a control freak." *Wrong words, Rachel.*

11

You're going to make him defensive. You'd never talk to one of your teens like that. "I'm sorry. What I meant to say—"

"No. You're right," Chris said. "I'm a control freak."

She turned to look up at him. His green eyes met hers. He gave her a sideways smile, the smile that had won so many hearts in high school. The smile that had won hers.

"Well, we've made progress," she said. "We have agreed on *something*." She returned his smile, but it didn't reach her eyes. "Horses are big animals. Too big for us to physically control. But Angel here will listen to your commands. She'll *let* you control her, because you will build a bond of trust with her. And that bond starts with brushing."

Chris didn't say anything. He just nodded. Then he put the brush back on the horse and started again.

"Keep with the grain of her hair," she said. "You can brush her entire body. She likes it."

Rachel watched him brush for about five minutes. His hands shook a little, and he seemed nervous. It occurred to the psychologist part of her brain that he was calling this "stupid" because he was scared. Rachel might hate him, but she should at least treat him with the same respect she would any other client. She was supposed to be *helping* him, after all. She would try harder.

When he came to the withers at the base of Angel's mane, the mare curled her lip up in pleasure. Rachel laughed. "See? You're making a friend!"

"Is this all we do?"

"Nope. I think we'll tack her up so you can ride her."

Rachel went to get the saddle, looking at her watch. Only thirty-five more minutes to go, and then she'd be free of Chris Adler forever. She could do it.

Chapter Two

Chris had been through a lot of therapies for anxiety, and the last thing he needed was to have *Rachel Walker* of all people trying to fix him. That girl—he supposed she was a *woman* now—hated him like nobody's business. And who could blame her? After what he had done to her in high school, he had hated himself too.

That was one of the reasons why he had joined the army. He ran from his responsibilities, and then he ran some more. When there was no place else to go, he signed up with Uncle Sam. But even the Middle East wasn't far enough away. No place is when it's yourself you're running from.

Rachel took his hand, and her touch pulled him away from his thoughts. He tried to ignore the electricity that ran through him from the contact. It surprised him how his body reacted after all these years. Then Rachel put his hand palm down against the horse and placed her hand over his. Was this the skinny girl he had invited to the party that night? The one he had wooed into coming with them because she had the connection he needed to score some booze? But that wasn't the only reason he had invited her.

He buried the memory before it could go any further. He cleared his throat, closed his eyes like she wanted him to, and tried to "feel" the horse.

After a moment, he *did* think he felt the horse. Maybe it was all in his head, or maybe it was just the warmth of the animal, but standing there in the quiet barn, with a warm, breathing horse under his palm, *did* feel a bit comforting.

After a few moments of standing there quietly, they brushed the horse some more, and then he watched as Rachel put the riding equipment on the mare.

"It's called a saddle and bridle," she said, when he asked. Then he felt stupid because everybody knew what a saddle was called.

The embarrassment made him nervous, and he started silently repeating the mantra his therapist had taught him: *I'm okay. I'm okay. I'm okay.* Which was a bunch of crap because he *wasn't* okay. *Please God,* he prayed. *Give me the peace that passes all understanding.*

He took a couple of deep breaths, which he hoped were too subtle to be noticed, and felt himself relaxing. A little.

He'd try not to be concerned right now about what Rachel thought of him. He was here to heal, and, judging by her attitude, this would be the only session he had with her. He would get another therapist next time. He could get through this *one* day with her. He could tell by her tense shoulders and lack of eye contact that she was only doing this because she was a professional. She'd undoubtedly had tougher clients than him. Only, not ones with such personal baggage.

"Let's take Angel outside to the arena," said Rachel. She handed him the reins and showed him which side of the horse to stand on while he led her. The mare responded well, following him at a slow amble, chomping contentedly on the metal bit that Rachel had put in her mouth. The outdoor arena was a round pen made of wooden fencing that stood in front of the barn, off to the side of the driveway. Rachel closed the gate and latched it. "This is a therapy saddle," Rachel said. "You'll notice there isn't a saddle horn like you've probably seen in Western TV shows. It's also not an English saddle, like the jumpers wear. This saddle is thinner, and made of a softer material than leather so you can feel the horse better. Go ahead and climb on. You should mount from the left side."

He didn't want her to know how inexperienced he was, so he tried and was pretty pleased with himself when he made it into the saddle without any trouble. The mare wasn't overly tall, but he had never mounted a horse before.

"Good job," she said, and clipped a cotton rope onto the horse's bridle.

"Wait. You're going to *lead me around?*" he said. "Like I'm a little kid?"

She looked up at him. He had forgotten how blue her eyes were.

"Yes." She didn't say it curtly, but she wasn't being overly compassionate, either. "Just let the reins lay on her neck for now. I'll teach you how to use them later."

He wasn't too sure about dropping the reins. Common sense told him these were the things he

16

needed to control the horse, and right now, being in control was a big necessity for him.

"It's okay. I've got her." Rachel said. She adjusted the buckles on his stirrups until they were the right length.

Again, he didn't want her to think he was afraid, so he reluctantly dropped the reins.

She began to lead the horse clockwise around the ring. He tried to settle into the rocking motion of the animal. He wasn't too sure what he was doing here.

"What's this supposed to do?" he asked.

"Just relax and close your eyes," was all she said.

Shouldn't she explain how horse therapy worked? Or 'hippo-therapy' as it was called in professional circles. That's the term his doctor had first used, and he thought he was going to go to the zoo to play with hippos. Which would be better than *this*. He didn't have anything against the horse, but he could feel Rachel's anger seeping out of her. He watched her rigid back as she walked beside the horse's head. Was she really still mad at him after all these years?

Apparently so. And it bothered him. He wanted to tell her he wasn't the same man. He needed for her to forgive him.

"I….uh…" he started.

But he wasn't sure how to say it. *I'm not the same guy that I was in high school,* sounded stupid.

Rachel ignored his attempt at conversation.

He took another deep breath. *I'm okay.*

"Are your eyes closed?" she asked, not turning to look at him.

He closed his eyes. "Yes."

"Good."

She didn't say anything more. He sat there with his eyes closed, the warm evening sun shining down on him. It was one of those perfect days where the weather was just right. A little too hot at midday, but now, at 6 p.m., the sun had warmed the air to a perfect temperature. He could hear some voices far off inside the barn and an occasional snort from a horse. But here, in the arena, it was quiet. He concentrated on the noises around him, and heard the wind rustling the leaves of a few trees. He thought about opening his eyes to see what kind of trees they were, but the sway of the horse's body was hypnotic.

He let his body relax and move with the horse. The sway was gentle, almost like a massage, as her muscles rippled under him. He could feel them through the saddle, feel the warmth of her sides against his calves.

"Lay your hands on her neck," Rachel said softly.

His hands were on his thighs, and, without opening his eyes, he slid them forward until they were on the base of Angel's neck. He felt the warmth of the mare under them, felt her muscles rolling under his palms, giving and contracting as she walked.

Her gait was four-beat. *One. Two. Three. Four. One. Two. Three. Four.* He counted each footfall in his head. *One. Two. Three. Four.* He listened, swaying with her rhythm and counting as they slowly circled the arena. Him, the horse, the rhythm beneath him.

He was so intent on following the rhythm of the mare that he almost forgot Rachel was there. Until she stopped the horse.

Reluctantly, he opened his eyes.

He expected her to ask him a few questions, like how did it feel? Did he like it? Did he want to keep riding? (He was surprised that he *did*.) But she wasn't even looking at him. She was looking down the driveway where a truck was kicking up some dust. It was coming toward them, pulling a trailer behind it.

"Looks like somebody's bringing in a horse," Rachel said, almost to herself.

"Is the owner getting a new one?" Chris asked. The truck slowed as it neared the arena, then followed the curve in the driveway to the right and around to the front of the barn, where it stopped.

"I don't know. She didn't say."

They watched as the driver got out, a tall, thick man with a cowboy hat. A thin, willowy woman jumped down from the passenger side and walked around to the front of the truck, where Kim met them.

"I wonder what's up," Rachel said.

Chris wondered if his session was over. He was about to ask, when Rachel looked at her watch. "We've been at this about forty-five minutes. I think that's good for today," she said. She came around to the left side of the horse. "You can get off now."

Chris wasn't sure what he expected, but he felt like he was being dismissed. Usually in a therapy session, there was some sort of wrap up, with goals to be worked on in between sessions. Maybe she'd tell him after they put the horse away. And wasn't he supposed to get a full hour?

"Swing your leg around behind you," she said, and explained how to dismount. He did, a bit clumsily, but not too bad.

"Okay," she said, briefly meeting his eyes. "You did a great job. I probably won't be your therapist next time. I think Angel likes you though, so I'll request her for your next session, unless you want another horse."

"No, Angel is great," Chris said.

"Okay then," Rachel said, busying herself with the horse's reins. "I wish you well."

He didn't really want to leave it like that. There were so many things he wanted to say to her, so many ways he had replayed that night in his head.

"Rachel," he said.

But then they heard a loud clang, followed by some scrambling. They looked in the direction of the horse trailer. The cowboy had let the back down. A dirty, light-brown horse was struggling to get down the ramp, while the woman who had been in the truck held a rope that was attached to the halter on the horse's head.

The horse took a step, but her front knees buckled and she fell. Scrambling on the metal, she righted herself quickly, took another step, swayed, and fell again. She half slid, half stumbled her way down the ramp until she was standing in the driveway, legs splayed, eyes wide with fear.

"Oh my gosh," Rachel whispered.

The horse looked like she hadn't eaten in months. She was so thin Chris could count her ribs. Her legs were black with caked mud up past her knees, and her mane and tail were in knots. But the worst part was her hooves. They were so long they had curled up. Chris didn't know anything about horses, but he knew that was wrong. She tried again to walk, and it seemed to hurt her. A lot.

Chris felt a knot form in his throat.

Rachel quickly took the tack off of Angel and hung it over the side of the fence. "Come on," she said, opening the gate for Chris to follow her through. She closed it behind her, leaving Angel in the arena.

Chris followed Rachel to where the three people were standing by the shaking horse. They approached, walking very slowly, but the horse looked at them warily.

"Kim?" Rachel said. "What on earth…?"

"The Humane Society asked if I would take her," she said. "They rescued several horses earlier today. They found this mare in a stall standing on about three feet of manure, nearly starved to death. She had a bit of dirty water in her bucket, but no food in sight."

"How long was she…like that?" Rachel said.

Chris saw that Rachel had gone pale, and he heard a tremor in her voice.

"A neighbor called because of the stink coming from the farm. Said the owner never seemed to go to the barn. The horses haven't been cared for in a long time judging by the condition of their hooves. There were six of them. We took in one. She's the worst off."

Chris had seen cruelty in the Middle East. Kids, animals…starving. Mistreated. He felt the sting of tears in his eyes. He angrily brushed them with the back of his hand.

"What can we do?" Rachel asked.

"I've got a stall set up for her, and the vet is on her way," Kim said. "We'll save her."

"If she can be saved," said the cowboy. "She's so weak that she can barely stand."

21

The horse tried to take a step, and her front knees buckled again. She almost went down. Chris had to turn and walk away. He stood over by the bushes, his back to the group for a moment, and took a few deep breaths, willing the tears away. His overall stressed-out self made him emotional. He hated it.

He heard them talking, something about vets and feed. But he tuned them out and concentrated on breathing.

I'm okay. I'm okay. I'm okay.

He felt his heart rate slowing a little. He couldn't have a full-blown panic attack. Not here. Not in front of Rachel.

After he pulled himself together, he walked back to the others.

"Sorry. The dust got in my eyes." He hoped they believed the lie.

Rachel glanced at him, but her hands were on the horse's halter. "You can go now, Chris," Rachel said. "We'll call you to set up your next appointment."

They were trying to persuade the horse to walk toward the barn, but she was fighting them. Sweat rolled down her sides, and she was shaking. She looked kind of like someone having an anxiety attack.

Then, she stopped, fell on her side, and couldn't get up. After a few struggles, she lay there, gasping in lungs-full of air, shivering.

"We need to get her inside," said Kim, looking up at the sky, which was turning darker. "We're supposed to get a storm around midnight."

"I have a tarp in the truck," the cowboy said. "If we can get it under her, maybe we can slide her in."

"That could hurt her," Rachel said.

"We'll have to be careful. Make sure the tarp moves, and not the horse," said the woman. "That's going to take some muscle."

"Our muscle is gone for the day," said Rachel. "Kim and I are the last two here. Our other therapist left a few minutes ago. I saw her car."

"I can help," Chris said.

He had no idea what he was signing up for, but it was clear they needed help to save this horse.

Kim stood there, hands on hips, watching the mare for a moment, then nodded. "Go get the tarp," she said to the cowboy. "Let's get this horse inside."

Chapter Three

Rachel watched as the two men, along with the woman who had also come in the truck, lifted first the front, then the back of the horse so she and Kim could slide the tarp under her. Chris got right in there, despite his lack of experience with horses, and didn't seem to mind getting dirty and bloody as he helped to lift and scoot the mare onto the tarp. The mare had given up on fighting and lay still, defeated and breathing heavily. After she was safely on the tarp, they slid it along the twenty feet that was left of the driveway, and into the barn, where, with some difficulty, they got the entire horse in the big box stall that Kim had prepared for her.

Under the dirt and grime, she looked like a palomino. Her coat was light gold in color, and her mane and tail looked like they might be cream colored under the filth. It was impossible to tell if she had any markings on her legs because the muck covered them up past her knees. Her face was caked in so much crusted dirt that Rachel couldn't see if there was a star or a blaze.

The whole ordeal was a dirty, messy, and somewhat terrifying job.

She wasn't sure what to think of Chris jumping in and volunteering like that. It wasn't something the Chris in high school would have done. He always ran from challenges. And it was clear that the condition of the mare bothered him, judging by the way he had teared up. She knew that wasn't from dirt getting in his eyes.

Rachel felt kind of light-headed looking at the horse. She never got used to this. Kim had taken in a few abused animals over the years: two horses and Granny the goat, who was now their barn mascot. But never, in all her years around horses, had Rachel seen an animal this neglected.

And she couldn't get Kim's words out of her head, how the mare had been found in her stall, standing in nearly three feet of manure, starving.

Rachel couldn't imagine what this horse had been through.

Kim left the barn and went outside with the cowboy and the woman. Rachel was alone with Chris.

The horse was laying on her side, breathing heavily. The two of them stood side by side, watching her over the stall door.

"She's so weak," Rachel said quietly.

"Yeah."

She glanced at him, standing there to her left. He was watching the horse intently. There was some dirt from handling the mare—and probably manure— streaked up his arms, and some straw had gotten in his hair. She thought about brushing the straw from his hair. She remembered how it felt, back when he was young. She had run her hands through it a few times.

"Okay, I'm back," Kim said, coming to stand beside the two. "The vet is on her way. She should be here in a few minutes."

"You got this horse from the Humane Society?" Rachel asked.

"Yes. They called earlier today. She was part of a horse rescue up north of here. I told them I'd take this mare because she was one of the few who didn't seem to have a respiratory infection. I can't risk making the others in our barn sick. And she was one that was going to need twenty-four-hours watch for a few days. Not many other people are willing to foster a horse that requires that much work."

"Is she going to make it?" Chris asked. His voice was low, uncertain.

"She will," Kim said with more confidence than Rachel felt. But that was Kim. Always positive.

And Kim *had* to be, given the farm's current financial situation. Things were not going well at the moment. Insurance companies were fighting payment for several of their clients, calling hippotherapy "recreational" instead of medical. Kim was owed $3500 from the insurance companies and needed it for horse feed and vet bills. She could charge the clients out of pocket, or let them go, but Kim would never do that. She would help who she could, when she could. Until she couldn't.

"What's her name?" Rachel asked.

Kim shook her head. "I don't know. But whatever it is, or *was*, she needs a new one."

They watched the horse for a few minutes, none of them speaking. The mare's eyes closed and they saw her sigh. She had either given up, or was relaxing. Probably the first.

"Faith," Kim said, breaking the silence.

"What?" Rachel said, startled.

"Faith. I'm going to name her Faith," Kim said. "Faith can move mountains. Faith can heal. And what we need right now is faith."

"Faith?" Rachel heard her voice crack. Faith was the name of the teen she had worked with three years ago. The teen who had broken her heart. The teen she had failed.

"No," she said before she could stop herself. Hearing that name every day would be too much for her. A name she had pushed to the back of her mind. A name of someone she had cared about deeply, but couldn't save.

A name that had *changed* her.

"Not sure about your faith?" Kim said, raising an eyebrow in question. Things were never black and white with Kim. She always looked deeper.

"No. Not sure about the *name.*" There was no way Kim could know about Faith. Rachel had never told her. "I mean…it's okay. It's fine."

Rachel felt her cheeks coloring a bit.

She could feel Kim looking at her, waiting for more. But Rachel kept her eyes fixed on the horse.

"I like it," Chris said. "I think it fits her."

Rachel felt a flash of anger. Who was *he* to have an opinion? This wasn't his farm or his horse. But when she glanced at him, he seemed sincere, not like he was trying to pick a fight with her.

Rachel shrugged.

"Okay," said Kim. "Faith it is."

The vet came and treated the mare. She gave her a pain killer that made Faith sleepy, stitched up a few of the cuts she had gotten, probably in transit, and applied salve and a few bandages. She also gave her a vitamin shot and some fluids through an IV. She told them that someone should stay with the horse that night.

After she left, Kim pulled out her phone and opened the calendar. "I was planning to go into town tonight to stay with my parents," Kim said. "Dad has cataract surgery in the morning, and I need to drive them to the hospital at 6 a.m."

"I can stay," Rachel said.

Her fist client at the clinic wasn't until 11 a.m. tomorrow morning. They decided that Kim would drop off her dad (surgery was at 7 a.m.). She'd have her parents back home by 10:30 and be back to the farm shortly after Rachel left for the clinic.

"Do you want to go home first to get a few things?" Kim asked.

"No," Rachel said, waving her off. "Go. They need you. I'll be fine."

"There's soup in the kitchen. Bottled water. You know the ropes. Use that cot in the observation room."

"Thanks."

Kim turned to Chris and laid a hand on his shoulder. "I appreciate you staying. We couldn't have done it without you."

He nodded.

Kim left and went up to the house to wash up, which left Rachel and Chris alone.

"Thanks for your help tonight," Rachel said. "You probably need to get going." She nodded toward his arms. "And wash up."

"Yeah," he said, giving a little laugh. "I'm pretty gross."

"There's a sink in the observation room if you don't want to drive your car like that."

She led Chris to the observation room, a place where parents sat during sessions to watch their kids ride. It had a long window that overlooked the indoor arena, and it was heated in the winter and air conditioned in the summer. It also served as a break room for the volunteers. There was a microwave and a stash of canned soups, protein bars, and drinks. Bottled tea, energy drinks, and bottled water filled the small fridge.

Chris soaped up to his elbows and rinsed thoroughly in the big sink in the observation room. After he was done, Rachel came over and did the same. Then she went to look at the microwavable containers of soup. Chicken noodle. Clam chowder. Minestrone.

She chose the chicken noodle, pulled the top open, and put the soup in the microwave.

"Well, I guess I'll be going then," Chis said.

He was lingering for some reason. Rachel just wanted him to *leave* so she could get back to the horse and eat her soup in peace.

"Yep," she said, not meeting his eyes.

"I guess I'll see you next week."

"Doubtful," Rachel said, busying herself with finding a drink. "You'll have another therapist." There was no way she was working with him.

"Oh."

Why wouldn't he leave? She picked the purple electrolyte drink out of the fridge. She wanted tea, but the caffeine would keep her up if she drank it this late in the evening. She was hoping to get *some* sleep.

She turned to check her soup, and he was still standing there. She nearly bumped into him.

"I wanted to apologize," he said. His green eyes looked at her pleadingly. His lock of hair hung over his left eye, just like it had in high school. He had his hands thrust in the front pockets of his jeans. He looked uncomfortable.

She stopped, taken aback. "For what?"

He dropped his eyes to the floor. "For high school. For what happened."

"Well, apologies don't fix it, now, do they?" Rachel snapped. Her sudden anger surprised her. He raised his eyes up to meet hers, and she saw the hurt she had caused. Part of her liked it.

"No, apologies won't fix it. But I need for you to know that I'm different now. I found Jesus and—"

"I don't care if you found the Pope himself. None of it matters," Rachel said. She crossed her arms. She could feel the heat rising in her face. She struggled to keep her voice low and even. "Anyway, it's in the past. We're all adults now and have moved on with our lives."

"I was a jerk."

"Yes."

"I lied and I—"

"Chris, why are you doing this *now?*" The microwave beeped. Her soup was done. She stepped around him to stir it.

He didn't say anything more. She stuck a finger in her soup. It was still not quite warm enough, so she set the microwave for another minute.

Then she turned to look at him.

"I don't really have time for this," she said, letting the annoyance creep into her voice. "I have a sick horse to tend to, and I'm starved. *Go home.* I appreciate your help tonight. You were great and all, but this isn't your farm, or your horse, and you need to leave. We're closed."

They *were* closed. But she also knew her words were harsh. All he had done tonight was to be polite and to help. It had been no small task getting the mare into the stall. Kim was right when she said they probably wouldn't have been able to do it without his help.

He nodded. "You're right. I'm sorry. I'll go now. I enjoyed my session. Thank you for your help today."

He turned and walked out. She watched him go, and he closed the door behind him. For a moment she almost called him back, so she could apologize. But no. Not to Chris. Then the microwave went off, and she went to get her soup. She grabbed a plastic chair in one hand, the soup in the other, tucked the drink under her arm, and went to the mare's stall.

The mare—*Faith*—was still sleeping. Bandaged, she was lying flat out on her side, and Rachel watched her breathing for a moment, counting her breaths per minute. Twenty. Just right. The vet said she'd be groggy most of the night, but would be able to stand if she wanted, which was good. If a horse laid too long on one side, its intestines could twist, and that was usually fatal. Rachel's job tonight was to make sure she moved a little bit.

Rachel sat down in the plastic chair, outside the stall, with her back up against the stall door. Her soup was too hot to eat so she blew on it and listened to the voicemail from her mom. It was about her sister's baby shower. *Again.* She decided to answer it tomorrow.

Pushing that unpleasant topic out of her mind, she thought about Chris.

The man she saw today didn't match the teen she had known in high school. Oh, he was still good-looking. That handsome, dashing, can-have-any-girl-you-want type of good looking. He had been a catch, and charming, which was why she had been so flattered when he had started paying attention to her.

She had started at Winchester High School during the second half of eleventh grade, a terrible time to transition. But her dad had been transferred from his job in Ann Arbor, Michigan to the smaller town of Winchester, near the west coast of the state. Winchester was opening up a new hospital and it needed an administrator.

The town was supported mostly from a bottle-making factory, giving it a strong blue-collar population. With the new hospital open, there was a definite shift in economics, with some upper class families of doctors and administrators moving in. Hands down, Rachel's was one of the more affluent families in town.

In eleventh grade, she had been brooding, missing her best friend Anne back home. She also missed her horse. Rachel had been taking riding lessons from a local stable since she was five, and when she turned thirteen, her parents started leasing her a horse to show. Blaze was a tall bay gelding with a white streak down his face, earning him his name. She still missed that horse.

Her phone buzzed in her pocket. She looked at it. Her mom again. She might as well answer. Her mom was relentless.

"Hi, Mom."

"Rachel! I thought you had fallen off the face of the earth!" her mom said.

"Sorry. I was busy. Kim got a new horse in."

Her mom blew past that. "Your sister wants to go register for the baby shower tomorrow night. We'd like for you to join us."

"Ohhhh, I have to work," Rachel said, trying to sound bummed.

"But it's only a volunteer position. You can skip out for one night. Surely they'll understand. It's not like it's your *day* job."

"I have clients," Rachel said.

"April is going to be so disappointed." There it was. The mom-guilt. "It seems you're always choosing horses over family. I always hoped you'd outgrow that."

"I'm not choosing horses over April. I have a commitment. That's different." This was a discussion they had repeatedly had since she was young. She felt a flash of anger. "Why didn't you buy Blaze for me when we moved?" She regretted it almost as soon as she said it. It wasn't an easy topic between them.

"What? Oh, not this again. You remember, his owners didn't want to sell him. He was a great schooling horse and they needed him."

"But you didn't really try."

"We did. We made an offer."

She remembered. The offer was low. Her parents could have afforded more, but they wanted her to "outgrow" horses and move on to something else.

Every day after school, she had gone to the stable to ride, and on Saturdays she often participated in local schooling shows. She was a good rider, and she and Blaze got along well.

"You moved on to other things in Winchester," her mom said. "You were busy getting used to a new school."

"Look how that turned out."

Her mom ignored that. "I guess we'll go without you."

"Where?"

"To register for the baby."

Oh, not that again!

"Guess who I saw today," Rachel said, desperate to change the subject from the baby shower.

"Who?"

"Chris Adler."

There was a long silence on the other end of the phone. Rachel regretted mentioning his name the moment she said it.

"Did you run him over with your car?"

She laughed a little bit. "No, Mom. He came to the farm for a session."

"For what? I can only imagine. He had a lot of problems."

"I can't say."

"That's ridiculous," her mom said. "It's not like Chris will even know you're talking about him." Rachel could just see her rolling her eyes.

"He's a client. I do have a bit of integrity."

Her third month into school, near the end of the eleventh grade year, she was running late for fifth hour, turned a corner too fast, and ran smack into Chris. Her books dropped and scattered across the floor.

"Oh, gosh, I'm so sorry," she had said, bending down to pick them up. Chris had squatted down in front of her, gathered her books, and handed them to her. She was suddenly embarrassed by the shiny horse sticker she had put on her notebook.

But he hadn't seemed to notice. Then he had met her eyes. She still remembered their brilliant green, and how they twinkled.

"Hey, Rachel," he said.

She had no idea he even knew her name.

"Hey," she said, then stood, smoothing her denim skirt. "Thanks."

He stood, still watching her eyes, then, without breaking eye contact, nodded toward the stack of books she was holding.

"You like horses," he said. It was a statement, not a question.

"Uh, yeah. I used to." *Was he making fun of her?* Her sister April teased her all the time, calling her horse crazy.

"So does my brother Dillon. He rides at the local stable, and on Mondays I drive him there after school for his lesson. You'll have to tag along some time."

Then he smiled. She noticed his teeth were perfect. He gave his head a toss so that the lock of hair momentarily shifted out of his eyesight, then fell right back.

"Sure," she said. It was all she *could* say.

He nodded. "See ya, cowgirl."

Then Chris Adler turned to go, and she had stood there and watched him saunter off to class.

"He ruined your life," her mom said into the phone.

But he had offered her horses. She wondered later if she would have pursued him if he had not.

"He took me to the riding stable that one day, remember?"

"I do," her mom said. "A waste of time."

Chris had stayed in the car for Dillon's entire lesson, but she had wandered around the barn, petting the horses. It had eased some of her heartache for Blaze, and she hoped to keep coming back. But the following week, Dillon quit riding to pursue football.

Faith snorted, bringing Rachel back to the present.

"It's late, Mom. I have to go."

"Okay dear. Good night. I'll tell April you're thinking about joining us."

Rachel pocketed her phone and stood, peering over the stall door at the mare. The horse still slept, her sides moving in and out slowly, her body lost in a relaxed, oblivious state from the sedative. She was so thin and weak, but the IV fluids had filled her out somewhat, so her skin didn't look so slack.

Tonight, Faith could rest. But tomorrow, she'd have to wake up and fight for her life. She'd have to eat, drink, rest, and repeat until she had her strength back. Rachel hoped she had the will to survive. Sometimes, that's what was missing. Sometimes, horses were so broken emotionally that they couldn't be brought back.

She opened the stall door and knelt down in the thick, clean straw by the mare. She took Faith's pulse; it was good. She placed her hand on the mare's neck and felt the warmth under her.

"You can do it, Faith," she said. "I'll be here for you, to help. I won't let you down."

She sat back down and took a sip of her soup. Now it was cold.

Why had she told her mom about Chris? She certainly didn't *want* to talk about him. She wasn't going to waste any more time on him. She had done enough of that in high school.

She cringed to think of how bad she had crushed on him. When she had gotten dressed in the morning, she tried to pick out something she thought he'd like. When there was a school event, like a dance or a fundraiser, she tried to figure out if he was going or not before she decided if she was. There was always a chance he'd speak to her again. And he did. He'd say, "Hey, cowgirl," when he passed her.

Then something happened over the summer between eleventh and twelfth grade. Rachel started to fill out, and, suddenly, she had curves. Her hair got thicker, and her mom let her put highlights in it. And she replaced her glasses with contact lenses.

When she entered the twelfth grade year, she was suddenly noticed. Not just by the more popular girls, but also by the boys. She went to all the high school events, working on the homecoming float and helping decorate the gym for the dance. She was even asked to dances a few times by some of the guys. By Snow Coming, basketball's "homecoming," she was chosen to be one of the royal court, although another girl was chosen as the queen.

She was starting to be happy here in Winchester. Her grades were up, she had friends, and colleges wanted her.

Then, in March, she stayed late after school to work on a set for the school play. Her mom got a flat tire so she couldn't pick her up. It was cold outside, and the school building was locked up. While Rachel sat outside on the school's bench, waiting for her dad to come a half hour later, trying to stay warm, a car pulled up to the curb.

"Hey, Rachel," Chris Adler said, rolling the window down. That lock of sand-colored hair fell over his eye, and he brushed it aside. "You need a ride?"

Chris was just getting out of practice and was offering *her* a ride home.

She nodded and went around to the passenger side door and got in.

"Thanks. It's freezing out there!" she said.

Chris looked over at her, waiting for her to buckle her belt. He smiled that charming smile of his. "I'm having a party on Saturday. You want to come?"

Rachel felt her cheeks grow red and tried to hide her smile. She was sitting in Chris Adler's car, he was smiling at her and inviting her to a party! Her crush!

His charm, his wit, his attention was all directed toward her. She never stood a chance.

Faith stirred, and Rachel gently rubbed her neck.

"And now he's back," she said quietly. "I won't let him ruin my life again."

She sat there for a long time, her hand on the horse, wondering who was gathering strength from whom. And she wondered why she had ever thought it was a good idea to let go of horses for so long.

Chapter Four

Chris opened the door of his apartment, threw the mail on the kitchen counter, and went to take a shower. As the warm water washed over him, removing the smell and the dirt from his experience at the barn, he kept thinking about Rachel.

It seemed like she had turned out okay, despite it all. She looked great, and here she was, volunteering at Three Heart's Ranch. He didn't get a chance to ask her what she did outside of the ranch. She hadn't been wearing a wedding ring, so he thought maybe she wasn't married. Or, she was, and it was in getting fixed. Maybe the stone was loose.

He didn't know what to think.

But she sure was mad at him. And she had every right to be. He had taken the coward's way out years ago. He had used her, and left her hanging high and dry when they got caught. He had sold her out.

As he was dressing, his doorbell rang. He jumped. Who could be here at this time of night? He glanced at his phone. 10 p.m. There was a text from his brother saying he was bringing pizza.

He pulled the white t-shirt over his head and answered the door.

"Bro." Dillon was standing there with a boxed pizza in his hand.

"Mom sent you to check on me?"

Dillon nodded. "Yep. But I'm supposed to act like it was *my* idea to visit."

"Thus the pizza."

"Barbeque chicken, your favorite." Dillon was still dressed in his coveralls from the factory. Two years younger than Chris, Dillon had married the girl next door, and they had three little kids.

He invited Dillon in, and poured them both a glass of pop. Then he opened the box and took a bite of pizza. It was fresh and hot.

"Not bad."

"It's from a mom and pop place in town. I thought I'd try it out. So how *is* this new town treating you, anyway?"

Chris' move to St. Ives hadn't been popular with his family, but his last therapist thought the smaller, quieter town about twenty miles away would be a good place for him to heal. His parents wanted him back in Winchester, close. Especially his mom, who worried about him constantly. He couldn't blame her. He had put her through a lot. Not only had he nearly been killed in Afghanistan, but he had returned home only to go through a long string of bad relationships in a near-constant drunken state.

"The town is okay," Chris said. He really liked it here. The quiet atmosphere was just what he needed. His therapist had been right. "I started the horse therapy I was telling you about."

"And?"

Chris shrugged. "You'll never guess who I met there."

"Who?"

"Rachel."

"Rachel *Walker?*" Dillon said. "Doesn't she *hate* you?"

"That might be the understatement of the year."

Dillon took a bite of pizza and chewed thoughtfully. "You can't really blame her."

Chris nodded in agreement.

He hadn't given that night much thought until a year ago, when he had given his heart to Jesus. Before that, he had only been running. And now, here she was, bringing back all of the guilt and reminders of the jerk he used to be.

The first day of senior year, she had chosen a seat up front in first hour math class. He always sat in the back. When she walked past him to find her desk, he noticed the sway of her hips, the thickness of her hair, and wondered who the new girl was. Then she turned to talk to a friend and he saw that it was Rachel Walker, the skinny girl he had taken to the horse farm last year.

After that morning, he started seeing her at school events. He had been dating Jeanine for a while the previous year, but then they broke up. Ashley had been his girlfriend over the summer, a brief but fun relationship. Ashley moved away, and it was too hard to keep in touch. He wasn't ready to become serious. But Rachel fascinated him, so he started asking around about her. She came from a well-to-do family. Her dad was a hospital administrator or something. Not rich as in millionaires, but comfortable, and because they often had work guests over for dinner, her dad kept a bar stocked in the den. That was the word around school.

"Is she still pretty?" Dillon asked.

Chris nodded. "Even prettier."

Dillon took a drink of his pop. "Forget about it, Chris. She's never going to get over what you did to her. Let that one go."

Chris had wanted to know her better back then. She was gorgeous, smart, and someone who was starting to move in the same social circles he was. And he, as the captain of the football team and basketball team, and as the homecoming king, wasn't about to let another guy get to her first. He wanted her to be his.

It shamed him to think about how shallow he had been.

When he saw her sitting on the bench in the cold, he thought he'd offer her a ride home. It was an innocent enough offer. He'd get to know her better, see where she lived, let her know that Chris Adler was indeed interested. Then he heard himself inviting her to his party. It was exclusive; only the most popular kids went. And they kept it that way because it would be in Rob's shed out back of his parents' beach house. The shed was about twenty miles out of town, and Rob had the key. When his parents weren't there, the kids would sometimes go there to drink. But since the town was small, and people talked, it was hard to get booze.

He found himself asking Rachel if she could bring some whisky. And maybe a few beers.

She hesitated, and he kept eye contact, making sure to really pay attention to her. Girls liked that.

She had wavered. They were all underage, and she had a reputation for being a good girl. She didn't put out and she didn't drink, at least that was what he had heard about her. But after only a moment, she said "sure," and it was on.'

"Are you still in love with her?" Dillon asked, choosing another slice of pizza.

Chris snorted. "I was never in love with her."

But he had been.

"She was in love with you."

"I know," Chris said quietly.

He had used her. From March through May, he had picked her up about twice a month and driven her out to the shed. She always provided the booze, but never drank. He wanted to kiss her. Oh, how he wanted to kiss her. And Chris Adler could have any girl he wanted. But she was their ticket to a good time, and if he blew that…what would his friends think? He wanted to play it cool, so he continued to flirt with her just enough to string her along.

But she got under his skin.

"If we had dated…"

"You would have ruined it," Dillon said. "And there would have gone your ticket to free booze."

Chris met his brother's eyes. He felt the years of shame weighing down on him again.

"I was a jerk," he said.

"You were."

Dillon had been the nicer brother. He had treated Miriam well, and they were now married. And happy. Chris had only destroyed people.

"You had a lot of pressure on you, bro. You were our ticket out of that town. Dad wanted you to get a football scholarship and go out and make us rich." Dillon shook his head. "I'm glad it was you. I could never have handled the pressure."

From age five, Chris had played football.

"Don't disappoint me, son." His dad had said those words so many times, he had lost count. A steady girlfriend would have been trouble. "Don't let your feelings get in the way of the goal."

The goal was to win. At any cost.

But the cost had been too great, and almost lost Chris his soul. Almost? No, it had. He had sold his soul on prom night for a football scholarship.

"Mom still has your prom picture," Dillon said.

"I had a lineup of girls who wanted me to ask them," Chris said, remembering.

"The head cheerleader. What was her name?" Dillon mused. "The leggy brunette."

"Megan."

"And yet, you asked Rachel."

When he picked her up, he couldn't take his eyes off of her. She was beautiful in her light blue, low cut gown, with her hair done up in some kind of a fancy style. He noticed how blue her eyes were, and how much he loved her laugh.

Dillon was right. He had been in love with her. For a brief moment that night, as Rachel took his hand and her smile lit up, he had felt like he wasn't alone for the first time.

"You coming to the party tonight?" he asked into her ear later as they danced. He pulled her closer. She smelled so good.

"What party?"

Nothing official had been scheduled. Security was tight and the teachers were on the lookout tonight more than ever for booze or anything illegal.

"Me and the guys, and Emma and Katie. We're going to drive through some fast food joints. It'll be fun. I can drop you off after the prom, and pick you up at 1 a.m. I'll be down the street waiting in my car. And bring us a few bottles of something, okay?"

He felt her back tense under his hands. "Not tonight. They said anybody caught won't get to walk at graduation."

"Rach..." he said. He let his hand caress her lower back. "Nobody will know. Prom will be long over, and you'll be tucked safely away in our car. I promise not to drink and drive. If I get drunk, I'll give you the keys."

She still hesitated, but he knew she had a weakness for him. "I won't let anything bad happen, I promise," he cooed into her ear. And then, he bent his head and kissed her. It was their first kiss. She tasted sweet and delicious, and, for the second time that night, Chris felt himself waver. How nice it would be to just go outside, walk around slowly with this girl, and hold hands.

As the song ended, she pulled away from him slightly. Looking into his eyes, he could see he had won her over. Again.

"Okay," she said.

His buddy Brogan came up to him then. "We on for tonight?" he asked in a low voice.

Chris looked at Rachel and nodded.

"We are."

It was a move he regretted to this day.

The phone on his kitchen wall rang, and Chris jumped, the memories of the past scattering. It rang again. Dillon reached behind him, grabbed it, and handed it to Chris.

"Hello?"

It was a sales call. At 10:30 p.m.? Angry, Chris hung up and handed it back to Dillon.

"A robo call about the upcoming election." Chris heard his voice tremble.

"You okay, bro?"

Chris nodded. He saw this his hands were shaking, and put them under the table.

"You should probably get going," he said to Dillon. "I'm wiped out and want to hit the sack."

Dillon nodded, and stood.

"You can tell Mom that I'm fine."

Dillon smiled. "I will. I have no idea why you want to live out here in this small town though," he said. "You know there's a place for you with Miriam and me and the kids."

"I know."

Dillon looked at him for a moment.

"You're not going to let Rachel mess your head up, are you?"

"No." But it was too late for that.

The brothers gave each other a quick hug, and Dillon left.

Chris put the extra slices of pizza in the fridge, leaving one more out to eat. He wondered why Rachel lived here in St. Ives. And what she had done over the past nine years, since they had graduated. He didn't follow her, or anyone really, on social media. He had heard that she went off to college, but he didn't know where or what she studied. Again, he wondered if she was married. But what did it matter?

It's not like he could turn back time.

He got ready for bed, and then lay there in the dark, thinking. His mind went back to that night, after the prom.

They were all sitting in Galloway Park, off a remote dirt road, under the dark canopy of the pavilion. It was around 3 a.m.

Rachel was on Chris' lap. He wasn't sure how she had gotten there, because he was feeling a buzz at this point, but he remembered he could feel the warmth of her through the jeans she was wearing. She wasn't drinking. She was just sitting on his lap, and he was wondering if he should slide his hand up under her shirt or not.

There were six of them. The two girls, Katie and Em, because they were dating his two friends, Sean and Brogan. Sean was drunk, and Brogan was smoking weed. Katie had had a few drinks, but Em was just taking a few hits of Brogan's joint. And they were talking about summer and where they were going to work.

He still remembered what Rachel had said. Rachel had a job lined up at the hospital. She wanted to be a psychologist. Her dad had gotten her an internship, something through a program for high school students entering college in the fall. And she was planning to attend University of Michigan, where she had gotten a partial scholarship.

A dark figure started walking toward them. They thought it was another student joining them, because Chris had invited Kevin, but he never showed.

The figure started jangling his keys. "Hey, what are you kids doing?"

Brogan swore and tried to put out his joint.

Suddenly, a flashlight came on and pointed in their direction.

"Stay where you are!" said a voice. "Police!"

Chris jumped up so fast he dumped Rachel on the hard cement floor under them. He remembered the ground spinning. He was drunk.

"Ouch!" she said, scrambling to her feet. But he was already running.

For some reason that he still couldn't remember, Brogan had his car keys. They all piled in the car. All except Rachel. He looked back, and she was limping badly.

"Rachel, come on!" he shouted.

"I can't!" she said. "Wait for me!"

"Get in, dude!" Brogan hissed.

He remembered thinking of school expulsion, how if he lost his sports scholarship he'd never get to go to college. He heard his dad's angry voice in his head.

Rachel's parents had money. They'd get her in somehow. She'd be okay.

He felt someone—Katie maybe—grab him and pull him in the car.

"Go!" Chris said, slamming the car door behind him. Brogan peeled out, and Chris glanced back, watching as Rachel sat down on the bench. He knew she was busted.

Running away and leaving her was one of the lowest things he had ever done. But later that night and the next day, he did something even worse.

Oh Lord, why did You let me mess up so badly back then? I really hurt her! Please Lord, please give me the opportunity to make things right.

He noticed his hands were still shaking from when the phone had scared him. He was so easily startled now. He took a few deep breaths. Five is what his previous therapist told him. Five slow breaths in one minute would change the level of carbon dioxide in your system and the chemicals in your brain. It would calm him. At least, until the next thing startled him. And there would be a next thing. There always was.

He got up and walked into the living room, grabbed the remote, and flipped on the TV. He sunk back on the couch and bit into his pizza. There was a house remodeling show on, but he wasn't paying attention to it.

He remembered how Rachel had loved horses, even back then.

That brought his mind to Faith, the light-colored mare that had come in to Three Hearts so badly neglected. He saw the devastated look in Rachel's eyes. And he saw the determined look in Kim's. He had seen that look before. That was the look of a woman who had faced pain and decided not to let it destroy her.

Suddenly, he very desperately wanted to know how Faith was doing. Would she survive the night?

Please God, let her be okay.

He didn't know why, but it was very important to him that she made it. He imagined her in her stall at the farm they had rescued her from, starving, wondering when people were going to come and help her. Probably frightened. Alone.

Like he had been in Afghanistan.

"I'm okay," he said aloud, because it helped when images of war came to his mind.

He laughed then, because now, here he was talking to himself. He needed to get out and do more. Maybe this horse therapy would be good for him.

He decided he would stop in and check on Faith tomorrow, to see if she had lasted the night. And maybe he'd see Rachel. If he did, God just might open up a way for him to finally apologize.

Chapter Five

Rachel was glad for caffeine, and took a long drink of her iced tea. The night had been cold, the cot uncomfortable, and her mind busy with thoughts about Chris and resurfaced regrets, so she barely slept.

She looked at the teen sitting across from her. His dyed black hair was long, hanging just below his shoulders, and he had lined his eyes in black. The black concert t-shirt he was wearing had an obscene word on it, but most of it was covered up by his thin, black, faux leather jacket. He wore black skinny jeans with holes strategically ripped in the fabric. They must have cost a fortune.

His name was Scott, but he went by Boot. Because, as he told her on their first visit, anybody who messed with him would get his. And they were combat boots.

Rachel was toying with the corner of a page in her notebook. Unlike many of the teens she worked with, Boot always had something to say. Most were solemn and quiet, depressed, or rebellious, sitting with their arms crossed and sneering at her. It usually took a couple of months before any of them would open up.

Boot had been silent and brooding his first visit, but she soon realized it was a cover up. He was a bright kid with a lot to say, and when he discovered that this was a safe space, he opened up.

Boot came from a bad home situation and needed somebody to listen. His parents were very rich, working constantly, and nobody had time for him. So, he had rebelled. His mom brought him in because he started wearing all black, lining his eyes, and "sulking" as she put it. Instead of taking the time to figure out what was going on with him, she and his dad had sent him to therapy.

"They think there's something wrong with me," Boot had said on his first day.

"Is there?" Rachel had asked.

He shrugged his thin, bony shoulders. "Maybe."

Teen punks all seemed to have a "cause" they were passionate about, and Boot had embraced "Freedom from Education" as he called it. He said schools were full of mind-control and forced him to learn things that were pointless, in an atmosphere where he was locked inside for nine hours a day and starved for sunlight.

In truth, he was just bored. Bored and lonely.

But today, Rachel was having trouble listening to him. Her mind still kept wandering to Chris. His appearance had really rattled her, and she couldn't figure out why she was letting it bother her so much. After all, he had done something stupid to mess up her senior year, but it wasn't like he had killed anybody or stolen her car or anything.

"Then I sewed my head on with dental floss," Boot said.

"What?" She tried to smooth the corner of paper she had been folding. "I'm sorry. It's just…I'm sorry." She smiled, and ran her hand across her notebook. She pretended to take some notes. She looked across at him. He was watching her through narrowed eyes.

She knew she couldn't fool this kid, so she just decided to be honest. He already had enough problems with people not thinking he was worthy of their time and attention.

"The thing is," she said. "I'm having trouble focusing today. This guy showed up in my life and I hate him."

Boot's eyes got wide. "You *hate* him? Wow. That's intense."

"Hate might be a strong word," said Rachel. But really, it wasn't. "This place where I volunteer, well, they want me to work with him. I can't go into the details, but I really don't want to work with him."

Boot shrugged. "So don't. It's a free country. And if you're a volunteer, it's not like they'd fire you. I mean, they probably need, like, TONS of people like you and only have a few. So just say no."

Rachel sighed, feeling the tension in her shoulders. "I know. I did try saying "no," but that didn't work. The woman in charge is very stubborn. But I will next time. I'll stand up for myself."

Boot was watching her carefully. As a therapist, she hadn't told him much about herself before. She probably shouldn't now, so she tried to change the subject.

"So, did you invite your Dad to your open mic night?"

Boot had written some verse (he refused to call it a poem) and put it to music. He was going to play it at a local mic night at the coffee shop. He had read it to her (because his parents wouldn't let him bring his guitar in and he refused to sing a capella) and it was really pretty good. It was about school and the stupidity of conformity in education. She didn't agree with a word he said, but she had to admit that he said it very well.

Boot shrugged again. His bangs fell over his eyes, and he brushed them back. "Yeah. But he was busy. He said poetry is for...." Instead of saying more, he shrugged again. "I *told* him it wasn't poetry. It was a *statement.*"

His dad was afraid that Boot was gay. He wasn't. But what bothered Rachel was the distaste his father showed. He made it clear that his love was conditional.

"How did it go?" she asked.

Another shrug. "I decided not to go."

This surprised her. Boot usually "did his thing," no matter what his parents thought. Or, more often, *because* they didn't want him to do it.

"Why?"

"So tell me about this guy of yours."

"Don't change the subject. This session is about *you.*"

"It doesn't have to be."

"It does. Your insurance company sees to that."

"But what we talk about here is confidential, right?"

Rachel nodded.

"So, they'll never know. Is he someone from your past?"

Rachel couldn't hide the smile at Boot's logic. "High school."

Boot nodded. "The institution of retarded learning."

"We don't use that word in here," Rachel said.

"The R-word? Since when are there so many rules? That's what I don't like about school. There are so many rules limiting who you can be as a person."

Rachel tried again. "So, are you mad at your dad?"

"Nah. That takes too much energy." He fished into his jacket pocket and pulled out a pocket knife. He opened it up and started cleaning his fingernails.

"You're not supposed to bring weapons in here," Rachel said before she realized she had just hit him with another rule.

He glanced up at her, and they both smiled as it occurred to them at the same time.

This kid wasn't dangerous. Far from it. He dressed tough and talked tough and, yes, even carried a knife, but she knew he was sweet down inside. She only wished his parents could see it.

"Look, Boot," she said, glancing the clock behind him. "Your session is about up. The part I was listening to today made me feel like you're starting to not care about your parents and whether they love you or not."

"That has always been the case, Ms. Walker."

She shook her head. "No, it hasn't. You *pretended* it was, but we both know it wasn't. But this sudden apathy worries me."

Yet another shrug. He concentrated on cleaning his thumbnail.

"Why the turn around?"

He sat up straight and closed the pocket knife with a snap. "Look at the time," he said, glancing at his phone. "It has been nice talking with you." He stood, gave a cursory bow at the waist.

"Boot, sit down. You have three minutes left. Let's not leave it like this."

"*Ms. Walker.* My dad doesn't care whether I'm dead or alive, you know that. So why should *I?* He isn't going to give me money for college unless I 'clean up my looks' and study law. I don't want to study law. And we both know my grades aren't going to get me any scholarships. My future is looking a bit like it sucks."

"Your future is what you make it." She could see he was really going to leave. She grasped for something. "And I owe you about fifteen minutes because that's when I zoned out. Why don't you come twice this week. I have an opening tomorrow."

He laughed. "Only if we talk about your boyfriend."

Rachel frowned. "He's not my boyfriend."

He raised an eyebrow. She glanced at the clock again. She didn't have another appointment right away. He was baiting her. She shouldn't take it.

"I wanted him to be," she said. "Once."

"In high school?"

"Yes."

"Were you a rule-follower back then too?"

Rachel looked across him, considering. "Okay. The brief version is I had a crush on him, and he invited me to the prom. Of every girl in school, he picked *me.* He was the captain of the football team—"

"Why does every girl go for the jocks? I don't get it."

"And he was handsome. He convinced me to bring booze to a party afterwards. My dad kept it in his liquor cabinet to entertain work guests with, so I had easy access."

"So you *are* a rule-breaker!"

Rachel remembered it like it was yesterday.

"Did you get caught?"

"Yes."

"What happened?"

"We got caught. He turned on me, ratted me out, and I didn't get to walk at graduation."

"He *told* on you?"

Rachel nodded.

"Wow. What a jerk."

"Yep. And the worst part is, I thought he liked me."

Boot sat there for a moment in silence, and she watched his face cloud over. "Why do you supposed he didn't like you?" The question was directed at her, but she knew he was talking about himself and his parents.

She shrugged. "I guess I didn't meet his qualifications. I wasn't a cheerleader. I wasn't one of the 'popular' girls. I had friends and did well enough, but…" She shrugged again. She really didn't know.

She saw Boot struggling with something and hoped he would stay. Then, as if he had said too much, he got up. "I gotta run. Lots of do." He was at the door.

"So I'll see you next week?"

He didn't turn back to look at her as he opened the door, but she saw a slight nod of his head as he walked through and shut it behind him.

Rachel briefly wondered if Boot was suicidal.

But no, she shouldn't go there. Not all kids were about to kill themselves.

Or were they? The small teenage girl, the one called Faith, had slipped through the cracks.

That's when her marriage had died. After Faith did.

The year previous to Faith's death, Rachel had three miscarriages. Then, she couldn't get pregnant. After testing, she learned she had primary ovarian insufficiency, which simply meant she had run out of eggs. In her *twenties*. It was rare, but apparently true. She was devastated, and so was her husband. They talked about adoption, but he didn't want to adopt. He talked about using a donor.

Then Faith had died. Rachel had been counseling the girl for two years when her parents came home one evening to find Faith dead from an overdose of sleeping pills.

Rachel sunk into a depression after that, and it was too much for her husband. Within six months, he had found another woman, filed for divorce, and was gone.

A tear rolled down her cheek, and she angrily wiped it away, cursing Chris Adler for returning to her life and causing old memories to resurface. If he hadn't sold her out, she might have gone to the University of Michigan instead of the smaller college. She never would have met her ex-husband. She would have maybe had a different job, had never met Faith, had never ruined so many lives.

Part of her logical brain knew it was unfair to blame Chris for everything, but she did. Her anger and hurt ran so deep, she needed a target.

And that target was Chris.

For years, she had replayed that night over and over again in her mind, wondering how things might have been different if she hadn't brought that alcohol. Or even met Chris at 1 am. when she was supposed to be in bed after prom. Hindsight was twenty-twenty, her therapist told her. No use crying over spilt milk.

Chris and his friends had left her to get arrested. They had *left* her! Angry and trying to protect herself, she had ratted him out when the cops asked who she was with. She started spewing names with no regret. They had, after all, left her behind.

The lone cop happened to be patrolling the park that night, not really looking for trouble. He had run across them by accident and smelled pot.

She still remembered the anguish and disappointment on her parents' faces when they came to pick her up at the jail. She wasn't drinking, but she was surrounded by bottles of booze. Bottles she had stolen from their liquor cabinet.

Her parents had the sense not to confirm those were *their* bottles. So, she wasn't in any legal trouble for supplying alcohol to minors. But when the school principal and vice principal met with her and her parents the next day, they had already done their homework. They had asked her friends some questions and someone had told.

"You know the penalty for partaking in alcohol on prom night," said the vice principal.

She remembered wondering why he used the word "partaking." But that's what he had said. "Partaking."

"I wasn't drinking," she said. And an alcohol blood test had confirmed that. But she had supplied the booze.

"We can't tolerate this kind of behavior," said the vice principal. They said if she told them who else was involved, she might get off with less detention.

So she told names. All of them. Every single one who was with her that night. Everyone who had left her behind.

When each of them was brought in for questioning, they had had time to work out their alibis. Chris was offered a deal. The right to graduate, and no expulsion, if he told who brought the alcohol. Not only did he talk, but he told them that Rachel had been a regular supplier to the high school parties.

In the whole confusing mess, Chris' two friends got two days of detention. The two girls got nothing. And Rachel got three days of detention and lost the right to walk at graduation. Somehow, the charmed Chris Adler walked away with no repercussions. Rumor had it that was because his football scholarship was so important to the school. It would make the small-town high school look good. Or because his dad had a secret meeting with the principal. Nobody ever found out for sure.

She had gone to the graduation and parked her car in a back corner of the parking lot of the stadium. She sat there and watched her classmates file out, hugging their parents, some of them tossing their hats high into the air. She sat there for hours, waiting until the parking lot was empty before she turned on the car and headed home. She decided to drive through the school parking lot one last time.

There was Chris, leaning against the brick wall out back of the gymnasium, a beer in his hand. Sean and Brogan were with him, smoking something. They were all still dressed in their graduation gowns.

She pulled up to Chris and rolled down her window.

"I hate you," she said.

He shrugged, and took a long, slow drink of his beer. "You should have been smarter, Rach." He held up the beer bottle in a sort of toast. Sean and Brogan snickered. Angry, she rolled up her window and drove off, hoping to never see Chris again.

The detention hurt her grades, went on her record, and the University of Michigan pulled her scholarship funds. She switched to a cheaper university closer to home that was still offering her a scholarship.

And that's where she had met her husband. *Ex-*husband.

It was a train wreck from there.

Chapter Six

Chris woke early and went for a run. He alternated between three and five miles every morning. Today was five, and he ran along the bike path that wound past his apartment and down through Cedar Park. There were some other early morning joggers, a few people out walking their dogs, and a mother pushing a stroller.

He wanted to work off that extra slice of pizza he'd eaten last night after Dillon left.

He thought about Rachel and Faith as he ran. He did what he called a Prayer-Run; this was his time with God. He'd wake up, read a few scriptures, and then meditate on them and pray as he ran. Sometimes, he'd pray for the people he passed on his run, like the mother with the stroller. She looked exhausted, and her baby was fussing. He prayed for the old man who opened the produce store at 6 a.m. every morning. He always had a smile and a nod for Chris, but he seemed lonely. He prayed for the baker next door in Don's Donuts, and the woman on the corner who owned the knitting shop.

This morning, he was praying for Rachel, Faith, and Kim.

Please God, forgive me for what I did to Rachel, Chris prayed. He had prayed this before and he knew that he was forgiven. Scripture promised that God forgave and forgot. There was no record keeping; he was absolved. If only he *felt* freer from the guilt.

Then he prayed for that poor horse. *And Lord, please help me not to hate the horse's owner so much,* Chris said. Because he did. Anyone who could do that to an animal...

He wondered if Faith had lived through the night. Kim had seemed determined that the mare would heal.

His mind wandered to Kim, and he wondered what her story was. He prayed for her, asking God to help her in whatever way she needed, and he prayed for protection for the farm.

He felt good after his prayer run. He went home, showered, spread some jam on a toasted freezer waffle, and left for work.

Chris worked at the local hardware store. He had started there two weeks ago, and was still getting to know his way around. The owner, Cal Burton, or Mr. B as everyone called him, was nice enough. An older man, probably close to seventy. He seemed okay with Chris' PTSD when he put it on the application, but, so far, Chris hadn't had any "spells." When he did, the story might change. Most people didn't know how to handle their employees having panic attacks at work.

His job was simple: stocking the shelves and answering questions if a customer needed help. Chris had worked construction in the army and had gotten pretty handy with tools. Working at this hardware store was the most stress-free job he could think of. And stress-free was what he needed.

"How's it going?" Mr. B asked. Chris had just unwrapped a sandwich and taken a bite.

"It's going." The day had been long and slow, but he liked it that way.

His mind kept going back to the horse, Faith. He shared her story with Mr. B.

The old man shook his head. "Gets to me how some people treat life," he said. "Ain't got a lick of sense."

"I was thinking about calling the farm to see how she is," Chris said. But what if she had died?

"Why don't you?"

Chris shook his head. "I'm not sure I want to know."

"Hmm," was all Mr. B said.

Even though he had no attachment to the horse, even though he had only spent a short time with her, Chris thought it would be too upsetting to find, while he was here at work, that she died.

He'd call when he got home.

But when his shift was over, he found himself wanting to *see* her. He also had a feeling that Rachel would be back out for the same reason, and as much as he didn't want to admit it, he wanted to see her as well.

He drove straight out to the farm after work. He hoped the hole in the muffler didn't scare the horses.

He parked his rusted Chevette and went into the main barn. Kim was sweeping the aisleway. She smiled when she saw him.

"Chris!" she said. "How's it going?"

"Fine," he said. "I was just here...I came by...I just wanted to check on the horse." Suddenly, he was embarrassed. His session wasn't for a week and it seemed silly that he had driven all the way out here.

"Faith is doing great," Kim said. She stopped sweeping and wiped some sweat from her forehead with the back of her hand. "She's awesome, in fact. She got up this morning and ate some grain! And she's been nibbling at her hay all day."

"Wow," Chris said. It surprised him how immense his relief was. He couldn't afford to lose anyone else. Not even a horse he barely knew. "That's great."

"The farrier—that's our guy who shoes the horses—came out this afternoon and trimmed her feet. Rachel stayed with her all night."

Chris wanted to ask if Rachel was here now, but that seemed too obviously an inappropriate question.

"Would you like to see her?" Kim asked.

Did she mean Rachel? Then he remembered they had been talking about the horse.

"Yes," he said.

He followed her down the aisleway and across the empty indoor arena to the stalls on the other side. As they approached, he saw the mare stick her head over the stall door. Her ears perked in his direction.

"Hey, Faith!" he said, and gave a little wave. To his surprise, the horse made a low noise in her throat.

Kim laughed. "She's talking to you!" she said. "She nickered. I think she remembers that you helped save her."

"Really?" Chris said. He walked up to the stall, careful to move slowly. Faith rolled her eyes up, showing their whites. She backed up a bit.

"Here," Kim said. She dug her hand into the pocket of her coveralls and produced a plastic baggie with sugar cubes in it. "Give her one of these."

Chris took the baggie and opened it.

"Flatten your hand, palm up, and put one on your palm," Kim said. "She can't see your fingers, so you want to be careful to keep them flat."

Chris did as she said, and the horse watched him carefully. Slowly, he raised his arm toward her, his palm up, the white sugar cube sitting there. He held it there for a few moments, but the mare stayed back, wary.

"She's interested," Kim said quietly, "but a little frightened."

"You can't blame her for having trust issues," Chris whispered.

Faith's nostrils were quivering as she smelled the treat. She stretched her neck out a little bit, trying to reach it without coming too close.

Several minutes went by and Chris' arm was starting to get tired. Slowly, carefully, he drew his arm back and set the sugar cube on top of the stall door. He and Kim both stepped back a few feet.

The mare watched them, and after they were out of arm's reach, she took a step forward. Then another, until she was close enough to reach her neck out and get the sugar cube. She stretched a bit and her upper lip quivered. Then her big, pink tongue came out and licked it. She took it in her teeth and stepped back, watching them while chewing.

Chris smiled. He had made a friend.

"She likes you," Kim said. "She hasn't let anybody else get this close to her all day without cowering in the back of her stall. "

"Really?" For some reason, this made him happy. His life had been such a mess for so long that this little bit of good news almost brought tears to his eyes. Gosh, he was an emotional wreck. His therapist didn't like it when he said that about himself, but it was true.

"Really," Kim said. "We had to give her a mild sedative to trim her feet."

Chris rubbed his eyes. To change the subject, he asked Kim about her farm.

"How long have you lived here?" he said.

"Fifteen years."

"This is an amazing place."

Kim nodded, her eyes still on the mare.

"So, what do the three hearts stand for?" It was a question that Chris had wanted to ask since he first saw it.

The driveway passed under a large, arched wooden sign. The farm's name was on it, and right in between the words "Hearts" and "Ranch" were three hearts. The middle one was painted light purple, and the other two hearts were painted white.

Three Hearts Ranch.

"My family," Kim said.

"Oh, do you have kids?"

Kim was quiet for a moment, then she reached for the baggie of sugar cubes. Chris handed them to her. She took another one out and gave it to Chris, then she stuffed the baggie and both of her hands into her pockets. When she spoke again, her voice was light and unemotional.

"No. Not anymore. We moved here, my husband and I, when Carrie was ten. This was our dream home, and we were going to raise Quarter Horses. I was going to give riding lessons. My husband made the sign. He did a lot of work on the barn. We didn't have the indoor arena then."

She inclined her head, motioning for Chris to offer Faith the other sugar cube. He slowly put it on top of the stall door. Faith watched him carefully. Her nostrils quivered as she smelled the treat. He took his hand away, and she slowly stretched her neck out again and, with her lips, grabbed it off the stall door. She backed up and chewed from a safe distance.

Kim smiled and Chris met her eyes. He couldn't hold back his own smile. "You're hooked," Kim said.

"Hooked?"

"On that horse."

Chris looked back at Faith. He wasn't sure what Kim meant, but he knew he was having fun. He couldn't remember the last time he had smiled so easily.

"The hearts stand for the three of us," Kim said. "My husband named the farm and carved them in the sign. Then Carrie got brain cancer. It was an awful two years. Chemo, surgeries...after she died, we were lost. Bryan couldn't take it and he killed himself a year later. An overdose of some painkillers he was taking for a bad knee. I can't blame him. We were barely existing. For over a year, we hardly spoke, hardly ate...it's a terrible thing to lose a child. Especially in such a bad way. We lost track of each other. I was suffering so much that I didn't see how far he had gone."

She was quiet again.

"I'm sorry," he said. "I can't imagine."

"After Bryan died, I figured I could lay in bed until I died too, or I could do something with my life. Carrie was amazing. She was this bright, shining light who just drew people to her. I knew she would never want me to wither away. So, I got up and turned this place into a safe space where people could come to heal. The first thing I did was paint the hearts that my husband had carved on the sign. The purple one is mine. The white ones on either side of it are for Bryan and Carrie. They're watching over me. My angels."

Kim looked at Chris and smiled. "But that's enough about me. I'm okay now. That was fifteen years ago. This farm means the world to me, and it brings me joy every day to see how the horses help people."

Chris didn't know what to say.

But Kim didn't let it get awkward. "I think you should help me with this mare," she said.

"With Faith?"

"Yes. She's going to need a lot of work."

"I don't know a thing about horses."

"You can learn. She needs you. You're the first person she's reached out to. She's asking for your help."

Chris looked at the mare. Faith looked back, her head cocked to the side, watching him out of one wary eye. But, she was watching him closely, looking for more sugar.

"Hello, girl," he said. "You want to be friends?"

"Can you come out here any days after work?" Kim asked.

"Um..." Chris didn't have much going on in his life *besides* work. Nothing, really.

"Sure," he said. "I'd love to. I could come every evening if you need me to." And he meant it. For the first time since his accident, he felt he might be useful. "I only work part-time, so I could come during the day too, on certain days."

"Good. It's settled then. Just come out and do what you're doing. Offer her sugar cubes. Apple slices. Talk quietly to her. That's all. Just make friends with her. The rest will come in time."

Kim turned to go. "I need to get back to work," she said, and left him standing at the stall. When she was at the end of the aisle and about to turn across the arena, she said over her shoulder. "If you have any questions about horses or horse care, Rachel is the perfect person to ask."

Chris was about to tell her that Rachel wasn't going to want to help him, but Kim was gone.

Rachel. He had a feeling she wouldn't be too happy about this. But maybe this would give him a chance to make up for what he had done to her.

Somehow.

Chapter Seven

Rachel thought about what Boot had said as she drove out to Three Hearts Ranch that evening. If Kim asked her to work with Chris again, she would simply say no. She could then avoid the ranch the evening Chris was there, and her problem would be gone.

Feeling better that she had made a decision, she was excited to see Faith. Kim had texted her earlier to tell her that the mare was doing well; she was up and eating some hay.

It was 5:30 when she pulled in the dusty lot. She saw Jennifer, the other ranch counselor, out in the arena working with a young boy who had cerebral palsy. She couldn't remember his name, but the bliss on his face said how much fun he was having as he gripped the mare's mane, his eyes closed tight.

Rachel fished in her pocket for the bag of carrots. She walked into the barn and turned to go down to Faith's stall, but what she saw made her stop short. There was Chris, standing at the stall door, and Faith was almost close enough for him to touch. The mare watched him with big eyes, but they no longer held fear. Only curiosity.

Rachel should have been glad that the mare was making progress, but instead, anger swelled up in her. She was mad that Chris was here, that Chris was messing around with the mare, and that Kim obviously knew about it. Rachel was usually the one to help the rescues that Kim brought in.

She straightened her shoulders and took a deep breath before walking toward them. She had to be calm. She didn't want Faith to pick up on her anger.

"Hi," she said softly. Both Chris and the horse jumped. It was then that she remembered he was a veteran with PTSD. Probably best not to sneak up behind him.

"Oh, hi," he said. His green eyes were sparkling. "Look how good she's doing!"

"I know already," Rachel heard her voice come out, clipped. "Kim texted me."

"And she's gaining some trust," Chris said, as if he hadn't heard the tension in her voice. "Watch." He placed a sugar cube on the top of the stall door. Faith waited until he drew his hand away, then she stretched her neck out as far as she could, lifted the cube with her lip, and drew back to chew and watch them.

It was amazing, really. Yesterday, this mare had barely been able to stand and was terrified of them all. Today, she was not only standing, but taking treats. And she didn't seem that afraid of him.

"That's nice," she managed to say.

Chris seemed happy. Relaxed. Different, already, than the stiff, uncomfortable man she had met yesterday. The horse was healing Chris as he was healing her. This was the way it was supposed to play out at Three Hearts Ranch.

"Kim said your evening session is still sick. She said you might be able to give me one again, tonight. On Angel."

Rachel felt the frustration surge in her again. He *knew* how she felt about him! Why would he even ask?

"That is, if you want to," Chris added. He turned to look at her briefly, then turned back to watch the mare.

"I thought your insurance only paid for once a week," said Rachel.

"It does. Kim said this one would be on the house because I've been here for a few hours volunteering."

"Fine."

He raised an eyebrow.

"I mean…*fine*," she made her voice softer. But it wasn't fine at all. "Excuse me for a moment."

She went to find Kim. It took a few minutes, because Kim was up at the house. Rachel knocked on the screen door and heard Kim yell from the back of the house. "Just a minute!"

She waited, and Kim came out with a stack of towels tucked under her arm. "Oh good. You can take these to the barn for me. That'll save me a trip. Come in."

She opened the screen door and Rachel went in.

Kim's house was small. A tiny kitchen and living room led to a hall with one bathroom and the two bedrooms. Kim said she didn't need much because she spent most of her time in the barn.

Her kitchen was a mess. The counters and table were covered with papers, and file cabinets lined the walls of the living room. Kim kept saying she was going to get the basement finished so she could put her office space down there, but there was never the time or the money.

Kim handed Rachel the towels. They were still warm from the dryer.

"What's up?" she asked.

"Why is Chris with Faith?" Rachel said.

"He's working with her," Kim said. Kim walked over to the table where a big bowl of fruit sat. She grabbed an apple, rubbed it on her shirt, and took a bite.

"But *I* usually work with the rescues," Rachel said, realizing how childish she sounded.

Kim turned to look out the window, and Rachel saw her trying to hide a smile. "I know. But you have a partner on this one. I still want *you* to be lead horse whisperer." She looked at Rachel then, and let the smile spread across her face. She had started calling Rachel "the horse whisperer" nearly two years ago when they had first met, and Rachel had instantly calmed down a frightened gelding. "But Faith needs to get used to men again. It was a man who hurt her, so it's going to be men she's most afraid of. And Chris needs Faith as much as she needs him, although he doesn't realize that yet."

"But I hate him!" Rachel said. The words were out before she could stop them.

Kim swallowed her bite of apple and their eyes met. She saw a puzzled look come into Kim's gaze. "Why?"

Rachel shrugged, and was embarrassed to feel tears sting her eyes.

"This is an awful strong reaction from someone who was just a jerk to you in high school. What did he do to you? Is this something I need to worry about?"

Chris wasn't violent. He never was. He had never made any inappropriate moves with girls that weren't uninvited, nor had he ever maliciously hurt anyone. He was just a selfish jerk.

"No," Rachel said. "

"So this was just embarrassing high school stuff?"

How could she say that his decisions had ruined her life?

She nodded but kept quiet.

Kim frowned. "I need to know more."

Rachel sighed. "He pretended to care about me so I'd bring alcohol to a party after the prom. We got busted, he ratted on me, and I lost my scholarship to the University of Michigan. So I went to a smaller college where I met my ex. It's a long story but that's the short version."

After she said the words, Rachel felt petty. It really *wasn't* a long story. That was basically it. So why did it hurt so much? She dropped her gaze to the floor as the blood rushed to her cheeks.

Kim was quiet for a moment. She often took some time to think before she spoke. Probably something Rachel herself should work on.

"Okay then." Kim said. "This man needs you. He needs this horse. I've been doing this for many years, and I have a gut feeling about this. And I think as soon as you get your head out of the past, you will too. I also want you to work with him tonight on Angel. He has been here for a few hours. He stacked hay, cleaned stalls, and has more than earned his keep. Give him some time on Angel, help him relax before he goes home for the day. And try to let go of some of that anger. Then maybe the both of you will sleep better tonight."

Rachel started to argue. She remembered Boot's words that she didn't have to put up with this. But she couldn't figure out the right way to say no. Not to Kim.

"I'm just a volunteer," she said quietly, and it sounded feeble.

Kim regarded her for a moment. "Rachel, you are *way* more than 'just' a volunteer. You are the lifeblood of this place. Your students love you. The horses love you. I love you." She let those words hang in the air for a moment. "And there's a man out there fighting for his sanity. He *needs* you. You're a professional. Of all my staff, you are the only one who has the tools to help him. So get to work."

She couldn't hold Kim's gaze any longer. She dropped her eyes, mumbled "okay," and headed out the door. In her heart, she knew that Kim was right. Kim usually was. So, she'd put on her professional hat and give Chris one more riding session. Then she could send him home so she could have some time alone with Faith.

How hard could it be?

Chapter Eight

Chris followed Rachel and Angel into the tacking up area. Rachel worked with him again on brushing the horse and showed him how to look at Angel's feet to make sure there were no stones in them. Then she taught him how to saddle Angel and how to put her bridle on. All of this took about twenty minutes, and never once did she meet his gaze. She moved about in a professional, detached manner.

He tried not to let it bother him, but it was making him antsy. He felt like he had to walk on eggshells around her, and because of his anxiety, it wasn't helping.

Rachel led Angel out to the arena. They were the only ones outside again, and it was quiet. The last student had finished up her session, and the last volunteer was just leaving in her car.

Chris mounted the mare, and Rachel started leading him clockwise around the arena. "Take your feet out of the stirrups and just let them dangle for a few minutes," she said. He did as he was told. Then, she told him to rest the reins on the mare's neck and feel Angel under him. He closed his eyes and placed his hands on Angel's neck. He miraculously felt himself begin to relax.

The session went surprisingly well. Rachel even smiled a few times when he made what she called "progress." He had no idea what kind of progress he was making, but the horse continued to plod slowly around the arena, and he felt his muscles unwinding. All of the physical work around the barn had been good for him as well.

Finally, it was time for him to dismount. He did, and Rachel took the reins from him.

"Great session," she said. "I'll get her untacked. You can go home now."

She turned, dismissing him.

It felt cold. He wanted more, but wasn't sure what "more" he wanted. And he wanted to see Faith one more time before he went home.

"So, how did I do?" he asked.

"You did great," Rachel said again, but didn't turn to face him. She started to unlatch the gate. He stepped over and put his hand on hers to stop her. He had to get on better ground with her.

"Rachel," he said.

She looked at him then, and finally met his eyes. "What?"

"Let's talk about this. If we're going to have to work together, we need to talk."

"There's nothing to talk about."

"There obviously is. You're really mad at me."

She jerked her hand away from his. "And why wouldn't I be?"

"I was a jerk. I get that. I know that. Yes, I messed up your life, and I messed up a whole lot of lives with my selfishness. I was only thinking about *me*. But it was just a graduation ceremony."

"*Just* a graduation ceremony?" Rachel said. She heard her voice raise an octave. "I worked hard for four freakin' years to keep my grades up so I could graduate with honors and get into the college of my choice. My parents were so proud. They wanted to see me walk across that stage and get that diploma. And you took that away from them. And away from me."

He was taken aback at the anger in her tone. He knew she was upset, but there had to be more to this story.

"And I'm so sorry about that. It was just a ceremony. The diploma is what we wanted."

"Like it mattered to you. You were barely graduating anyway."

"Hey, that's not fair! I had a football scholarship!"

"And what happened to *that?*" she asked. She crossed her arms, still holding Angel's reins. The horse seemed unconcerned with their argument. Angel's eyes started to close.

Should he tell her? How he had drank and partied his scholarship away? How he had broken a few more hearts, stringing girls along and leaving them when he got bored?

He had never been able to get Rachel out of his head. Not even after all the drinking. Once, he had tried to apologize to Rachel, but her parents wouldn't tell him how to find her. He had no idea where she had gone to college. When he finally found her through a few friends, he had just signed on the dotted line to join the army and figured why bother at this point?

Then, when he returned, he drank himself too deep inside a bottle to care about anyone.

"It didn't turn out so well," he said quietly. "So I joined the army. Ended up in Afghanistan. And now that's why I'm here."

He saw her anger waver.

"So, I wanted to apologize," he said. "I'm sorry. Please forgive me, and let's work this out so we can work together."

The lines of her mouth hardened again. "I don't want your apology," she said. "No apology could fix what you took from me!"

He was confused. It happened so long ago, and they were just stupid kids. "All I did was rat you out and make you miss graduation."

Rachel stepped back from him. Angel opened her eyes to see if she was supposed to follow. But Rachel only turned, took a few steps, then spun back around.

"You *ruined* my *life!*" she said. "Because of you, my parents wouldn't pay for my college when I lost the scholarship from U of M. The school still offered me a partial scholarship, but my parents punished me by withdrawing all of their funding. So, I went to my second choice college, where I met…"

She stopped at this point. Her eyes filled with unshed tears, and she angrily brushed them away. "It doesn't matter."

She started to leave, but Chris stepped in front of the gate.

"It *does* matter," he said. "Where you met *who?* What happened to you in college?"

"Get out of my way." Her voice was hard.

"Rachel, please…"

"Get. Out. Of. My. Way."

He stepped back. She opened the gate and led Angel through, and he watched the two of them disappear into the barn.

Where she met *who?* Who had hurt her so much? Was she blaming him for *that?*

He sighed and realized that his hands were trembling. All of the relaxing he had achieved on Angel was gone. He closed his eyes and practiced some of the deep breathing that his counselors had taught him. When he felt steady again, he walked into the barn, the opposite direction of where Rachel was untacking Angel. He would say goodnight to Faith, and then head home.

Faith saw Chris and perked her ears in his direction. He approached quietly, and fished for more sugar cubes. He only had one left in his pocket. He placed it on top of the stall's half door.

Faith's nostrils twitched. She stretched her neck out, snuffing at the treat, but she couldn't quite reach it.

"I'm not going to hurt you," Chris said, keeping his voice soft. "It's your bedtime snack."

Faith took a step toward him.

"That's it. Come on," he said. He was standing right next to the stall door. If she took the treat, she'd have to practically touch him.

Faith hesitated. Then took another step. Then she stretched her neck out again, moving her muzzle toward the treat. She paused to sniff Chris' sleeve.

Then she snatched the cube with her lips and retreated back two steps to chew it and watch him.

He smiled, and counted that a small victory.

He heard footsteps behind him.

"Why are you still here?"

It was Rachel. Still angry. He felt the calm drain from him again. He turned to face her.

"What did he do to you that you hate me so much?"

She froze at the words. He had hit home. A man had hurt her, and she blamed Chris. She blamed Chris because he had ruined her graduation, which had caused her parents to withdraw college funding, and she wound up somewhere else.

She protectively wrapped her arms around her torso. He felt her close herself up. He had said too much. Her eyes drifted to Faith.

"I saw her take the sugar cube," she said softly. "She likes you."

He turned to the mare, who was watching him carefully.

"I'm out of treats now, though," he said, holding his empty hands palm up.

Rachel came to stand beside him at the stall door. She rested her arms on it. Faith snorted.

"Hey, girl," she said softly. "You still hungry?"

The mare's eyes went from Rachel to Chris, then back to Rachel.

"I have some carrots," she said, and dug into her front jeans pocket to pull out a baggie with three baby carrots in it. "Just a few left."

She took one out. Faith, who had already learned that baggies contained goodies, watched her carefully.

Rachel put a carrot on the stall door and stepped back. Chris stepped beside her and they watched.

"See how her ears are pricked forward?" Rachel said. "That means she's curious. She's listening."

Faith picked up her foot and pawed the ground.

"And she's impatient," Rachel laughed. "She wants it, but now there's another human to worry about."

Faith snorted again.

"Come on. It's okay," Rachel said. Chris and Rachel stood there quietly, side by side, and Faith took a step toward them. Then another. She stretched forward, snatched the carrot, and then backed away, chewing.

When Faith was finished, Rachel slowly raised her hand out in front of her and opened her palm. She had a carrot. Faith's nostrils quivered.

Rachel stepped forward and extended her arm over the stall door.

Faith tensed.

"Watch her ears," Rachel said quietly.

He did. They swiveled like a radar. Back, forth, sideways, but always coming forward again in that curious motion.

"She's still curious. If she was angry, they'd be flat back. The fact that they're swiveling means she a little nervous. But her eyes are on us. Look."

Faith's eyes kept traveling toward the carrot on Rachel's palm.

After what seemed like forever, but was probably only a few minutes, Faith took a step closer.

"Hello pretty girl," Rachel said.

The horse pricked her ears at the sound of Rachel's voice.

"Come on," Rachel said. Her voice was soft, melodic, encouraging.

Faith took another step.

Rachel leaned forward just a little bit and blew a slow breath out from between her lips. Faith's nostrils twitched, then enlarged. Rachel blew again. This time, Faith blew back a little puff of air.

"That's one way horses talk," Rachel said.

"You're talking to her?" Chris whispered. "What are you saying?"

"Hopefully that I'm a nice woman with a yummy carrot."

Chris smiled. Faith took another step until she was standing within reach. Then, slowly, she extended her head toward Rachel's palm and carefully lifted the carrot with her lips. She retreated back to chew, snorting as she went.

Rachel smiled. "Success!" she whispered.

Faith chewed, swallowed, then on her own, took a step, then a second one, toward the stall door. Rachel produced another carrot and held it palm up. Faith snorted again, her ears swiveling, then she reached forward and took it. Again, she retreated to the back of the stall to chew.

"Here," Rachel said. "My last carrot." She reached for Chris' hand. She turned it over and put the carrot on his open palm. "Keep your fingers together and your hand flat so she can't accidently get any fingers when she eats."

That would be bad, Chris thought. He did as she said so he didn't lose a finger.

Faith watched the whole thing from the safety of the back of the stall. But this time, she moved forward more confidently. She stopped when she was just out of reach.

"Blow," Rachel said.

Chris did. He felt a bit foolish, but he leaned forward just a little, like he saw Rachel do, then blew gently toward the mare. Faith responded by flaring her nostrils and blowing back. Then, she took another step and ate the carrot. This time, she stayed by the stall door while she chewed.

"Should I try to pet her?" Chris asked.

"No. Not yet," Rachel said. "This is enough for tonight."

Faith finished her carrot and looked at Chris, ears pricked. "That's all we have," he said to the horse.

She watched them expectantly for a moment or two, then walked to the back of her stall. She looked tired.

"We should go so she can rest," Rachel said. "Kim told me that the vet said that Faith is okay to spend the night alone. She's doing remarkably well."

"That's awesome," Chris said.

"Yeah. It is."

They turned and walked down the barn aisle together. Rachel turned out the light, and Chris pulled the big metal door closed behind them.

"Hey, thanks," he said when they reached their cars. "That was pretty cool. I think she's trusting us more."

Rachel unlocked her car door and barely looked at him. "Yep. Good night," she said, her voice back to that clipped manner. She opened her car door and climbed in, shutting it without another word.

She started the car and backed out, driving down the driveway without so much as a wave.

Chris sighed. Well, he had done what he could. He was happy that Faith was doing so well. It felt good to finally make a difference. He hung on to those good feelings, climbed into his car, and drove home.

"Thank you, God," he said. "Thank you for Faith. Thank you for Angel. And God, can you please be with Rachel? I think she really needs you right now."

Chapter Nine

The next morning, Rachel was having trouble staying awake during their weekly staff meeting at the counseling center. Her boss, Greta, was talking about insurance issues and new diagnostic codes, but the dull topic wasn't what was putting her to sleep. What was putting her to sleep was the fact that she had hardly slept last night.

She had been awake thinking about Chris.

If Kim was insistent that they work together, then Rachel would simply have to figure out a way to keep their past issues from bothering her. After all, she had counseled countless people about getting along with their coworkers and toughing out difficult employment situations. Chris just got to her more than he should. He was back in her life, apologizing and acting like he had changed. Well, maybe he *had*. But that didn't matter. Not to her.

She had learned the hard way not to count on people. Drew had taught her that.

The memory of her ex-husband didn't help to calm her down. She knew he certainly wasn't wasting any energy thinking about *her*. He was with his new wife, living up the coast in Traverse City. Rachel tried not to keep tabs on him, but she had looked at his Facebook page a few times. His new wife was blonde and pretty, and they looked happy together in their wedding photos. Drew certainly hadn't wasted any time.

She noticed, then, that the other counselors were leaving. She pushed back her chair and Greta held up a finger.

"Rachel? I need to go over a few things with you before you go."

Rachel sat back down. As her co-workers dispersed, she wondered what she had done wrong *now*. She liked Greta, and working here for the past five years had been a good experience. But since her divorce, and since the tragedy with one of her teens, she just couldn't seem to get her head back into her job. She was sure that Greta only had so much patience.

Greta closed the door so the two of them were alone. This was the room where Greta met with her clients. A long, green couch lined one wall, and two high back chairs sat across from it. Rachel was on the couch, so Greta took the chair across from her. The white noise machine was running, because Greta had a client coming in at 9 a.m., in just fifteen minutes. This felt more like a counseling session than a meeting with her boss.

"How are things?" Greta asked.

By "things," Rachel wondered if she meant her mother, her grief, or her job. "Things?" Rachel said. She shrugged. The motion reminded her of Boot. "Things are good."

Greta watched her closely for a moment, then changed the subject. "I want to talk about Scott's parents."

"Boot."

"What?"

"He likes to be called Boot. He's going to legally change his name when he turns eighteen."

Greta paused, as if considering remarking on that, then changed her mind. Rachel knew she was being both tolerant and patient.

"*Boot's* parents," Greta said, emphasizing the name, "want to know why they haven't seen any changes in their son. If anything, they believe he is getting worse."

Of course. When the clinic received a complaint, the problem always came from the parents. Never the kids.

"I've only been working with him for six months," Rachel said.

Greta nodded. "I know. I tried to explain to them that these things take time."

"What exactly do they think is wrong with their son that he's getting worse?" Rachel said. "What do they mean by *worse?*" She could feel her skin prickling and the heat rising to her face. She used to be able to separate her feelings better. But, nowadays, she got so angry at the parents. It seemed they all wanted a quick fix: a pill, a therapy, *anything* to make their kid more compliant, more 'normal', less weird. What they *really* wanted was something easy, because they were all taxed out with their own busy schedules and didn't have time to walk alongside their child. They didn't have the energy to parent, so they expected her to do it for them.

Greta paused, thinking carefully. She was a good counselor, and Rachel knew that in this case, Greta was on her side. "He's withdrawn and rebellious. That's all they say. And his dad is afraid that Scott— *Boot*—is gay."

Rachel snorted. Within the first two sessions, Boot had told her about three different girls he was interested in. But right now, she almost wished he *was* gay, just to spite his parents.

"Well, all of that is confidential," Rachel said. The only thing she had to reveal about her kids was if they were going to be a danger to themselves of others. "Tell them he's doing fine, and that we're making progress. Tell them to give us six more months. Or maybe three. But probably six."

Greta nodded again. "Good enough," she said. "I promised them I'd talk to you. And now I have."

Rachel started to rise, thinking she had escaped anything more personal. But Greta held up her finger again, signing her to wait.

"I noticed you've been distracted the past couple of days. Did you even hear anything I said in the meeting this morning?"

"I'm not distracted," Rachel said, then realized that by immediately going on the defensive, she had clued Greta in that she really *was* distracted. She felt herself redden. Greta knew a lot about her and had acted as a sounding board and something of a counselor to her over the past three years since Faith died and Drew left. "Maybe I was a little. There's this guy at the farm I know from high school."

Greta smiled. "A man from your past. How intriguing!"

Rachel frowned. "Not like that. He's just...he was a jerk to me in high school, and now I have to work with him at the farm."

"The farm has been your escape," Greta said. "Your safe place."

Rachel felt her phone vibrate in her pocket. Probably her mother.

"Yes," she said, reaching in to push the silence button. "It was." Rachel glanced across at Greta. She didn't want to get into a discussion about Chris. "It's not a big deal," she said dismissively, and forced a smile. "It's fine."

"Rachel, you're a very good counselor. But I need for you to be *on*. I know you've been through a lot, but you need to promise me that you're at your best. You're dealing with some pretty serious cases."

Rachel nodded. "I am. I'm at my best."

"And you would tell me if you weren't?" Greta asked.

Rachel nodded. Greta didn't linger on the subject, so Rachel was free to go. She had lost some client files last year that nearly got her fired. She had mixed them up with some older files and accidently shredded them. Before that, on two different occasions, she had overslept and missed two appointments, but Greta let it go because Rachel was grieving her divorce then. And just last month, she had scheduled two clients at the same time. Nothing big, but enough to put her on Greta's radar.

Back in her office, she looked around. She had a bookcase full of books, one plant, and a photo of

Angel on her desk. And, of course, there was the eight by ten framed print of Jon Bon Jovi that the teenagers often teased her about. She was a big fan of his music—her guilty pleasure—and she and Boot had discussed his music at length one day. Remembering the discussion made her smile. Boot had said she was only interested in him because he was a good-looking rock star, nearly her dad's age, and that was pathetic. She argued that he loved westerns and much of his music centered around cowboys, which tied to her love of horses, and that's what drew her in.

But in truth, she could admit (never to Boot!) that Bon Jovi *was* kind of handsome.

She laughed out loud.

Her phone vibrated. Another voicemail from her mom. That made four since after their chat yesterday evening. The woman was relentless. Rachel figured she'd better listen to one of them to be sure it wasn't an emergency or something. Although, it never was.

"Rachel," said her mom's voice into her ear. "I need to know about the shower gift. Please call me! My goodness, I have no idea if you are even alive or not." She could hear the irritation.

Rachel texted her.

Busy morning. I'll call you this afternoon.

She hit SEND.

The morning didn't get any better. Her 10 a.m. client was whining, and there wasn't really anything to whine about. The young woman was convinced she was depressed, but Rachel knew after five months of counseling that it was because the girl was spoiled and was no longer getting her way now that she was in college with roommates. Instead of working on depression, she needed to be learning how to handle disappointment and work well with others. But the girl didn't want to hear that. Her 11 a.m. was the overweight child of a single mother. The child ate for attention, and Rachel had been trying to get that across. But today, the mother wanted to know if insurance would pay to send her child to "one of those fat camps." Rachel wanted to explain that good meals and some attention would most likely solve the problem, but she had tried that before and the mother wouldn't listen.

Her 1 p.m. had cancelled, so she had two hours free. She decided to drive out to the farm to see Faith. She wanted some time alone with the mare, and she figured Chris would be back out there this evening. He seemed like he had gotten attached to Faith already.

Which was a strange thing. Rachel wondered when and why this self-centered guy had grown a heart.

Rachel parked her car next to a beat up Chevette. She had seen this car here, two previous times. She wondered if Kim had a new volunteer. She realized then, that she didn't know what Chris' car looked like. She tried to remember what he had climbed into last night, but she had been trying so hard not to look at him that she hadn't paid attention.

But he would surely be at work today, right?

Feeling edgy, she got out and walked to the barn. She was still dressed in the light green, cotton summer dress that she had worn to work that morning, but she had traded her flats for barn boots.

She took a deep breath, inhaling the scent of barn and horse, of the outdoors, and the freshly mown grass from Kim's lawn. The place was quiet. Kim didn't have a lot of clients during the day. Most worked or were at school. Rachel loved being at the ranch in both the middle of the day and late at night, when she could be alone with the horses.

Angel saw her and whinnied from the field next door. "Hi, Angel!" Rachel said, but didn't take the time to walk over and see her. She only had a short time before she had to be back to work, and she wanted to spend it with Faith today.

The barn was quiet and dark when she went in, but she could see there was nobody in the aisle. She was relieved that Chris wasn't there.

She walked toward Faith's stall. The five stalls before her were all empty. It was a nice day and all the horses were out.

She approached quietly and peeked in the stall.

There was Chris. His back was to the stall door, and he was carefully applying salve to Faith's side, to the places she had been cut during transport. The mare was standing quietly, letting him do it. He didn't have a halter or lead rope on her. It was just the two of them, and he was quietly talking.

"See? Doesn't that feel better?" he said, his voice just above a whisper. "I know how it feels. I've had my skin torn up pretty badly before. But this will fix you up. And then I have some sugar cubes for you."

Faith saw Rachel, and quietly perked her ears, but didn't seem to mind that she was here. Rachel didn't move or speak because she didn't want to break the bond. As annoyed as she was at seeing him here, she was thrilled that Faith was receiving the care she needed.

Chris capped the tin on the salve and ran a hand softly along the horse's neck. Faith turned her head toward him, touching him lightly with her muzzle. He turned to leave, then, and saw Rachel. He jumped, then recovered and smiled.

"I didn't hear you come in," he said.

"I just got here. I tried to be quiet. I didn't want to startle her."

Chris let himself out, locking the stall door behind him. "Kim asked me to put salve on her cuts," he said. "It took me two hours before she trusted me enough to let me touch her." He arched his back and rubbed it. "That was a long time to stand! I just stood still and finally she came to me."

Rachel took a deep breath. *She* had wanted to take care of the mare today. And he had been here *all morning?* This man who seemed so passionate and caring was not the same guy she knew in high school.

"That's nice," Rachel said.

She met his eyes briefly, then looked down at his hands. "Kim loves that salve. She says it heals anything."

"Yeah. She called me to come in this morning. She has some meetings up at the house, and Faith needed some care."

"She left you alone with her?" Rachel found this hard to believe. Chris had no idea what he was doing. He could get himself killed.

"Yes. Well, no. Keith is around some place. I think he just cut the lawn."

And now he knew the name of their landscape guy?

"You shouldn't be alone with a horse."

Chris narrowed his eyes. "But weren't you just about to be? That's why you came here, right? To see Faith?"

"That's different. I know what I'm doing."

"I was careful," Chris said. "She's not violent or anything."

Rachel's temper flared. She should have just stayed at the counseling office. "Why are you here, anyway? Don't you have a job or something?"

Chris frowned. "Why are *you* here? Don't *you* have a job?"

"I do, and I should get back to it," Rachel hissed. But first, she wanted to see Faith. "Can I have a few moments alone with her?"

Chris looked at her for a moment, but didn't challenge her. "Sure," was all he said. He turned and walked down the barn aisle.

Rachel looked at Faith. Unbidden, tears ran down her cheeks, and she angrily wiped them aside. This farm was her safe place. This was where she came when the rest of her life was getting her down. But now, Chris was here, and she didn't feel safe anymore. She didn't want him here, reminding her of her past, of what she had lost. She didn't want him here messing around with *her* horse, doing *her* duties. She knew it was ridiculous to be this jealous of a man and a horse, but she couldn't help it. She felt as if he was doing it on purpose, to see what else he could take away.

Which was ridiculous.

She wiped her eyes again and closed them, taking a few more deep breaths. She put her hands up against her face, hiding her eyes. She didn't want Chris to come back and see her crying.

She felt warm breath on her hands, then a soft, velvety muzzle rubbing against them. She opened her eyes and peeked through her fingers, and there was Faith. The mare had approached her and was now pushing her forehead up against Rachel's hands.

Rachel stood still, feeling the warmth of the mare against her. They stood there together, sharing comfort. It was as if Faith sensed Rachel's distress and wanted to offer her something in return.

In the distance, Rachel heard a car start and knew it was Chris pulling out of the lot. He was gone. She was alone, now, with her horses, at her farm. Kim was up at the house and wouldn't be back down to the barn until this evening. She used afternoons for paperwork.

The mare kept her head against Rachel's hands, then pressed her forehead against Rachel's face. Rachel closed her eyes. She could feel Faith moving, breathing, resting with her, and soon, Rachel felt her own heart rate slowing to match the calmness of the horse.

It was these horses that rescued her and loved her when no one else would. She was never good enough for anyone else. Her parents. Her ex-husband. Her friends. Her job. But here, the horses didn't judge. They didn't know what mistakes she had made or how inadequate she was. They just loved her unconditionally.

And Faith, who had no reason to ever love another human again, was showing her compassion.

Rachel slowly moved one of her hands and ran it down Faith's nose.

"Thank you," she whispered.

Faith brought her nose up to Rachel's face, and her nostrils flared slightly. Rachel breathed back into them softly. Faith pricked her ears and gently nuzzled Rachel's cheek, causing Rachel to smile.

"I love you, too," Rachel said. And suddenly, as often happened when she was at the farm, things felt right with the world.

Chapter Ten

Chris was upset. He clutched the steering wheel hard as he drove. He knew he shouldn't let Rachel's words bother him, but they did. She was clearly a hurt, angry woman set on blaming him for how miserable her life had turned out. Why should he care? Why should he care what she thought about him?

But her accusatory tone: *"Don't you have a job?"* had hit hard.

Because the fact was, no, he didn't. Not really. His gig at the hardware store was only about fifteen hours a week. Not enough to pay the bills and certainly not enough for any extras like health insurance or retirement.

His "joblessness" was one reason he was in therapy. His PTSD was so bad that if there was too much stimulation at work, too many phone calls, or people talking, or even bright, fluorescent lights, it was too much.

He had lost his last job because someone had spilled their pop. He was working as a waiter. There had been a lot of noise that day—too many demanding customers, too much stress trying to keep all the orders straight, and then the spilled pop. It was the straw the broke the camel's back. He pretended to go get a rag to wipe it up and, instead, took off his apron and walked out the back door. He had never returned.

Chris brushed the memory aside as he stopped at a red light near town. Today was not a work day, and he had no idea what he'd do now. He had planned to ask Kim if there was anything else to do at the farm, but he had let Rachel upset him. And then, he had run.

He picked up some groceries to kill time. At home, he went online to look up recipes that used chicken breast. He made an olive oil and herb marinade and put it in the fridge for later. Then he did a load of laundry, but was still restless.

He decided he needed to talk to Rachel, to get everything out in the open. It may get him kicked out of Three Hearts Ranch, but he had to take the chance. He couldn't go on like this.

He knew she'd be there tonight, working with a client. He had seen her name on the chalkboard. Before he could change his mind, he grabbed his keys and headed for his car.

She was in the arena when he arrived, working with a small, brown-haired little boy, who looked to be about ten years old. The kid was very quiet, holding tightly to Angel's mane as a woman Chris didn't know led the mare. Two side-walkers walked, one on each side of the horse, to make sure he didn't fall.

Rachel was asking the little boy to take his hands off the horse's mane and to hold them straight out beside him, like an airplane. The kid hung on tight, as if he didn't hear her.

"I have an idea," Rachel said brightly. "Why don't you hold my tennis balls for me?"

The leader stopped Angel, and Rachel dug some tennis balls out of a bucket near the door and took them to the kid. He wouldn't make eye contact with her. She stuffed a tennis ball into her pocket and reached for his hand. He didn't look at her, but he let her unfold his fingers and free them from Angel's mane, then fold them back around the tennis ball. She walked around to the other side of Angel and did the same thing with his left hand. Now the kid was sitting there, holding a tennis ball in each hand.

"Hold them out to your sides, like you're an airplane," Rachel said.

He shook his head, no.

"Come on, Timmy," she coaxed. "I know you can do it. I know how much you want to be a pilot someday. This is your chance to start training. You need to work on your balance first, before you can get in a real plane to fly it."

Her voice was gentle, encouraging.

Timmy shook his head, no, again.

Rachel nodded to the horse's handler, and she started walking Angel again, slowly. The kid opened his eye wide and looked panicked.

"You're okay," Rachel said. "Balance with your core. Remember how to tighten your tummy? I know you can do it. You've been working hard on your strength."

The kid finally looked at Rachel, then straight ahead, clutching the tennis balls in a death grip. But slowly, as the horse moved around the arena and he realized he was safe, he began to relax. By the second time around, he looked at Rachel briefly, and smiled.

"See? What did I tell you!" Rachel said. "I'm so proud of you, Timmy!"

Chris saw a woman through the observation window, her hands to her cheeks, tears in her eyes. He guessed this was Timmy's mom, and that Timmy had just crossed some milestone.

"Very good!" Rachel said. The session lasted for five more minutes, then, Rachel had brought Angel into the center of the arena. She hadn't seen Chris yet, and he was glad. He was enjoying watching her work.

"You want to dismount by yourself today?" Rachel asked, taking the tennis balls from the boy and pocketing them. Timmy hesitated, then nodded. With the help of the side walkers, he kicked his one leg free of the stirrup, swung it over the horse's back, and slowly dismounted.

"Yay!" Rachel said. "You did fantastic. You want to give Angel a treat?"

The little boy nodded again. One of the side walkers had gone to get a bucket. Rachel handed Timmy a few pieces of carrot, and he dropped them in the bucket. Then she gave him the bucket, and he set it down in front of Angel. The horse put her head in, and Chris could hear munching.

Timmy's mom came out and talked to Rachel in low tones for a moment, while Timmy and the side walkers fed Angel more pieces of carrot. Then, Timmy's mom smiled and hugged Rachel.

"I'll see you next week!" Rachel called, waving to Timmy and his mom as they left. That was when she saw Chris standing by the door. Her expression darkened immediately.

"Let's talk," he said to her.

"I have nothing to say." She turned her attention to the woman who had been leading Angel. "You can put her in her stall, Kara. Thanks!"

Chris walked into the arena, meeting her in the middle. They were alone now.

"You asked why I was here today," he said. "You asked if I had a job. The answer is no, I don't really have a job, not a proper full-time job, which is why I was here all morning. I work about fifteen hours a week down at the hardware store, where this nice old man named Mr. B puts up with my anxiety disorder by pretending not to notice. I've lost every other job I've had since I've been back from Afghanistan. *Every single job.* I don't like noise. I don't like people. I don't like enclosed rooms or stress or too much stimulation like music and cash registers beeping. I can't focus enough to do anything serious, like engineering or math or even writing. So, right now, I'm doing the best I can at the hardware store by working with my hands. I find things for people, and I offer advice on tools."

Rachel started to say something, but he interrupted her.

"So I'm here for therapy for anxiety, or PTSD, or whatever you want to call it," he said. "You *know* that, and yet you insist on hating me every single minute no matter what I do or say, regardless of the fact that any sort of confrontation makes me antsy and puts me on the defensive. So in fact, you are hurting my recovery."

He saw her eyes change then, and, for a moment, there was sympathy. But it was gone the next instant.

"You were always so good at being smooth, at getting whatever you wanted," she said. "How do I know you're not back at your old games?"

"Because the old Chris is gone," he said. "He died in the desert when the Humvee blew up, and it took six months in a hospital, feeling sorry for myself and wanting to die, then another several months drowning those sorrows in alcohol, before I realized how loved I am. And so are you. God *loves* you, Rachel. Whatever happened to you, whatever you believe, that doesn't have to be your story. God loves you."

She snorted. "That's what changed you? *God?*"

"Yes. I made Jesus my Lord and Savior."

"That hardly fixed you if you're still so stressed." She regretted the words as soon as she said them.

"I'm not fixed. I'm *loved*. That makes all the difference."

Just then, Rachel's phone rang. The tone was "You make me crazy," by the BAND.

She yanked it out of her pocket and answered it.

"Mom," she said. "I texted you that now is not a good time. I have a session."

He could hear a muffled voice on the other end but couldn't tell what it was saying. Rachel's mouth was set in a hard line.

"I told you I can't make it," Rachel said.

More muffled conversation on the other end.

"Mom," Rachel said. She turned so Chris couldn't see her face. "I don't want to. Fine. You get something, and I'll pay you for it."

More conversation.

"You *know* why." He saw her shoulders tensing up. "I'm *not* feeling sorry for myself. Yes, I'm happy for my brother. Mom, I'm at work. I have to go. Bye."

She hung up. There was a log silence, but she finally turned around.

"My mom," she said.

"I remember her," Chris said. "Sounds like she hasn't changed."

That got a little smile from Rachel. "She's upset that I'm not helping my sister more with baby shower stuff. Then, she actually asked if I was going to show up at the shower! Of course I'm *going*. She's my sister! And this little girl will be my niece."

"Sounds cute," Chris said. "Babies and all. My brother has three kids. Remember him?"

"Yes," she said. "He was the nice kid in the family."

"He still is," Chris said.

Rachel's phone beeped with a text. She looked down at it, then her face turned a dark red and she crammed the phone in her pocket.

"Chris…just leave me alone. I need to go."

She walked out of the arena at a fierce pace, and turned down the barn aisle.

"Rachel, wait!" He trotted after her, wanting to catch her before she left. But, instead of heading for the parking lot, Rachel was walking toward Faith's stall. There, she crossed her arms on the top of the stall door and put her head on them.

He stopped and watched her from a distance for a few moments. They were the only ones on that side of the barn, and it was quiet. He could see Faith standing a foot or two back, watching Rachel, her ears swiveling back and forth.

Then he saw Rachel's shoulders shaking, and he heard a sob.

Whatever she had seen on that text had upset her. He walked up the aisle toward her.

"Hey," he said, and stood beside her. Faith turned her eyes to him, and her nostrils quivered. She was sniffing, wondering if he had brought any treats.

"You okay?" he asked Rachel.

She shrugged but didn't lift her face from her arms.

"Was it that text? Should I go get Kim?" He didn't know what to do. What if somebody had died, or maybe a boyfriend had broken up with her?

Rachel shook her head. Keeping her head on one arm, she pulled her phone out of her pocket and handed it to him. There was a text with a photo. He peered at it. It was an ad from a store for a crib decorated in pinks. It looked like some kind of a butterfly pattern on the material. Pastel butterflies. Above it, the text said: We're going to get them this. What do you think?

"So...you hate the crib set?" he said.

She made a noise, which he took to be a muffled laugh. She lifted her head, wiped her eyes with her hands, and turned to look at him.

"I do," she said.

"Pink butterflies aren't your thing," he said. He handed her the phone back. "But I assume there's more to the story?"

She nodded. "My husband left me," she said. "He hung in there for a while, and I thought he loved me. We both really wanted kids. I love them, I love working with them, and I had always wanted my own. So did he. We planned a big family…"

The tears started coming again. She wiped them with her sleeve. Then she fished into her pocket and came up with a tissue. She blew her nose.

"He left me," she said. "He's already remarried to some blonde he met at work."

Chris didn't know what to say. He settled on, "I'm so sorry."

"And my sister got pregnant right away. She had this awesome career going and didn't want a baby for a few years, and this one was unplanned. But they're so happy anyway. And she's even thinking of going to part time work so she can stay home with her. It's a little girl. I want to be happy for them, but my mom keeps pushing all of this on me…and I just don't…I can't…"

She started weeping then, really crying. Chris wasn't too good at emotions, so he stood there awkwardly, wondering what he should do. It seemed she needed a hug. So he reached out and put his arm around her, drawing her into him. She pressed her face up against his chest and cried.

He felt warm breath against his right arm, and it was Faith, pressing her nose against them, nuzzling at Rachel's hair.

Rachel laughed again, pulling back, and rubbing Faith gently on her nose. "Sweet girl," Rachel said.

She seemed to realize then that she was in Chris' arms, and she backed away. "I'm sorry," she said. "I don't know what came over me. It's just a stupid baby shower. And it's a couple's shower, which is even more stupid."

She wiped her eyes again, then turned to the horse. "Faith is really sweet."

"Sounds like he was a real jerk," Chris said.

"Who? My ex-husband?"

"Yes."

"Well, I wasn't in my best frame of mind when he left. He was as patient with me as one could expect."

"Love is patient, love is kind," Chris said, quoting the verse from Corinthians.

"Well, *his* love was neither," Rachel said.

"Love is supposed to be forever."

Rachel turned to him. "Who *are* you? And what happened to the Chris I knew from high school?"

"A lot happened to that Chris," he said. "I'm different, Rachel. I need for you to believe that."

"So, tell me," she said, "tell me what happened."

He sighed. He hated to talk about it. But he felt the Holy Spirit prompting him. Rachel was hurting, and she needed to know she wasn't alone. There was really no way to share his story about Christ, without sharing what brought him there.

"Okay," he said. "I guess I'll start at the beginning. Why don't you have a seat?"

Chapter Eleven

Rachel sat in the white plastic chair next to Faith's stall, and wiped her eyes with a tissue she found in her pocket. There was another chair across the aisleway, and Chris pulled it over next to her chair. Before he started talking, he reached into his pocket for a plastic bag of sugar cubes. Faith's eyes lit up, and she started working her mouth, salivating. He took one out of the bag and held it to her in his palm. Rachel noticed that he kept his fingers pressed close together like she had taught him. Faith didn't even hesitate. The mare gently plucked it from his hand and stood there chewing.

Chris sat down, leaning back against the stall door. Her chair was angled a little bit toward him. She watched him while he told her about his life after high school, how he had gone off to Grand Valley to play football on a scholarship, with plans to study sports medicine. There was something different about this Chris from the boy she knew in high school. His voice was softer, his eyes less confident.

"I got carried away with partying," he said. "My grades dropped and by sophomore year I was off the team. I got caught underage drinking at a party."

He came home and got a job at the bottle-making factory. He spent the evenings after work at the local bar, hanging out with the boys. He often went home with a girl.

"I was a jerk," Chris said. "But I was also a mess. I felt like a failure, and I carried around all this guilt. I was mean to so many people and used them to get where I was. I didn't even earn my football scholarship the right way. I had terrible grades and I was caught drinking more than a few times. Both of those should have gotten me kicked off of the high school team. That would have ruined my chances of a college scholarship. But because I had talent, everyone looked the other way."

"And charm," Rachel said quietly. "You had that charm."

Chris nodded. "Yeah. I had charm back then. And I took advantage of that too."

"I know," she said.

"About that—"

She cut him off. "So what happened?"

He looked at his hands for a moment, as if ashamed of the memory of how he had treated her, as if he wanted to say something else. But he continued with his story. "What happened is that I lost my job at the factory," he said. "At this point, my parents had had it with me. They told me I wouldn't get any more chances. So they kicked me out."

"Tough love," Rachel said.

"Tough love. I lived for a few months with a buddy of mine in Lansing and waited tables. He had friends come over on the weekends to play cards. One of them was in the army. We talked, and he kept telling me how awesome it was and how it paid for his college tuition. I could never imagine myself in the army, with people telling me what to do. But, then I drank too much one night, overslept, and lost my job at the restaurant. My buddy told me if I didn't pay rent, I'd have to move on. I was smart enough to figure out I needed to change my ways. So, I joined the army the next day."

"That was when?"

"Four years ago."

Rachel was twenty-six then. Still married. Working at the clinic.

"And they sent you to war," she said.

"Yeah."

Faith was getting impatient and nickered loudly. Chris pulled out another sugar cube and held up his hand, offering it to her. She ate it happily.

"I was deployed to Afghanistan," Chris said. "Joining the army was a good move. I stayed sober, worked hard, and didn't have much time to get into trouble. But I had regrets, and I carried those with me. I regretted how I had treated people. How I lied to get ahead. How I threw away my college scholarship." He looked at her. "And, I regretted how I had treated you."

Rachel swallowed and looked away.

Chris cleared his throat. "So, I was in Afghanistan, and I was pretty close to the guys in my platoon, and one guy in particular. His name was Freddie and he was a Christian. He was from Arkansas and had this cool accent." Chris smiled at the memory. "He played a mean game of gin rummy. We talked a lot, and he told me about his family and his life growing up on a farm. And about Jesus. He talked a lot about Jesus. He said that Christ offered us salvation and forgiveness from our sins, and that we could accept that gift and start over. One night, we were huddled in a shelter, with a bomb raid going off outside, and Freddie asked me if I wanted to make Christ lord of my life. I did. Right then and there surrounded by bombing, I prayed and accepted Jesus into my life. And it changed me."

Rachel didn't know what to think about that. Her grandma had been a church-goer, but her own family rarely went. After all that had happened to her, she had given up on God. She never attended church herself, and she couldn't remember the last time she had prayed.

"Then…" Chris cleared his throat again. Faith leaned her head over the stall door and bumped his arm playfully, as if reminding him that she was there. He smiled and pulled out another sugar cube. This time he handed it to Rachel. She noticed his hands were trembling. She stood up, took the sugar cube, and offered it to Faith. The mare munched contentedly.

"Then, a few days later, we got called out to a town to clean up after a raid," Chris said. "On the way there, our Humvee was attacked. A firebomb… it flipped us, and the explosion killed four of the six of us instantly. Me and Ralphie, another one of my friends, were rushed out of there ,and Ralphie died on the way. I'm the only one who made it. Freddie was driving. He was killed instantly."

Rachel kept her eyes on Faith. Her own life was difficult, but to go through that…to see your friends die so violently, must have been awful.

"I'm sorry," she said quietly.

"It's okay," Chris said. "I was a mess for a while. But I know where Freddie is, and I know I'll see him again someday. That was a consolation to his parents when I talked with them."

Chris sighed and stood. They watched the mare. The barn was quiet. A few birds chirped outside.

"So, I regret how I treated you, and I'm sorry," Chris said.

Rachel felt tears in her eyes again. She had been waiting to hear those words for nine years. And she believed he meant them. "You need to quit apologizing," Rachel said. "And I've been unfair. I've blamed you for so much," she said. "I was so angry at seeing you again. It just brought everything back."

Faith asked for another sugar cube. Chris pulled one out and offered it to Rachel. She shook her head. "Your turn."

He fed the mare, who crunched it and immediately asked for more by nuzzling his arm.

"So, you met your ex at college?" he asked.

"Yes."

"And you went there because your parents pulled your funding from the University of Michigan?"

Rachel nodded. "I lost the full scholarship they were offering me."

"Because of *me*."

Again, she nodded, keeping her eyes on the horse.

"So, basically, if I hadn't messed up your graduation, you'd have gone to Michigan and never met your ex. So you blame me for the way your marriage turned out."

She smiled. "I actually blame you for the way my *entire life* turned out. Crazy, huh?"

"Not really. I blame me for a lot of things too."

He laughed, and she laughed with him, but she felt a pang of sadness at his words. He was hurting, and she had been adding to that hurt.

Kim's voice called out, startling them.

"Rachel? Can you come to the house for a minute? I have to tell you something." Kim was standing at the end of the barn aisle, silhouetted by the outdoor light. Her hands were on her hips. "You too, cowboy. Come with her. I may need you both."

Chapter Twelve

Chris looked at Rachel and raised an eyebrow in question, wondering what Kim wanted with them. Rachel shrugged, but she looked worried as she walked up the barn aisle beside him and out into the bright sunshine.

Chris heard Faith whinny after them. "She misses us already," he said.

"Yes. It's a miracle. She's doing amazingly well both physically and mentally."

Kim's back screen door squeaked as they walked through. Chris had been inside briefly when he filled out the insurance papers. Kim had interviewed him about why he was here and what he wanted out of the program. He had sat at her kitchen table and wondered about the mess. Now, he understood why Kim had so many papers and stacks around her kitchen. She was running this business alone and had little time for anything else. Even tidying.

Kim handed each of them a bottled water and motioned for them to sit at her little kitchen table. She took a chair across from them. She smiled, causing creases around her eyes, and Chris saw how tired she looked. Then, she ran her hand through her short, graying brown hair, leaving it a mess.

"You're both doing a remarkable job with Faith," Kim said. "The vet was here this morning to check up on her, and she allowed Dr. Tremper to come right inside her stall and touch her."

"Faith is amazing," Chris said. "She really seems to want to be friends with us."

"It's true," Rachel said. "She lets us hand-feed her now, and she even whinnied after us when we left."

Kim picked up a pen that was laying on the table and started clicking it. "The vet said her skin sores are healing well. If you have a time today, can you wash off her legs? Maybe tomorrow the two of you can give her a full bath. Then, we can see what color she really is."

Chris thought bathing a horse sounded like quite a job. He glanced at Rachel, but she was watching Kim closely.

"So, what's the real reason you called us in here?" Rachel said.

Kim sighed and put the pen down. Then she picked it up again and opened a notebook that was in front of her. There were columns of numbers down the page. It looked like a ledger.

"I guess I'll just come out and say it," Kim said. She glanced down at the notebook, then closed it and looked across the table at them. "I'm about to lose the farm," she said.

"What?" Rachel leaned forward. "I mean...I know you're not getting some of the insurance claims but..."

Kim interrupted her. "That's not all. Remember last month when that man came here to discuss licensing?" Kim turned to Chris to explain. "We lost two of our counselors last spring. We operate here on a tight budget so many of them are underpaid or volunteer, like Rachel. They moved on to greener pastures, and I can't blame them. They needed a paycheck."

She sighed again. "So, he said I need more licensed counselors for what I'm doing. A certified riding instructor isn't enough. I can't afford to hire anybody. And then there are the vet bills from this spring."

Rachel turned to Chris. "A few months ago, we had some bad horse care. Kim had hired this guy to feed in the mornings so the horses would be ready for our first clients at 8 a.m. He came to feed in a hurry a few times on his way to his other job and only gave them hay and not their grain. We didn't know until we saw they were losing weight. Our poor horses were working all day without much breakfast."

"And that lowered their immunity," Kim said.

"Kim talked to him about increasing their grain a little bit, and I guess he felt he was about to get busted. So, the next day, he *did* give them their grain, but it had sat for so long unused, and water had gotten into it from a leak in the roof above. The grain soured and the horses got sick. Plus, their stomachs weren't used to such a rich diet after several weeks of not getting any grain."

"Several of them foundered and got colic. Two had to be put down," Kim said.

"And the rest...well, the vet treated a dozen horses so you can only imagine the costs," Rachel said. "We're still paying off the bills."

"Geez," Chris said. He couldn't believe the cruelty of people. You'd think after a stint at war he'd no longer be surprised when humanity showed their worst side. But he was. "So what happened to the guy who made them sick?"

"Kim is in a law suit, but that costs legal fees, and it doesn't look like we'll get anything. He lives in a trailer and doesn't have a good job."

"And now the state is going to close us down if we don't hire another counselor," Kim said. "Our workload is too heavy for our staff."

"There has to be a specific ratio of caregivers to clients," Rachel said. "I'm only here very part time."

The three of them were quiet. Chris didn't know what to say, but he had this strange, panicky feeling in the pit of his stomach at never seeing Faith again. "What will happen to the horses?"

Kim shrugged. "We'll have to find them homes."

"Can't you sell some of them to get some money?" Chris asked.

Rachel laughed. "Most of our horses are rescues. Nobody will want them. You'd have to *pay* people to take them!" Rachel rubbed her face. "Oh Kim, I'm so sorry. There has to be something we can do."

"I have four weeks to come up with the mortgage money and, if we want to continue equine-assisted therapy, to hire a full-time, licensed counselor," she said.

"Or…" Rachel said.

"Or I have to foreclose and shut down the business."

Her words hung in the air of the little kitchen. Chris propped his elbows on the table and put his head in his hands. What a mess. He had finally found a place that was starting to make him feel safe and now…? Now he was going to lose it?

"What can we do to help?" he said. "You said you may need our help."

Kim opened her notebook again. She hesitated as she looked at the numbers on her page. "Chris, I thought maybe you could find us someone who can do some repairs around here for cheap. Since you work at the hardware store."

"What needs to be done?"

"Fence repair. Odd jobs, like the wheelchair ramp needs some work, and one of our wheelbarrows has a broken axle. The tractor needs some oil. Stuff like that."

"I can do that," Chris said. He liked to be outside, working with his hands, and he had helped his dad work on cars a lot. He had also done a lot of repair work in the army. Things broke, and sometimes you had to fix them with what you had on hand.

"Really?" Kim said. She looked grateful, but also like she had hoped he would say that. "I can't pay you much."

"We'll work it out," Chris said.

Kim looked at Rachel. "I need a counselor. I know your day job is demanding and you work full time and then you volunteer here. But I was wondering if you might be able to put in some hours on Saturdays?"

"Sure," Rachel said, without hesitation.

"I know Saturdays are your day off," Kim said. She looked at Chris. "Rachel is here most evenings, so I hate to take her weekend away from her."

"It's okay," Rachel said. "I love being here."

"I can't pay you," Kim said. "Not at all."

Rachel laughed. "So, I'm getting a raise on my current salary?"

"A one hundred percent raise on what you are currently making," Kim said.

"You know that doesn't matter," Rachel said. "I want to help."

"Thanks, guys," Kim said. "I appreciate it. Hopefully it will only be for a few weeks until I can get some more clients or some income another way." She closed her notebook and stood, signaling that the meeting was over.

Chris took a swig of his water bottle and screwed the cap back on. He stood. "Well, if we're finished here, let's go wash off Faith's legs. I want to see what she looks like under all that mud."

Chris watched as Rachel carefully put the halter on Faith. The mare stood quietly and allowed it to be buckled on her head. It was like she understood that they weren't going to hurt her, that they were only here to help her. Faith even lowered her head a little bit to make it easier for Rachel to buckle on the halter.

Chris opened the stall door, and Rachel slowly led Faith out. The mare was still very weak and seemed shaky on her feet as she walked. The mud and manure caked on her legs probably didn't help the situation.

Stepping carefully on her sore feet, Faith followed them outside. The evening was warm. They went around to the back of the barn. There was a faucet with a hose attached and a poured concrete slab about twelve by twelve feet in size with a drain in the middle of it. A green bucket stood next to the faucet and contained what looked like an assortment of brushes and a shampoo bottle. There was a rack above that with several towels hanging from it. The whole area was apparently made for washing horses down.

Rachel handed Chris the lead rope. "Hold her while I adjust the water."

He took the rope. Faith stood quietly, breathing a little heavier just from her walk. Her head hung low, as if her body was too tired to hold it up.

Rachel turned the water on low, and it made a hissing sound as air blew out of the hose. Faith jerked her head up, her eyes wild.

"It's okay," said Chris. He didn't know what to do, but instinctively, he put his hand on her neck and stroked her. She edged closer to him until her shoulder was right up against his. It was the equivalent of a cuddle. Apparently, he made her feel safe, and she wanted his protection. He smiled. It felt good to be needed.

Rachel adjusted the water so it was coming out at just a little more than a trickle, then held the hose up for Faith to investigate. The mare stretched her neck out and snorted at it, then must have decided it was okay because she started to relax again. Rachel let the water run on the cement and slowly moved it closer until it was running on Faith's front legs. Faith didn't seem to mind.

"Let's just wash her legs today, like Kim suggested,' Rachel said. "I don't want to reopen the sores on her body. Plus, it's evening, and she'll get cold if her whole body is wet."

Chris nodded. "She doesn't have a lot of fat on her to keep her warm."

Rachel pulled a brush out of the green bucket, along with a bottle of shampoo. She squeezed a little of the shampoo onto her brush and started to gently scrub Faith's right front leg. Faith stood quietly, her head down a little bit.

Slowly, the dirt and manure started to come off. Rachel rinsed and then shampooed the leg again. This time, when she rinsed, Chris could see a white stocking running up to Faith's knee. Above that was a golden color.

Rachel took her time and scrubbed all four of Faith's legs. Then, she turned the water off and grabbed a towel from the rack. "Want to dry?" she said.

Chris nodded and exchanged the lead rope for the towel. He carefully wiped down all four of Faith's legs while Rachel held onto the mare. The hair was shiny and clean, a stark comparison to the rest of the horse. When he was done, he stood back to have a look. Faith's hair was a beautiful golden color, and all four of her legs had long white markings up to her knees.

"She's pretty," he said.

Rachel was smiling. "She sure is. She's a palomino, with four white socks. And I think she has a white star on her forehead. Wait until we get her mane and tail washed. You'll see how pretty they are. They'll be a cream color, almost a white."

Faith's head was hanging low, and she was resting her hind foot, the toe tilted up.

"That's how they stand when they sleep," Rachel explained, noticing he was looking at her back leg. "She's very relaxed."

Chris hung the towel up on the rack to dry. Rachel handed him the lead rope. "Why don't you take her back to her stall?"

He nodded. Faith pricked her ears and gave Chris a playful bump with her nose.

He laughed. "I'm starting to see why you love these creatures so much."

"Horses are awesome," Rachel said.

He led Faith back to her stall. He noticed Kim had cleaned it out while they were gone and put fresh straw down. Faith sniffed at it, then stuck her nose in her food bucket.

"She's hungry," Rachel said. "*Again!* I'll go get her some hay."

Chris stayed with the horse. He slipped the halter off her head, and Faith pressed her forehead up against his chest. The warm contact felt good, and he wanted to put his arms around her big neck, but he was afraid he'd startle her.

He thought about what Kim had said and wondered what would happen to Faith if the farm went under. Would anybody else be this patient with her? Would she trust anyone other than Rachel and him?

Chris sighed, trying to push those worries away. God had a plan, and he would have to trust in the Lord to make it all okay. God worked all things together for those who loved Him. That's what the Bible promised.

He closed his eyes and said a prayer for Faith, whose forehead was still pressed against his. The horse's eyes were closed, as if she too were praying. The two of them were standing that way when Rachel came back with the hay.

Chapter Thirteen

The next day, Rachel sat in Greta's office, twirling the shoe on the end of her foot. She had slipped off the flat and it hung carelessly on her toe, where she dangled it while Greta talked. She recalled that her high school English teacher used to do this, and it brought a smile to her face. She had always loved English class. Maybe she should have been an English teacher.

"Are you even listening to me?" Greta said. Rachel stirred from her memories and peered across the coffee table at Greta. She was back on the couch, which was a bit too deep for her. She felt lost in it. On the coffee table was a box of tissue and a small crystal candy dish that held red and white striped mints. She preferred chocolate.

She sighed loudly before she realized that was rude. "Yes, I heard everything you said. Boot's parents are only giving me two more weeks with him. That's not enough time. You and I both know that."

Greta was watching her carefully, and, for a moment, she reminded Rachel of Kim. Was everybody forever analyzing her? Was she that messed up?

Now Greta was playing the silence game. All good therapists knew that if you remained silent long enough, the empty space would grow uncomfortable and the client would talk. Well, Rachel could play at that game. So they started at each other for a good minute. Maybe a minute and a half.

"Fine," Greta said, a slight smile playing at her lips. Rachel knew she had won the game, and tried to hide her own smile. "Use your two weeks wisely."

Rachel nodded and stood, smoothing her skirt.

Back in her own clinic room, she closed the door and sat down at her desk. She sighed. "What now?"

Then she spied the Bible shelved on her bookcase, among her psychology books. Her grandmother had given it to her a few months before she died. Rachel went and pulled it off the shelf, blowing the dust off of it. She had loved her grandmother, but at the time she had just given it a cursory flip through the pages, then put it away. What did she need with a Bible?

She set it on her desk and opened the cover. On the inside, her grandmother had written, *Faith can move mountains.*

She started turning pages. There was nothing else spectacular about the book. It was leather-bound in mahogany, the pages thin. There were no bookmarks. No letters tucked inside.

She started to flip through it rather quickly, then saw a verse underlined in blue pen.

Jesus replied, "Because you have so little faith. Truly I tell you, if you have faith as small as a mustard seed, you can say to this mountain, 'Move from here to there,' and it will move. Nothing will be impossible for you." — Matthew 17:20

Faith. That word—that name—seemed to be everywhere these days.

She turned a few more pages and saw another underlined verse. The line was shaky, like her grandmother's hands had been unsteady when she drew it.

"Now faith is confidence in what we hope for and assurance about what we do not see." – Hebrews 11:1

And one more:

"And the prayer offered in faith will make the sick person well; the Lord will raise them up. If they have sinned, they will be forgiven." – James 5:15.

She flipped through the rest of the pages to the end, and found three more, all verses about faith.

She closed the Bible and sat there for a moment, wondering why her grandmother had focused on that particular topic.

She heard the front door of the clinic chime. Someone's client had arrived. She glanced at the clock.

It was lunch time, so she put the Bible back on the shelf and went into the small kitchenette that served as their break room. She pulled her salad out of the fridge. She had made it last night, along with a sliced apple and a chocolate chip cookie.

"It's not a low-carb lunch if you eat cookies," her mother had told her many times. But it *was*. Rachel figured it was low carb if you avoided bread and croutons so you could *have* the cookie. Why did she eat low carb anyway? It was something her mother had brainwashed into her for years and years, and she had always thought it was the way to go. Maybe she'd order a pizza for dinner. She poured the vinaigrette over her salad and stirred it. She ticked off her failures in her head. Boot's parents wanted another therapist if she didn't produce results in two weeks. She had a twelve-year old girl she seemed to be getting nowhere with. It was discouraging.

Sure, there were positives. Her eating disorder kid was doing better. The little boy who was getting bullied and acting out had found other ways to channel his anger, and his parent had listened to her and put him in another school where he seemed to be thriving.

But what was she doing? Her work used to mean so much to her, but for the past two years, her heart just wasn't into things here. She felt numb. She had once likened herself to someone just passing the time. But passing the time until *what?*

Was that why her grandmother had underlined so many verses about faith? Was she trying to work through something, passing time, and looking forward?

Rachel thought of Chris and what he had said about God. Did she really believe in God anymore? After her marriage dissolved, her own womb was barren, and the beautiful young teen girl she had failed….

But Chris said that God loved her. That she could rewrite her story.

She thought about his hand touching hers when he handed her the sugar cube. His hands were so warm and strong. He was still as good looking as he had been in high school, only better. More filled out and manly.

She remembered one time he had picked her up first on their way to a party. By that time, she had been hanging out with him for about two months. Oh, how she wanted him to kiss her! But, for some reason, he had never tried. He was so carefree with other girls and always had at least two fawning over him. She knew he had had several girlfriends.

He probably didn't think she was cute.

She had worked extra hard that night to look good. She had on her favorite jeans and a soft angora sweater that she loved because it was both warm *and* accentuated her curves. It was the same blue as her eyes, and she knew she looked good in it.

She had curled her hair, then run her fingers through the waves so they were soft and broken apart, giving her hair more body.

She had put her makeup on carefully. Not too much, so it looked like she was trying. But enough to bring out her eyes and lips.

It was dark when Chris picked her up. She had started getting a ride there with her friend Emma, who worked evenings at the Coney Island. She had lied and told her mom she was going to Emma's house for a few hours to do homework. Emma dropped her off at school, where Chris picked her up.

It wasn't that she didn't want her parents to meet Chris. It was just too complicated to explain why she was hanging out with him. They weren't dating, just "hanging," so she wasn't sure at this point what to call him.

"What do you have for us tonight?" he asked, giving her his thousand dollar grin. His green eyes sparkled.

She pulled the bottle of whisky out from under her jacket. Her dad had a heavily stocked cabinet and she had chosen one in the back. It would take a while before he missed it.

"All right!" he said and gave her a high five. Sometimes she thought maybe he only hung out with her for the booze she provided.

He put his car in gear and peeled out of the parking lot. The pressure forced her against the seat, and she laughed.

"Where we going tonight?" she asked. It was too cold to be outside at the park, and Rob's parents were up at the cabin.

"Sean's parents are on a ski trip, and he and his sister have the house to themselves. We're going there."

The house was a small little bungalow on the outskirts of town. Sean met them at the door. Music was playing inside. Chris' friends Sean and Brogan were there with their girlfriends. Jessica, a cheerleader, and a few of her friends were also there, and one girl Rachel didn't recognize. Chris always invited somebody new, as if he were "trying" people out.

The night went like most others. A little drinking. Sean lighting up his joint and passing it around. A bit of music. Brogan and Katie were in the living room making out on the couch. But nothing bad. Nothing she felt uncomfortable with. That's why she kept coming. Tonight, she and Chris were sitting together on the couch, just about a foot apart.

Jessica may have had a little too much to drink that night. She came over and sat down in between Rachel and Chris, practically sitting on Rachel's lap so that she had to scoot over or get squished.

"Hey, handsome," Jessica said to Chris. She twisted a strand of her long, blonde hair around her finger and batted her eyelashes at him.

"Hey, beautiful," Chris said. He was feeling pretty good. Chris didn't usually smoke pot, but he had tried some tonight. His eyes were a little droopy and he was relaxed.

Then, without warning, Jessica leaned in and kissed Chris on the lips. He didn't seem surprised at all and leaned into it.

Rachel saw his hand come around and brace Jessica at the small of her back as she turned into him for a deeper kiss. Something came over Rachel then. Jessica's left hip was still on Rachel's leg. She swung her leg aside and sent Jessica toppling down on her bottom.

"Ow!" Jessica said, rubbing her hip. "What happened?"

Rachel shrugged. Jessica climbed unsteadily to her feet, and Sean came to help her. They went in search of more beer.

"I was in the middle of something nice," Chris said, leaning back into the couch. "Something..." his voice trailed off. His green eyes met hers. Rachel scooted over closer to him.

"Something?" she said softly. She was close enough so she could whisper it.

132

"Yeah…" His lock of sand-colored hair fell over his left eye. Gosh, he was handsome!

The usual cocky, sparkling look in his eyes turned serious.

"Rachel," he said. His words were a little slurred. "You're…beautiful."

And he leaned toward her.

She closed her eyes just as his lips touched hers. The world suddenly stood still. The music, the other voices, the smell of alcohol and pot, all faded into the distance. All she knew was that Chris Adler was kissing her, and his lips were amazing.

He gently pulled back, watching for her reaction. She wanted more, but wasn't sure how to ask. What did this mean? Did he really like her, or was she just another girl to Chris Adler? She had imagined this moment for months. She thought about it when she got dressed in the morning. She thought about when she went to bed at night, and, as she closed her eyes, she often pretended they had been kissing. And every time she saw him in school, and he gave her his charming grin, she thought about it then. About what it would be like to be kissed by Chris Adler, Winchester High School's golden boy.

Did he think of her like she thought of him?

She didn't care at the moment. She wanted more.

She started to lean toward him again, when he suddenly turned a funny color and his eyes got big.

"Gotta go!" he said, and made a beeline for the bathroom, where she heard him throwing up.

Lovely.

But despite the fact that he vomited, despite the fact that he didn't seem to remember anything the next day, Rachel had seen the look in his eyes when he kissed her. It wasn't the haughty entitled look he had with the other girls. It was different.

She meant something to him. Or, at least, that's what she told herself.

Until the night he turned on her.

Chapter Fourteen

Chris was at the hardware store shelving cans of paint. He found the weight of them comforting, and as he shelved the thirty-odd cans according to their brands, he was starting to feel the nice serotonin effects of a workout.

He started to whistle. It had been a while since he had whistled, a habit he had picked up in the army while doing mundane chores in basic training. Sometimes, he whistled a modern tune. Sometimes, he whistled the hymns that he was learning at church. He loved the old-fashioned ones the best. Today it was *Amazing Grace*.

Mr. Burton, the store's owner, came shuffling down the aisle. He was arthritic. His back ached and his hands were often swollen, but he was always in a good mood.

"When you get a chance, I need two one-gallon cans mixed up with this," he said, and handed Chris an index-sized card with a paint sample on it. "It's for their living room."

Chris put the last can on the shelf and took the card. The color was dark cranberry. He imagined a man-cave with a rifle-case and leather couches.

"I think that's too dark for a living room," said Mr. B. "Maybe a den or a basement, but not a living room."

In his head, Chris then replaced the man-cave with a family. Now, he imagined an entire family enclosed the darkness of the room, the kids needing lights to do their homework at 3 p.m. when the sun was still out. He shook his head.

"Beats me," he said. "I'm not an interior decorator."

He grabbed two cans of eggshell and followed Mr. B back up the aisle and to the counter where he would add the dye and mix it. While Mr. B went through the accounting book, Chris measured the color, added it to the paint, put the top back on, and put it on the mixer.

"Nice day, outside," Mr. B said to make conversation.

"Mmmhmm," Chris said, watching the paint can shake. The two of them didn't talk a lot. Sometimes Mr. B would tell him stories from the early days of the store, when his father owned it, and he was just a kid. But mostly, the two of them worked in companionable silence. Which was just fine with Chris. He preferred it that way.

"When you finish with the paint, help me move that ladder, will ya?" Mr. B asked.

Chris nodded. He had used it earlier to stack the extra flower pots up on the top shelves for Mr. B and it was still out.

The bell over the door rang, and four construction workers came in. They were wearing their hardhats, the unbuckled chin straps dangling under their chins. They each had on bright orange safety vests and brown work boots. Chris recognized them as some of the men who had been working on the new building across the street. He sometimes took his break on the bench out front and watched them work. They had made a lot of progress very quickly.

"Hello, fellas," said Mr. B. "Can I help you find something?"

"We're just here for more nails and a ½-inch screwdriver. Ted here dropped his someplace in the dirt and that sucker's gone."

The man who was presumably Ted said something Chris didn't hear, and they all laughed.

"Down aisle three," said Mr. B.

They heard the men laughing and joking as they walked along. "How many construction workers does it take to buy a package of nails?" one of them said.

"Four!" answered another. "One to buy the nails and the other three to keep him company—"

"—and buy the cold pop!"

They roared with laughter, and Chris and Mr. B looked at each other and shook their heads.

"They're in a good mood," Chris said. Mr. B agreed. Their laughter seemed really loud after the long morning of silence in the store. The paint had finished mixing, and Chris took it off the machine. He popped the lid off to see if the color matched the card sample. It did.

"When you finish that, can you walk back and help out the ladies in the fertilizer aisle?" Mr. B asked. "They've been there awhile. I don't think they know what they're looking for."

"Sure. But I should move that ladder first." Chris set the lid back on and reached for the soft mallet to tap it on tight as the four construction workers came up to the counter with their box of nails. They were still laughing and teasing one another, this time about somebody's girlfriend. The man named Ted, who apparently took the brunt of the jokes, pulled off his hard hat and playfully swung it at another man's shoulder in mock hitting. The man stepped back, and bumped into the ladder that had been sitting up against the counter, knocking it over. It landed on the linoleum floor with a deafening crash.

The noise startled Chris, who had his back to them. He jumped, spinning around to face the noise, and knocked over the paint can. Cranberry red spilled down the counter onto the beige linoleum floor beneath.

"Oh, man, I'm sorry, dude!" the man who had knocked the ladder over said. He stepped behind the counter, pulling a rag out from his belt loop, as if that was going to help.

The paint can was still laying on its side, the rest of the paint running out and pooling on the floor.

Chris felt Mr. B brush past him. The old man reached behind Chris and set the paint can upright. The other man was on the floor, one knee bent, trying to sop up the mess.

Chris stood rigid, noting his jacked up heart rate and racing breaths. Out of the corner of his eye, he saw two women emerge from aisle five, pushing a cart with a bag of fertilizer in it. Black dots swam in his vision.

"Is everything all right?" one of them said. Her voice seemed far away. He could hear someone else talking, a man's voice, maybe the man at his feet. Chris tried to move, to take action, but he couldn't. Then he felt a warm hand on his shoulder. "Son, why don't you go get a mop?" It was Mr. B's voice.

Chris nodded, and, as if the touch of Mr. B's hand gave him courage, he was suddenly able to move, to get his feet to propel him forward.

Somehow, he got out from behind the counter and headed down aisle four, toward the swinging dark green door in the back marked "Employees Only." He pushed through it and welcomed the quiet and darkness of the back room. He scanned for the mop, then saw the exit to the loading dock, unlocked it, and pushed through.

Warm sunshine enveloped him. There was a bench out back where Mr. B sometimes came to sit and chat with the contractors as they loaded their purchases.

Chris sunk onto the wood, the chipped paint brushing off as he sat down. He had been meaning to sand and repaint it for Mr. B.

He leaned forward, putting his elbows on his knees and his face in his hands. He concentrated on breathing in and out slowly and calming his heart rate.

It was funny how he knew exactly what the problem was, and yet couldn't quite fix it. This was a panic attack, a full-blown one, brought on by the sudden crash of the ladder, after the busy morning and continuous noise. But knowing what was happening didn't make it any less scary. Chris' nervous system was revved up, and he needed to calm it down.

Panic attacks felt like someone was shoveling sand into his lungs, while telling him to breath. He felt cold and hot at the same time, and a bit dizzy.

He sat there, breathing. Focus on something in the present. The sounds of a bird chirping nearby.

I'm okay, he said to himself. *I'm okay.*

He felt like he was talking to Faith. He fully understood fear. That was something he had in common with the horse. Ever since his Humvee got blown to shreds and killed his friends, he had been having these attacks.

"It's part of grief, part of survival guilt, and a big part of the never-ending threat of violence you encountered for a year over there," his therapist had told him. "Your nervous system is on edge. It'll go away, but it's going to take time and hard work."

That was four years ago.

Please God, please God, please God, was all he could pray right now. Scripture verses flitted through his head.

Be anxious for nothing...

Fear not, for I am with you...

He tried to imagine Jesus sitting next to him. It was an image his therapist had encouraged.

I will never leave you nor forsake you...

Eventually, Chris felt his heart rate slow. His breathing became more regular, and the dizziness subsided. He straightened up, stretched his legs out, and leaned against the back of the bench. He closed his eyes and let the sun wash over his face. He was okay now, the attack over, but he was left with an overall feeling of weakness.

As he relaxed, the old voices started up.

"You're not good at anything," they always said. "You can't do anything right. You messed up again."

He realized with a start that he had left Mr. B alone

with the paint mess and all those customers. And never got the mop.

"Oh no," he said, sitting up straight.

What a mess he was. He'd get fired for sure, now. This was what? His fifth job this year? And it was only August?

He thought about Faith and the ranch. Three Hearts was the only place he felt useful. This week he had done several jobs for Kim, and he hadn't had a single panic attack. He felt so good there, so valuable.

At least at the farm he was making a difference. Kim couldn't really fire him. She didn't pay him.

His thoughts were interrupted by Mr. B pushing the door open and coming out. He came over to the bench, and without saying a word, sat down quietly by Chris.

Mr. B took off the cap he was wearing and brushed his gray hair back with a gnarled hand.

"What's up, son?"

He said it quietly, keeping his eyes off Chris, looking across the alley and parking lot out back.

Chris glanced over at him. "I'm fired, aren't I?"

"Why would I fire you? That crash darn near gave me a heart attack too." He put his cap back on.

"But I left. I...ran off and left you in a mess. You can't count on me."

"The way I see it, you're right here. If you had left, you'd be in your car on your way home."

Chris didn't know what to say. He looked down at his hands. "I've been like this a long time," he said. "It has happened before. It'll happen again."

"It comes with the territory," said Mr. B. "I suspected what I was getting into when I hired you.

Especially the way your hands were shaking when you came for your job interview, and the string of short-term jobs you had listed on your resume."

Chris felt tears threatening at this unexpected grace and empathy. He blinked them away. "Those are the jobs I quit," Chris said. "The ones you *didn't* see listed, well, I got fired from those, sir."

They were silent for a while. Chris wondered what Mr. B was thinking. He knew Chris was a veteran, and he knew there had been an accident. What Chris hadn't told him was how it had messed him up emotionally.

"Do you believe in God?" Mr. B asked.

Chris glanced at him again. "Yes, I do. I believe in God. He is the only reason I'm still here."

Mr. B nodded, focusing on the road in front of him.

Chris suddenly felt like talking.

"When I was in the army, my buddy shared Christ with me. After I accepted Christ into my life, I really started to change. It's not like I was *trying to* change, I just did. You know?"

A small smile, a nod from Mr. B. He did know.

"I was great at football in high school," Chris said. "I could have really made something of my life. Instead, I messed up a lot of lives." He told him about Rachel. About that night. About working with her now. "And I messed up mine. I'm thirty years old and can't even support myself."

Mr. B turned his head to look at Chris. His dark eyes crinkled under the brim of his cap as he smiled. "Have faith, Chris," he said.

"I'm trying," Chris said. "I really am. But I've prayed and I'm still...like *this*." He pointed to his chest. "A mess."

"Faith is the assurance of things hoped for, the conviction of things not seen," said Mr. B. "Hebrews 11:1. That's one of my favorite Bible verses. My wife used to quote it to me a lot."

"Assurance," Chris said. "So that means I'm assured of my prayers being answered?"

Mr. B was quiet for a moment, thinking. "Not necessarily on this side of Heaven," he said eventually. "But that doesn't mean you aren't heard."

"I've prayed," Chris said again. He had lost count of how many times he had pleaded for God to take away the panic. "God hasn't healed me."

"Yet," said Mr. B. "The prayer offered in faith will make the sick person well; the Lord will raise them up. If they have sinned, they will be forgiven."

"My pastor says complete healing might not come until heaven," Chris said.

"Yes, but there are other kinds of healing. Hold on to that faith."

"So, you're a Christian," Chris said, a smile tugging at the corners of his mouth. He had suspected when he first started working here, just by the way of Mr. B's character. But he had never asked.

"Sure as shootin'. Now, let's go back in before somebody steals my merchandise. You ready to help me clean up the rest of that paint?"

"Yes, sir," Chris said, smiling. He stood and offered Mr. B a hand up.

As he walked the eight blocks home, Chris thought back about the incident at the store. There had been so many of these "incidents" that led to him losing his job. He just assumed Mr. B. would get rid of him, because he was a risk to have around. You couldn't have a man hanging around with power tools or standing on a ladder if he was going to suddenly panic. But Mr. B had been full of compassion and forgiveness.

And he was a Christian. That in itself made Chris feel a lot better.

Faith. That's what Mr. B said Chris needed. Faith. That word—both as a noun and as a name—kept popping up. He thought back to how Rachel had reacted when Kim named the horse Faith. What bothered her so much about that as a name? Was it somebody she had once known? Or was she bothered by the *concept* of it?

Chris stopped walking when he came to a bench near his house. He pulled the phone out of his pocket and sat down. A tree above him rustled in the slight breeze. The road in front of him ended in a cul-de-sac, where his apartment complex was, so there was very little traffic. He sat there for a moment, enjoying the quiet. Then, he opened the Bible app on his phone and typed in the word "Faith." Several verses popped up.

"Truly I tell you, if you have faith as small as a mustard seed, you can say to this mountain, 'Move from here to there,' and it will move. Nothing will be impossible for you." - Matthew 17:20

Faith could move mountains.

"For I am the LORD your God who takes hold of your right hand and says to you, Do not fear; I will help you." — Isaiah 41:13.

God was helping him.

"Trust in the LORD with all your heart and lean not on your own understanding; In all your ways submit to him, and he will make your paths straight." — Proverbs 3:5-6.

He needed to trust, and God would show him the way.

Did he really have the faith to trust God in *all* things? Or just some?

Chris read the verses a few times. The sun dipped closer to the horizon, and he realized he needed to hurry if he was going to have time to visit the farm that evening.

Second Corinthians 5:7. *So we live by faith, not by sight.* Freddie had shared that with him in the rabbit hole.

"How do I know I'm saved?" Chris had asked, after he prayed the prayer.

"Because God promises that you are," Freddie had said.

"But how do I *know?*" Chris persisted.

"It's not of your doing. God doesn't need to prove it to you, all you have to do is believe. And God is good. He will honor that."

Then Freddie had quoted to him 2 Corinthians 5:7: *"For we live by faith, not by sight."* Chris practiced that every day. It was the only way he got through some days.

He thought of the farm and his fear of where he would go if it closed. Of what would happen to Faith. He thought about Rachel and wondered how she would ever gain back the years she had lost, in part because of him.

What would become of them all?

But that's where faith came in. He didn't have to have the answers. All God required was for him to pray and move forward. God would handle the rest.

Faith. He just needed to have faith.

And then, suddenly, he had a plan.

Chapter Fifteen

Rachel walked up the dusty path at Three Hearts Ranch that led from the parking lot to the barn. Chris' car wasn't here, and she felt a mix of relief and disappointment. She quickly pushed those thoughts down.

She entered the barn and took in a deep breath of hay, horse, and wood chips. It was a smell that always brought her back to the fun days of her childhood, hanging out at the pony club near their home. She missed those days so much and should have bugged her parents to enroll her in a riding school here in their new town.

Her life might have turned out much better.

"Rachel, welcome!" said Kim in her usual, cheery manner. It was 10 a.m. and much too early on a Saturday for cheer. Angel stuck her head out her stall door and gave a whinny in Rachel's direction.

"Hey, Angel!" Rachel said.

"Sure, greet the horse and not me," said Kim, walking up the aisle to meet Rachel.

"Of course!" Rachel laughed. "How's my other girl today?"

"I'm fine," said Kim. She stopped and stood in front of Rachel, a twinkle in her eyes.

"I meant—"

"I know who you meant," Kim said, frowning in mock anger. "Faith is fine. She ate her entire tub of grain this morning and asked for more. You and Chris have worked miracles with that horse in just a week. Love heals."

"Love does," said Rachel, ignoring the twinge in her stomach when she heard her name paired with Chris'. It had been years since she had heard that. Rachel and Chris. She had to admit, she still liked it.

Except that he was a jerk.

Or maybe not.

"Did you hear me?" Kim asked.

"What?" Rachel forced her focus back on Kim.

"Yeah…that's what I thought," Kim said. She had that mischievous look in her eyes again. Rachel frowned, trying to ignore its implications.

"Your first client arrives in ten minutes," said Rachel. "She's eight. She has autism. Her mom is hoping the horses will bring her out of her shell a little bit."

Kim brought Rachel up to speed on the little girl and what work she had done so far with the horses. The girl would be riding Tommy, a fat, quiet gelding who could plod around the arena forever, as long as he didn't have to move faster than a walk.

"Sounds good."

"The second client is a kid you have worked with before who has opted for a Saturday session. You can look at the chart. You have an 11 a.m. after this little girl, then a break, then a teen at 1 p.m. The teen is new. Her name is Julia. Come find me before she gets here, and I'll show you the paperwork her mom filled out."

Before her first client arrived, Rachel had time to visit Faith. She walked across the indoor arena and into the other side of the barn.

"Faith!" she called out.

The mare peeked her head over the stall door, her ears pricked. When she saw Rachel, she whinnied loudly.

"Hey, girl!" Rachel said, thrilled that the mare was so happy to see her. She reached the stall, where she was greeted by a gentle bump from Faith's soft muzzle. She put both hands on it and kissed it. It was amazing how quickly the mare had come to trust her.

Faith bumped her gently again.

"I'll bet I know what you want," Rachel said. She dug into her pocket and pulled out the plastic baggie of baby carrots. She held a piece out on the palm of her hand.

"Here you go." The mare took it between her lips and crunched contentedly. Then she pricked her ears again and nuzzled Rachel's hand.

"One more. Then I have to save the rest for later."

She always brought carrots for her students to feed to their horses after their sessions. It made the horses happy, but also, the kids *loved* feeding the animals. The joy on their faces was always something she could count on at treat time, no matter how the session had gone.

Her two morning sessions sped by quickly and without incident. She finished at noon and went to the break area to use the restroom . It was a small but clean room, with a tiled floor, a fan that vented to the outside, and a real, working toilet. The sink was cracked from when the heat went off last winter and the water leaked. Because Kim hadn't been able to afford to replace it, they resorted to using sanitizing gel and wipes.

It was lunch time and she was hungry. She found a cup of microwavable chicken noodle soup in the break room, vented the top, and turned the microwave on for the designated amount of time.

"Hey."

The voice made her jump. It was Chris.

"Hey," she said.

"I'm here to work. Kim has me outside fixing a fence, but I thought I'd pop in, grab an iced tea, and see Faith."

"Faith is doing great," Rachel said. "Wanting her carrots, as usual." The microwave beeped. She turned back to her soup. "I'm glad you're helping Kim."

And she was. The words were generic, but she felt she needed to say something nice to him. She was trying.

Then something occurred to her.

"You work in a hardware store, don't you?" She turned to look at him again. He was dressed in faded blue jeans and a worn, red cotton t-shirt that stretched across his broad chest and showed the bulging muscles in his biceps.

"Yes," he said. He raised his eyebrows. She noticed again how green his eyes were. They had a twinkle in them now, sometimes a wariness, but never the haughty I'm-better-than-you look he used to have in high school.

"Have you seen the bathroom sink?"

"Yeah, what happened in there?"

Rachel told him how a small leak had led to water forming in the bowl, which had frozen, and then cracked the ceramic.

"All it needs is a new bowl," Rachel said. "Maybe you can get a discount since you work there? I can ask Kim how much she can afford."

"I'll see what I can do."

"Okay, thanks."

They were quiet, then. Rachel stirred her soup in the uncomfortable silence.

"Well, I guess I'll get back to work," Chris said. He opened the door to the mini fridge and reached for an iced tea.

"Okay," Rachel said. She took her soup to the small table and sat down. Chris left.

Well, that wasn't awkward at all. She was no good at fake niceness.

After she ate, she found Kim and asked for the paperwork on the teen. She took it back to the breakroom to read. Julia's mom had filled out the paperwork. She had written a lot, covering both the space Kim allotted for "explain why you are here" and carried it over, filling out the entire back of the page. As Rachel read it, her heart went out to the girl.

She was fifteen and would be a sophomore in high school this fall. Academic competition was tough, and to fit in at her school, she had to be Barbie-doll perfect (the mother's words). The girl had been in treatment for an eating disorder, as well as cutting.

Julia arrived at 1 p.m. on the dot. Her mother dropped her off, and left, whispering to Rachel that it was to give her space to work.

"Hey," Rachel said.

"Hey," Julia said. She kept her eyes on the floor. She was too skinny, accentuated by her tight jeans and fitted t-shirt. Her dyed blonde hair was pulled back in a ponytail.

"Let's go see your horse. I thought Angel would be perfect for you."

Angel was what Rachel thought of as a healer of the broken-hearted. Her sensitive nature often gave her a special connection to people.

Julia followed her slowly to the stall and watched as Rachel took Angel out. No phones were allowed during session time, so Rachel didn't have to worry about losing her teen to electronics. That was a strict policy they stuck to, and Julia had been asked to leave her phone with her mom.

"We're going to brush her first," Rachel said. "Do you want to lead her to the grooming area?"

Julia shook her head "no" and crossed her arms over herself.

Rachel ended up doing the brushing herself, because Julia wouldn't get involved. She sat on a bale of hay and picked at her fingernails. Rachel tried to strike up conversation, but Julia's answers were either a shrug or a "whatever."

Rachel saddled Angel. Maybe if she could get the girl on the horse, they could start to bond.

"Come on, Julia, follow me out to the arena."

Julia obediently followed her. She kept feeling her pocket, as if missing her phone. They had the indoor arena to themselves, and it was quiet in the barn. Only the occasional sound of a horse moving its feed bucket, or the twitter of the barn swallows that flew in occasionally, disturbed the silence. Hopefully, the peace and quiet would allow Julia's soul to settle a little bit.

"Let's get you up on Angel," Rachel said.

Julia watched as Rachel checked the girth, and then explained how to mount. Julia shook her head and looked around the arena.

"I don't feel like it," she said.

Rachel knotted the reins and looped them over Angel's neck, so they wouldn't fall and trip the horse. She turned to Julia.

"Angel won't judge you," she said.

Rachel wanted to say that she knew about the bullies at school, and how that made Julia feel small and defeated. But she knew that moving into psychologist mode wasn't what Julia needed. The girl had already had that and it hadn't worked.

Right now she just needed a friend.

"She's just a stupid horse," Julia said. The girl turned and walked away from the middle of the arena. There was a stool off to the edge that Rachel sometimes pulled into the middle to sit on if her sessions had gone long and her feet were tired.

Julia sat on it.

Rachel looked at the horse, then at Julia. "I'm going to get the bucket for carrots," she said. "Maybe you'll want to give her one."

She left Angel standing there and walked over to the corner where the supplies were kept. She picked up a small, blue bucket and turned to take it to Julia, but she stopped when she saw what was happening.

Julia had started to cry.

"This isn't going to work," she said. "Your stupid horse isn't going to help me."

But Angel was watching Julia carefully. Her ears were pricked, her head lowered, her nostrils quivering. She slowly started to walk toward Julia.

Rachel looked at the teenager. Julia's hands were over her face now, and Rachel heard sniffing as Julia's nose stuffed up from crying. Rachel saw the scars on her arms where she had cut herself. She saw the thin legs hanging off the stool, the tiny body that Julia had tried to force into a perfect, unattainable shape.

Angel was almost to the girl. Rachel hung back, quietly, and watched. The mare very gently touched Julia's hands with her soft muzzle.

Julia jumped, unaware that Angel had approached her. She put her hands down, her face streaked with tears.

"Go away," she said to Angel.

Angel gently placed her muzzle against Julia's chest and held it there. Julia froze, and sat very still for a moment, then slowly brought her hand up to the side of Angel's face. Angel took this as acceptance and pressed her forehead into Julia's chest. Julia seemed unsure, but then she put both arms around Angel's head, in a hug, and held her tight against her chest.

Rachel stood very still and quiet, watching as the horse offered the girl something that no human had been able to—unconditional acceptance. Angel didn't have any fancy words of wisdom to share, any behavior therapy to try, or a barrage of self-help strategies. She offered only herself.

For the next fifteen minutes, the girl and the horse held that position, with Angel standing quietly and letting herself be hugged. Julia cried. Eventually, the tears settled, and she pulled back,.

"Thank you," she whispered to Angel.

Angel butted Julia playfully with her nose, and Julia smiled.

Angel butted her softly again, and this time Julia laughed. The teenager looked around and saw Rachel.

"You said you have carrots?"

The hour with Julia had finished extremely well, and Rachel rode the wave for the rest of the day. She was happy. She wished that every hurting kid could come to Three Hearts Ranch.

What she did at the clinic was critical and had helped so many. But if she could pair it with this— this miracle—that had happened today, she knew she'd be able to save so many more.

Maybe she would have been able to save Faith. She still had dreams about that girl, about how she would see her and run toward her in a last minute attempt to stop her from committing suicide. But in her dreams, as in real life, she was always too late.

Rachel entered Faith's stall, talking gently to the mare. Faith pricked her ears, then went back to the hay she had been munching. She was unconcerned. Carefully, Rachel slipped a halter on her head and clipped the lead rope to it. She led her out of her stall.

"Let's go for a walk. It's a nice evening."

The sun was setting, and after a long day of sessions, Rachel wanted to take Faith for a walk in the evening breeze before she left.

As she led the horse outside, she saw Chris up ahead in the drive, working on the big tractor. He was laying on the ground, on his back, and working on something underneath it.

She led Faith up to him and stopped.

"Hey," she said.

She wasn't sure what made her approach him.

He slid out from under the tractor and sat up. "Hi!" he said, a bit too cheerfully.

"Faith wanted to visit," she said quickly.

"Hey, Faith," Chris said. It still chilled Rachel when she heard somebody use that name. She pushed the thought away before it could ruin her good mood.

He wiped his hands on a rag and stood up. He came over to them and scratched Faith on the neck. The mare curled her upper lip in pleasure.

Rachel laughed. "She has itchy spots tonight!"

"She certainly seems to be feeling better," Chris said.

"She is. Her feet are still tender, and she's very weak. You can see how she's breathing a little heavily just from walking out here. But she's fine. She's going to make it."

Chris smiled.

"So, I have an idea," he said.

Oh no, Rachel thought. *He's going to talk about our past again.*

"I wanted to run this by you before I told Kim."

Or maybe not.

"What's going on?" Rachel said.

"I think I have a way to save the farm."

Rachel raised her eyebrows.

"A fundraiser! Here at the farm. We'll have an event of some sort."

She smiled politely. "We've tried those before," she said. "They have always been failures. By the time we buy the food and pay for a tent or two, we barely break even. And they're a lot of work." She wondered if she sounded mean. She wanted to be encouraging. "But it was a good thought," she added.

Chris wasn't deterred.

"I looked online to see what you guys did in the past. I think we should do something different than a concert or pony rides. What if we auction off shares in the horses?"

"What?"

"I don't mean for real. I mean that people can adopt the animal, like they do for zoos. For example, I could buy a "share" in Angel, and pay $10 a month for her feed, etc. In return, I wouldn't actually *own* a part of her, but I'd get regular updates on her, photos emailed to me, notices of her birthday, etc. We could say, 'Angel needed a new blanket this winter and here's what your contribution bought her,' and we could send them a photo. It would be like a newsletter for each horse."

Rachel thought about it. So many of the kids who passed through here were sad to leave the horses behind when they were finished with therapy. And so many people who weren't clients loved horses and wished they owned one, but didn't have the space.

"It would be like owning a horse but without having to do the work," Chris said.

He had actually had a good idea.

"For this event, how would it work?" Rachel asked.

"I was thinking we'd have a picnic, so yeah, I guess we'd have to supply hot dogs or something. But I can probably get a place in town to donate. There's this new pizza place that my brother bought pizza from the other night. It was pretty good. I'd bet they'd to help us out in exchange for advertisement, you know, like a sponsor. And that's another idea!" Chris was really starting to look excited now. "Maybe we could sell 'My Horse Lives at Three Hearts Ranch' t-shirts with the names of our sponsors on the back!"

Rachel looked at this man who had changed so much.

"Hmm. That's actually a really good idea."

"You like it?"

"I do!"

"Great!" Chris said. "I'll tell Kim before I go home tonight. Which reminds me, I've got to get this finished before it gets dark."

"Sure," Rachel said. "Go ahead."

He was grinning like a kid. He ducked back under the tractor. Rachel turned Faith and led her slowly back to the barn.

A fundraiser. It sounded like a lot of fun.

Chapter Sixteen

On Monday morning, Chris picked up a few items Kim needed so he could finish some repairs at the farm. He was excited to get to work. Kim was on board with his fundraising idea, and he wanted to get the farm in tip-top shape before they had the event. They had decided to have it in late August, before the kids went back to school after Labor Day weekend. That only gave them three weeks.

He had promised to help Mr. B close up the hardware store, so he had to leave before Rachel got there. On Tuesday, he went to the new pizza place in town and asked if they'd be willing to donate pizza for the event.

"I'd love to!" said Marty, the restaurant's owner. "What a great way for us to get our name out there!" Chris ordered pizza, estimating a count of 100 people. He could always add more later.

"One hundred people!" Kim said, when he told her on Wednesday morning. "Aren't you confident!" But she sent out the email blast announcing the event, which Chris had worked hard writing the night before. People started RSVPing right away.

"I'm hearing from clients we haven't seen here in several years!" Kim said.

He gave Kim some flyers, and left some for Rachel. He'd hang the rest up around St. Ives tonight when he headed back home.

He hadn't seen Rachel since Saturday. As busy as he was, he still couldn't get his mind off of her. Now that she was back in his life, his old feelings toward her had started to creep back.

When he came in on Thursday morning, Faith had been bathed. He leaned on the stall door and fed her some treats, then ran his hand along her silky hair. She was a beautiful golden color, with a dappled coat, and a flaxen, almost white mane and tail. She had a white star on her forehead and four white socks on her legs.

"You are one beautiful girl," he said. He ran his fingers through her mane. It was free of tangles.

"Rachel showed up about twenty minutes after you left yesterday," Kim said. "We figured it was time to give Faith a bath. It wore the poor horse out, but I imagine she feels much better now."

"She looks like a completely different horse. What color is that?"

"She's a palomino," Kim said. "She'll be beautiful once she gets more weight on her. I was thinking she'll probably make a great therapy horse as well. She has a gentle nature, and she seems to love being around people."

"Which is hard to believe considering how people treated her," Chris said.

"She's forgiving."

"I could use more of that."

As if on cue, Rachel walked into the barn. She was wearing jeans and a t-shirt instead of her work clothes.

"My morning client canceled, and I don't have anyone else until after lunch," she said. "So I thought I'd come and check on our girl."

"She's beautiful!" Chris said. Kim looked at him and smirked, as if he was talking about Rachel. He felt his face redden. Fortunately, Rachel's eyes were on the horse, and she didn't notice.

"I need to get some paperwork done," Kim said. "Don't spoil Faith too much."

"That would never happen," Rachel said, rubbing her neck.

"Did she like her bath?" Chris asked.

Rachel shrugged. "She didn't seem to care. But she sure liked me rubbing her off with a towel afterwards. And now she's so soft. She really is a beautiful color. Not all palominos have those dapples on their coats. She's going to be gorgeous once we get more weight on her."

They watched Faith, who was contentedly munching on her hay. Rachel looked over at Chris. "There's nobody here right now, and you're on the schedule for today. Do you want your session now or after work tonight?"

It was the perfect summer day, with temperatures in the seventies, and a dry breeze blowing. The sky was a clear blue, and Chris had been looking forward to working on the flower garden outside. But this sounded better.

"We can do it now," he said. "But I thought you weren't going to be my instructor?"

161

Rachel shrugged. "Kim says I'm the only one qualified enough."

Chris laughed. "I'm not sure how to take that! Am I that bad?"

Rachel laughed too. She seemed relaxed today. She walked over to the tack room and grabbed a lead rope. He followed her outside.

Angel was in the pasture, at the far back.

"Angel!" Rachel called to her.

The mare picked her head up, still chewing her grass. Rachel took a baggie of carrots out of her pocket and shook it. Angel and two other horses started walking toward her. Then Angel tossed her head and started cantering.

"She's frisky today!" Rachel said, laughing.

The mare reached them, snorting, and buried her nose in Rachel's hand, gently taking the carrot. The two other horses arrived, both light brown, and asked for their share. After Rachel had fed each of them, she opened the gate and led Angel through.

She shut the gate and held out the lead rope.

"Here," she said.

"Me?"

"Yeah. Lead her from her left side. See her jawbone? Stay even with it and you won't get stepped on as you walk. You'll be ahead of her front feet, but she won't trample you if she runs off. Which she won't. Not Angel. And never, ever wrap the rope around your hand."

"Yeah. I get why that could be bad," he said.

Chris had to glance at the horse, watch where he was going, and make sure he stayed in line with Angel's jawbone. It was harder than it looked.

Rachel showed him how to tie Angel into the cross ties, so they could brush her. The cross ties consisted of two ropes hooked to separate walls, and one rope hooked to each side of the horse's halter, with the horse in between.

"Remember how we did the brushing the other day?" Rachel said, picking up a brush and demonstrating the rhythm.

"Yeah."

"I'll brush this side, you do that side."

She handed him another brush and watched for a moment before she went to work on her side of the horse.

Brush. Rub. Brush Rub.

He concentrated on the horse's skin underneath his hands and on moving the brush with the grain of her hair. Angel rested her back foot, which he now knew meant she was relaxed. Her ears softened and dropped. Pretty soon, her eyes started to close. She was clearly enjoying the brushing experience.

"What do you hear?" Rachel asked quietly.

Chris listened to his surroundings. "Nothing."

"Listen again."

He could hear the breeze outside, ruffling the leaves on the trees. The occasional bump of a water bucket against wooden walls. A barn swallow chirping. But that was it. He told her.

"And what do you smell?" Her voice was soft.

"Horse manure?"

She laughed softly. "Expand on that."

He closed his eyes as he brushed Angel's neck and took in the scents around him. Hay. The cool dirt outside the barn door. The warm smell of Angel, not unpleasant, and tinged with grass and fresh air from outside. The crisp smell of wood chips. He described this to Rachel, the best he could.

"That's why I love it here so much," she said. "The sounds, the smells, the fresh outdoors. It's very healing."

They tacked Angel up, and Rachel let Chris lead Angel to the outdoor arena. He climbed on. He was glad for the baseball cap and he was wearing. The sun was warm overhead, and it felt good on his shoulders.

"Close your eyes," Rachel said, "and feel the horse under you."

He did as he was told. Rachel led Angel, and Chris let the reins rest across the saddle horn. He placed his hands on Angel's neck, feeling her underneath him. He was soon lost in the rocking, swaying motion of the mare as she walked quietly around the arena, first clockwise, and then counterclockwise.

"Memorize what this feels like, how you feel now," Rachel said. "You can use it later."

Chris wondered what that meant, but he didn't want to talk for fear of breaking the slight trance he was in. He felt his muscles relax. He hadn't even realized how tense his shoulders were.

"Kick your feet out of the stirrups and let them hang loose," Rachel said after a while.

He did.

"Feel the gravity pulling them down. Just let them hang."

He briefly wondered how he would stay on if Angel startled, but the mare kept up a nice, steady beat.

One, two, three, four. One, two, three, four.

He was so relaxed, he almost fell asleep. When Rachel stopped Angel, they were back at the gate. He opened his eyes. "That's it?"

"That's it. You've been riding for a half hour."

"No way," Chris said. "That's so…wow."

He sat there for a moment longer, reluctant to get off. This was the first time he had felt that relaxed in…he couldn't remember. He patted Angel on the neck. "You're a good girl," he said.

"Do you remember how to dismount?"

Chris nodded and swung his leg around. Then, he was standing next to Rachel. He couldn't see her eyes behind the dark sunglasses she was wearing.

"How do you feel?" she asked.

He took in a deep breath and let it out slowly. "Awesome."

"Remember this feeling. Memorize it. Next time you feel anxiety creeping up on you, try to draw on this feeling. Close your eyes if you have to and pretend you are on Angel."

Chris nodded. He should have felt awkward now, in front of this woman who hated him. But he felt so relaxed from his ride that he didn't.

Rachel opened the gate and led Angel through. "I'll get her put back outside, and then I need to get back to work."

Chris followed her back to the cross ties and watched as she took the saddle off. He grabbed a brush and helped her brush the hair down on Angel's back.

"Why does this work?" he asked.

"Horse therapy?"

"Yeah."

"I think it's because of the bond with the animal. The horse is someone you can trust, when it feels like you can't trust anyone else. They give you their all, their complete attention. They aren't rushed for time. They don't judge." She paused and reached for a comb, running it through Angel's black mane. "And it's a sensory thing as well. The touch. The movement. It all works together. And, I suppose, it's having control of something, some part of your life, when everything else feels out of control."

He wondered for a moment if she was talking about him or about herself.

Rachel looked at her phone. "I need to get back to work. Do you want to help me put Angel back in the pasture?"

When he nodded, she handed him the lead rope. He concentrated on keeping close to Angel's jaw, not getting stepped on, and not running into anything. When he got to the gate, he unintentionally sighed.

Rachel laughed. "Was it that hard?"

"Hey, I'm just getting started," Chris said. "Go easy on a guy."

"He can take on the enemy as an army man, but leading a horse to pasture..."

"We all have our different strengths!" He laughed. It was good to see Rachel relaxing a little bit.

Her phone vibrated. She pulled it out of her pocket, and then sighed. "Not again," she mumbled. He saw her face crumple.

"Something wrong?"

Rachel shook her head. "It's my mom. It's about the baby shower."

"So what *is* a couple's shower anyway?"

He could see that Rachel rolled her eyes behind her sunglasses. "It's torture. Men and women come as a couple. The men don't want to be there, and the women don't really want the men there because they don't get the whole baby thing. So everybody is miserable. Except the mom and dad-to-be. They're so happy about the impending birth that they don't realize everybody else is bored with shower games and hates the fancy-baked cake from the bakery that has that too-sweet sugary icing."

"Sounds like a hoot."

"That's a kind word."

"So, who are you taking?"

"Me?" Rachel said. "No one. I would never put a man through that. I'll go and face my family alone."

He remembered how she had reacted to the photo on her phone and how difficult her relationship with her mom had been in high school. Her parents had been very controlling then. He wondered if they still were.

"I could go with you," he said.

Rachel's head swiveled around.

"I mean," he back-pedaled, "they probably don't want to see me. But I could. If you want somebody there in your court. If they get on your case, well, an army guy can be intimidating." He flexed a muscle.

She laughed.

"No. I don't hate you *that* much."

He cringed. "So, you do hate me."

Rachel stopped and turned. "No. I mean, not really. I never *hated* you."

Chris raised an eyebrow.

"Okay, so I did. But we're adults now."

"So, adults don't hate?"

Rachel laughed again. He was making her nervous. Why couldn't he just have kept his mouth shut? Why on earth did he invite himself to the shower?

"No worries. I'm probably the last person your family wants to see anyway," he said.

Rachel was silent for a moment. "Since you put it that way, maybe you *could* come."

She had always had a mischievous side. That's what he had loved about her. She was sweet, but crafty.

"If you're not busy, that is," she said.

"I'm never busy, unless I'm at work. When is it?"

"It's a week from Sunday."

"I'm in!"

Rachel nodded and climbed in her car. "Okay. I'll give you the details later. I need to get to work."

He shut her door and watched as she backed out. Then, he turned to go back to his chores.

He grabbed a shovel and found himself singing as he dug up the weeds near the entrance to the barn. They looked like they hadn't been touched in years. The perennials had been choked out by weeds, and the clay ground was hard and rocky.

He realized how relaxed and happy he felt. He thought about Rachel, and how she had warmed up today. He wondered if she was starting to forgive him, or if she was just being professional. He may never know. And because of their schedules, he wouldn't see her again until this Sunday.

But he had an outing a week from then to look forward to. *If* a shower was something to look forward to. But maybe then he could find out if she was truly starting to forgive him.

Chapter Seventeen

It was Sunday morning, and this was Rachel's last week to save Boot. His parents had given her only two weeks (not more), and she knew that after this week's session, they'd pull him out. She had met parents like his before, looking for a quick fix for their kid so they could get on with their lives. Boot was an embarrassment to their upper-class lifestyle, and his punk-style clothes made them uncomfortable when they had guests over. Heck, she figured it made them uncomfortable, even if nobody was there but them.

He was just a kid acting out, seeking love and attention, and they were pulling away from him instead of moving toward him. She had woken up early this morning with Boot on her mind. How could she get his parents to extend their contract with her? She was still thinking about him as she shopped for groceries.

She sighed, putting a bag of chips in her cart. Her mother would have something to say if she saw them when she came over next, but the carbs were a guilty pleasure Rachel was willing to risk.

Suddenly, she heard familiar voices in the next aisle. Her heart started racing.

She pushed her cart to the end of her aisle and peeked around the next.

It was *them*. Jill and Michael Reiner, Faith's parents.

They were dressed up, like they had just come from church. She remembered them as strong Christians. She hadn't seen them since the funeral, which, admittedly, she had only spent about five minutes at. Looking at the young girl in the casket was more than she could bear.

It was my fault.

Rachel heard the familiar words in her head, a mantra she had told herself all these years, even though the logical part of her brain knew it wasn't true. She had discussed it numerous times with Greta. But that didn't make her feel any better, didn't lessen the pain she felt.

She quickly turned her cart in the opposite direction and ducked down an aisleway. She didn't want to see them. She had avoided them for the past two and a half years, afraid to face their grief. She knew they probably blamed her. After all, they had sent their daughter to her for help, and Rachel had failed them.

She often questioned if she had been so caught up in her own grief over the miscarriages and loss of fertility that she hadn't paid attention to the signs Faith was sending. She had replayed those last sessions over in her mind so many times, she had them memorized. Faith sitting curled up in the chair in her clinic, twirling a strand of hair around her finger, promising that everything was okay. Apologizing for taking up Rachel's time. Worrying what her parents would think if she couldn't get better.

Faith.

Rachel pushed her cart all the way across the grocery store to the front door, glancing behind her once to see if they had followed. There was no sign of the Reiners. They hadn't seen her.

She looked at her cart. She only had a few things in it. Some chips, a loaf of bread, and a jar of pickles. Lunch.

She pushed it aside and headed out to the car. She'd come back another time when she was sure they were gone.

Rachel had a bowl of cereal for Sunday lunch. She was out of stuff for sandwiches. She scrolled through her phone and came across the photos her mom had sent of shower gift ideas for her sister. She decided on the pink floral crib set—a bumper pad, a little quilted comforter, and a mobile with cloth flowers to hang above the baby's crib.

She supposed she should call her mom.

Rachel finished her cereal and hit speed dial.

"Rachel!" her mom said, cheery as ever. "Did you get the photos I sent?"

"Yes, and they're very pretty!" Rachel was determined to be happy for her sister. Or, at least, to *act* happy. She didn't want to be the horrible person she felt she was.

"I thought so too. They painted the walls a light pink. They're really going all-out. I hope the doctor got it right!"

"The ultrasound imagery is 3-D nowadays," Rachel said. "It's pretty accurate."

"So you're coming to the couple's shower? Are you bringing anybody?"

"I'll be there," Rachel said. She didn't mention Chris.

"Of course you will," her mom said. "I need you to make up shower favors. I have these little clothes that we can fold into small triangles, like diapers, and people can pin them on their shirts when they arrive. Then, when we're playing the games, we'll ask people to unpin them, open them, and see what's inside. Somebody will have a small black stain (which you can doodle with marker) and it'll be a dirty diaper!"

Her mom laughed.

"Isn't that great? And that person will win one of the prizes."

Rachel listened as her mom told her about the prizes she had bought, and that she'd bring the materials over this week so Rachel could start making tiny diapers.

Rachel thought about her grandmother, and how she loved to play games.

"Mom?" Rachel said, interrupting.

"Yes dear?"

"I was looking through Grandma's Bible the other night. Why does she have the word faith underlined so many times?"

"Hmm. Let me try to remember." Her mom was silent for a minute, thinking. "I think it had to do with Grandpa's brain tumor."

This was news to Rachel. She had always remembered her grandpa as the epitome of health, until his heart attack took him. Grandma had passed away soon after.

"Brain tumor?"

"Yes. When your uncle and I were kids, Dad had a tumor. His symptoms started with vertigo, and it took the doctors a while to find the cause. I was only five, so I don't remember it well, but your grandma was scared. She was afraid she'd be left alone with two kids, and she really loved your grandpa. She started going to this little church, and I remember her taking us. Somebody there gave her a Bible, and she prayed every day that your grandpa would be healed. They cut him open, removed the tumor, and he was fine after that. So maybe that's when she underlined those passages."

"Hmm." Rachel said. "Why didn't *we* ever go to church?"

"Well, when I married your dad, he wasn't keen on church," she said. "We got married in the church, and went on occasion, but I guess we sort of got away from it. Your grandma always tried to get us to go."

Rachel remembered. Her grandparents would talk to her about God when she visited. One day, shortly before her grandma had died of a stroke, she had given Rachel her Bible. Rachel often wondered if she had known her time was about to be cut short in this world. Otherwise, why would she have given her the Bible?

"I never really looked at the Bible she gave me," Rachel said. "Until lately."

"You were young and newly married then. You were busy."

After they hung up, Rachel sat there, thinking about God and wondering why she had never pursued Him. She supposed it was because she had learned at an early age that the only one you could count on was yourself. She had found that out with Chris, and later, with her ex-husband.

But that didn't have to be the case. Wasn't that what she tried to tell her kids in counseling? That there was always *someone* out there you could count on?

Somehow, she had to let Boot know that he could count on *her.*

Sunday was her day off from both the farm and the clinic. But this evening she thought she'd go and check on Faith. She wanted to see how the mare was doing.

She was going over Faith's coat with a soft brush when Chris came by.

"Hey," he said, leaning his big arms on the stall door. "I was thinking."

"Not that again," Rachel said, but she smiled.

"I think you should quit your job and work here full time."

Rachel snorted, startling Faith. "I'm sorry girl," she said, putting a calming hand on her neck.

"No, really. You're good at this! At helping kids. With horses. The whole thing. And Kim needs a therapist."

Rachel sighed. "Do you have any idea how much I'd love that? That has been my dream since I started here."

"So, what's stopping you?"

"Money!" Rachel said. "Kim can't afford to hire me."

Chris waved a hand in the air. "There has to be a way to come up with enough money. What's your current salary?"

"What?"

"And I guess there's insurance. You'd need health insurance."

"I could pay for my own if I made enough." She had thought it through a lot, made the calculations, and even called insurance companies.

"What if you freelanced? Can you come in as a contract employee and still work at the clinic part time for your benefits?"

Rachel shook her head. "I've asked Greta before. There's a lot of paperwork, and I would need to clock a certain number of hours to get benefits. Besides, it would still have to be an unpaid position."

"Hmm." Chris was silent for a while, and she went back to brushing Faith. The mare was munching on her hay, chewing slowly and sleepily. In just a week and a half, she was already starting to fill out from the good nutrition. Her feet were no longer sore either, and she was gaining strength.

She thought more about what Chris had said. Oh, how she wanted to work here full time! But Kim had never been able to afford to pay her therapists, and now it looked like she might lose the farm as well. Sometimes, Rachel even dared to dream a little about having foster kids of her own, and bringing them here to heal.

"We need to save the farm before we think about my job," Rachel said.

"I'm working to make that happen." Chris told her he had secured them pizza for one hundred people, and free advertising. "Kim sent out an email blast to current and previous clients. We're already getting RSVPs."

"That's wonderful!" Kim had given Rachel flyers, and she had hung them up in her part of town. "This place helps a lot of people. Adults, but also a lot of kids."

"You love kids," Chris said. It wasn't a question.

Rachel nodded. "I do. I started out wanting to work with younger kids when I was getting my degree. But I really like working with teenagers now. Some of them really work their way into my heart."

Faith came, once again, to her mind. She pushed the thought away.

"What type of kids do you work with?" Chris said. "I'll bet you're good at it."

Not with all of them, Rachel thought.

"This particular kid has been with me for about six months, but his parents aren't happy with his progress, so I will probably lose him this week."

"Lose him?" Chris asked. "What do you mean?"

"His parents will pull him from our clinic and take him someplace else. They'll move him around until he's either what they consider cured, or he grows up and leaves home."

"What's he in for?"

Rachel laughed. "You make it sound like jail!"

He laughed. "I'm in for anxiety. PTSD. Trauma. What's this kid in for?"

"I can't discuss the details. Let's just say he's really a cool kid, but his parents don't see it. They want him to fit a certain mold."

"And he doesn't want to?"

She shook her head. "No."

"It's a lot of work fitting into a mold. Other people's expectations are a big burden to carry."

"I know." Her parents had always expected her to be perfect. To get good grades. Date the right boys. Walk at graduation. But what did Chris know about that?

"It wore me out," he said.

She frowned. "What? Being Winchester High's champion athlete?"

Chris laughed. "Being perfect. Do you have any idea how hard football practice is? Or how much hair gel I had to use to get my hair to do that thing?"

Rachel smiled. "I loved your hair." She looked at him. "It still does that thing. Falls over your eye. Has that little bounce."

Their eyes met. She had lost herself in those eyes so many times in high school. But he wasn't looking at her with the same confident, haughty look he had then. Instead, she saw something deeper. Sincerity, perhaps?

"Yeah, well," he ran his hand through the lock of sandy hair and pulled out a piece of hay. "*Now* look at me." He held the piece of hay up.

"There's nothing more handsome than a man who likes horses."

"Really?"

"That's what Kim says."

Now it was his turn to laugh. "I don't think Kim has time to notice men. I've never seen a woman more driven and busy."

Rachel put the brush away and ran her fingers through Faith's mane. Then, she gently put her arms around Faith's neck in a hug. Faith responded by lifting her head and nuzzling Rachel.

"Do you want to come for a walk with us?" Rachel asked Chris.

"Sure."

Chapter Eighteen

Chris opened the stall door, and Rachel led the mare out. Faith walked slowly, but much more steadily than she had even yesterday. The horse playfully bumped Chris with her nose on her way by.

"She missed you," Rachel said.

"She missed *these*," he said, producing a bag of sugar cubes from his jeans pocket.

Faith pricked her ears, and he offered her one off the palm of his hand. She took it gently and chewed happily.

They walked out of the barn. Rachel opened up the gate and led them onto a path that wove toward the back of the farm. The land stretched back pretty far, and ended in a row of trees. It was mostly grass, but big oak and maple trees dotted the fields.

"How many acres does Kim own?"

"Twenty-nine."

Chris whistled.

"I'd hate to see her lose it. She built this place with her family," Rachel said.

"She told me about that."

They walked quietly together for a while. Faith's ears were twirling in different directions as she looked around and listened. The walk was slow, and they had to stop twice on their way to the back of the acreage for Faith to catch her breath. Each time, Rachel put her hand on the mare's neck and said comforting things to her.

There was something soothing in the way Rachel worked with the horses,. She had soothed that little boy the other day. She had a gift.

"I do think you'd be great working here," Chris said. "This is perfect for you."

They reached the back fence line. The other horses were already inside for the night, and the sun was setting, casting streaks of golden light across the field.

"I'd love that," Rachel said, "but I don't like to get my hopes up."

"You need to have faith," Chris said. "Maybe God has a bigger plan for this place than you can see."

"Or maybe God just sits up there on his throne and watches as we struggle to survive."

Her tone was bitter. The soothing voice was gone.

"I'm sorry," Chris said. He changed the topic. "So tell me more about this kid at your clinic. What if you bring *him* to the farm?"

"I already told you, Greta says the paperwork is too complicated. There are lots of hoops to jump through and stuff. And his parents would never agree."

"Does it have to be on clinic time? What if you just invite him? You know, a person inviting a friend out to see the horse they are trying to save?"

"It's not like that," Rachel said. She looked across Faith's ears at him. He still couldn't get over how blue her eyes were. A strand of blonde hair had come out of her pony tail and was blowing in her eyes. She brushed it back behind her ear.

"But if you brought him here, maybe you could fix him?"

He saw the line in her jaw harden, and knew he had said the wrong thing.

"*Fix* him?"

"Well, I didn't mean…it's just that you are so good…"

"No, I'm not," Rachel said firmly and turned her eyes back to the horse. "And I can't just miraculously fix kids. I'm not some miracle worker. It's a process, and I do the best I can, but some of them I just have to let go."

"So you're going to let this kid go?"

"I have no choice."

"Seems to me like you do. It would be easy to simply invite him here to—"

She stopped and turned so she was facing him. "What do you know about anything? Everything has been easy for you, but that's not what us mortals live like!"

She started walking toward the barn again. He could tell she wanted to storm off, but Faith's slow gait kept her with him.

"Is that what you think? That everything has been easy for me?"

"Well, it sure was in high school."

"Was it really? It may have seemed like it, but it wasn't all a piece of cake."

She was frowning. This wasn't going the way he wanted.

"Look, Rachel, I don't want to argue with you. I'm sorry." He couldn't seem to get on her good side. "I don't even know this kid you're working with."

"No, you don't. And you don't understand how all of this works."

"You're right. I had no right to assume."

She was quiet.

"Forgive me?"

She looked over at him and was about to say something, when he heard gunfire. One. Two. Three shots. Without thinking, he dove in front of Faith and pulled Rachel to the ground. They fell hard and he heard her exclaim as her knees fell on the dirt, and he landed on top of her.

"Chris, what—"

But he was shaking, and his heart was pounding. He couldn't speak. He couldn't move. All he could think about was saving her.

"Chris!"

His heart felt like it was about to explode in his chest, and his mind frantically fought its way through terror.

Think! He said to himself. *Think!*

He was laying on top of Rachel, protecting her from the danger, and felt something sliding between them. The lead rope. Faith was pulling on her lead rope. He glanced up and saw the horse rearing on her hind legs, her front legs above them, her eyes wide. She pulled the rope free, turned, and ran, stumbling on the rough ground.

"Chris!"

This time it wasn't Rachel's voice. It was Kim's.

"Chris, it's okay!"

He turned his head the other way, his ear on Rachel's back. He could hear her heart. He could see Kim running across the field toward them. Her truck was in the driveway.

Her truck.

Slowly, pieces of the world around him started to make sense again. They were in the pasture field. Kim had just pulled in the driveway in her truck.

And it—

"It was my truck!" Kim said. "It backfired."

Chris rolled off of Rachel and laid there on his back, staring up at the blue sky. His whole body was shaking.

I'm okay.

But he wasn't. He tried the deep breathing that he had learned in all the years of therapy he had been through. In for four seconds. Out for six. In for four seconds. Out for eight.

Longer exhales than inhales would relax him.

"Chris!" This time it was Rachel's voice. It sounded like it was coming from a tunnel somewhere far away.

I'm okay. He tried counting some more as he breathed, but he couldn't focus. He couldn't count.

He tried to sit up, but his arms felt like jelly. Things swam in his vision.

"You're okay," Rachel said.

He shook his head. He wasn't.

Someone put a hand on him. He shook it off and tried to stand up, but he only managed to get on his hands and knees.

"Rachel," Kim said. "Come here." Her voice was soft. He couldn't see her. He had his eyes closed.

He waited for someone to come to him. For one of them to tell him it was okay, to feed him the lies that he would be okay, if only he'd get up, get a glass of water, breathe into a paper bag.

He had to tell them it wouldn't work. But he couldn't speak.

He waited. Then he felt it. Not a human hand. But a soft, warm breath on the side of his face. His cheek.

A soft muzzle.

Silky hair that smelled faintly of fruity shampoo.

Slowly, he opened his eyes. There was Faith, her warm brown eye looking into his, her cheek against his face. Her mane hung down, long and soft. He grasped it and carefully stood, holding onto the horse like she was his lifeline.

His legs felt like jelly. Faith moved into him gently, pressing her forehead against his chest, so that the arm that still held her mane wrapped around her head. She pushed into the hug and held herself against him. Solid, quiet, steady.

He held her mane in his hand, as her warm head pressed against his torso. Slowly he wrapped his other arm around it so that he was hugging her head against his chest. He bent his forehead onto her silky forelock, the soft hair between her ears. And he closed his eyes again.

He heard the stillness of the pasture, a lone bird chirping. He felt the breeze brush against him, lifting the hair at the back of his head. He breathed until he felt he was breathing with Faith, until he felt his heart beat slowing.

He had no idea how long he stood there like that, but when he opened his eyes and lifted his head,

Rachel and Kim were standing some distance away, quietly watching.

He let go of Faith's mane and took hold of her lead rope.

"Thank you," he whispered to her, and ran his hand along her neck, under her mane, feeling her against his skin. He petted her for a moment, until he was sure the shaking in his hands had stopped. Then he turned to the women.

"Truck backfired?" he said, a bit sheepishly.

Kim nodded. "Are you okay?"

"Yeah. I am now."

He looked at Rachel. There was a hole torn in the knee of her jeans, and her knee was bleeding.

"Did I do that?" he said, nodding toward her pants.

"Yes. But I'm okay."

Chris swallowed and moved to stand on the left side of the horse. Slowly and carefully, he and Faith made their way back toward the barn.

Chapter Nineteen

The next morning, Rachel set her cup of tea down on her desk and settled into her chair to wait for Boot. It was 9 a.m. No teenager functioned well at 9 a.m., but his parents insisted that was the only time they could get him here today. He had no car because they had taken it away last month in another ill-fated attempt to get him to change.

She glanced at her watch and crossed one leg over the other. The pain in her knee instantly made her uncross it.

Last night, Chris had put Faith in her stall and asked Rachel several times if she was okay. She insisted she was. She had skinned her knee and had a few bruises from when he took her down, but it had scared her more than it had hurt her physically.

He had mumbled an apology to them and gone straight to his car. He had never met her eyes.

He had had a flashback, brought on when Kim's old truck had backfired. She kept forgetting he had PTSD, because he was able to function pretty well most of the time. She wanted to text him to see if he was okay, but she didn't have his number, and she knew that Kim would never give it out due to privacy regulations. She also knew he needed time to get over the embarrassment and let his nerves settle. But what she *knew*, as a therapist, and what she wanted to do were often two different things.

She heard the little bell on the front door of her clinic chime. She heard the receptionist talking to Boot. Then, he walked through her door, closed it.

"Hey there!" He smiled and dropped onto her couch. He had a brown paper bag with him and set it beside his feet on the floor. Instead of pulling out his knife and flicking it open with his customary flare, he sat, hands folded in his lap, and looked across at her.

But that's not what troubled her the most. The black liner under his eyes was gone, and he was wearing a t-shirt and jeans. A light-blue t-shirt and *blue* jeans, instead of his customary black. She was relieved to see he still had the combat boots on.

She was speechless for a moment, then took a deep breath. "What's with the new look?" she asked.

"This?" He plucked at the front of his shirt, and shrugged. "It's easier."

"Easier?" Rachel raised an eyebrow and crossed her legs again. She cringed and immediately uncrossed it.

"Yeah. I got tired of being harassed. If I wear this, I get my car back next week."

"Hmm."

"Hmm? Is that a therapy response to stall for time?"

She laughed.

"And I guess you should just call me Scott today."

"Scott. So now you have a dual personality?"

She didn't receive the grin she was hoping for. Something was really off with him today.

He fished in his back pocket and finally produced the knife. He opened it and started working it under his fingernails.

"So what happened?" she asked softly.

"I told you. I got tired of it all. It's fine."

"I don't think it is."

His dark blue eyes met hers, and for a moment, she saw a flicker of fear. He wanted to ask for help, she knew he did. But then he smiled his winning smile and said, "Let's talk about your boyfriend."

"This doesn't work that way. Insurance doesn't pay for us to talk about me."

"We won't tell them."

She smiled, despite herself. "I'll talk about me if you talk about you."

He shrugged and went back to work with his knife.

"Well, first of all, he's not my boyfriend."

"Hmm."

Rachel laughed again. She loved this kid.

"And...I can't really talk about him because he, too, is my client."

"You said you weren't going to work with him anymore. That you hated him."

"If I hated him, he wouldn't be my boyfriend, right?"

Boot smiled.

Rachel sighed and set her pen down. "It's complicated. I *wasn't* going to work with him. I even told my boss I wouldn't work with him. But she said I was the only one qualified to help him. And, well, that's my job."

Boot nodded. "So you're loyal. You have integrity. You can put your work before your feelings."

Rachel nodded. "Hopefully. Now it's your turn."

He closed his knife. "I'm fine." He looked across at her. "I really am. I've thought about it, and I don't know what I was making such a fuss over. I mean, I have it good, right? I have a place to live. I'm not being enslaved or trafficked; I'm not strung out on drugs. My parents don't hit me. And if I shape up, my dad will pay for all of my schooling."

He shrugged again, then smiled a too-big smile. "I've got it made, Ms. Walker."

"What do you mean, 'if you shape up'?"

"You know. Just wear normal clothes. Quit hanging out in places, playing my music, and start thinking about a serious career, like my Dad wants. It's all good. I'm okay now. I just needed to give it some thought. I'm sorry I've wasted so many months of your time."

Rachel felt a chill in her stomach. This sudden change, compliance, his will to fight gone. The fake smile. The relaxed shoulders. The uncaring attitude.

The apologizing.

Was he going to kill himself?

She shook her head. She couldn't measure every client based on Faith, the one she had lost.

"What?" Boot asked.

"Nothing."

"You shook your head."

"I was clearing away the cobwebs."

"But seriously," Boot said, "I'm fine now. You've done a great job. My parents won't get you in trouble for wasting their money. And now I can—"

"Wait." Rachel said. "Get me in trouble for wasting their money?"

He froze. "What? No. I meant to say—"

"Boot." She cut him off.

"It's Scott now. My parents hate Boot."

They looked at each other for a moment over the coffee table. Rachel heard the ticking of her clock. It seemed unusually loud today. She might be imagining it, but there seemed to be a pleading in his eyes. A cry for help? She had to reach him.

"About my boyfriend," she said.

"The one who's not your boyfriend?"

"Yes. That's the guy. You asked what happened back in high school. I came from a home where everybody expected me to be perfect. And I was. I got all As. I dressed well. I ate my veggies. I did everything I could not to rock the boat. My parents weren't mean. I didn't have a terrible childhood. I just knew that people had certain expectations of me."

She paused.

"Then I met this not-boyfriend, and I was crazy about him. He wasn't good for me and part of me knew that. But he was soooo good looking, and when he looked at me…anyway. So, I started doing things for him that I normally wouldn't do for anybody else."

Boot made a face. "I hope you're not going to talk about sex."

Rachel laughed. "No. Gosh, no."

He sighed. "Thank God."

"He asked me to supply booze for some parties, because my dad had a liquor cabinet, and I knew where the key was."

"Mrs. Walker! You were cool!"

"I was stupid. But he was just using me. And then he turned on me. My parents, my friends, even my fake boyfriend, all just expected me to be and act a certain way. And I was miserable. Then, when I went to college, I met this guy, and I thought he really loved me. I slept with him. But my parents were always so, "Wait until you get married," so then I felt really ashamed about what I had done, and I was afraid no other guy would want me. I mean, I stole booze, lost my college scholarship because of it, and then slept with a guy in college! In my eyes, I was a mess. I had failed everybody I had ever loved."

Boot was quiet, listening.

"He was perfect. Good job. Nice looking. *Normal.* My parents loved him. And then, I married him. And it all fell apart after that."

"So, you're divorced?"

"He left me for a blonde with a boob job."

Boot laughed. "I'm sorry. I shouldn't laugh."

"No, it's funny. Looking back on it all. And the joke is on him because the boobs should have been the first warning sign. I hear she spends his money like crazy." She started laughing then, and the two of them were soon in tears. It felt good. She hadn't laughed about her ex in…well, ever.

After a moment, they quieted down.

Boot put his knife away. "I'm going to miss you," he said quietly. "I brought you a thank-you gift."

He reached down into the bag and pulled out a record album. "I thought you would like this."

He handed it to her. It was a copy of the album *Keep the Faith*, signed by Bon Jovi.

"This must be worth a fortune!" Rachel said. "I can't accept this."

"I picked it up at a record show. The signature is legitimate. I was sorting through my albums, getting rid of stuff."

"Wow." Rachel ran her hands over the cover. "This is amazing. Thank you."

Boot shrugged. "It's not a big deal."

"Boot, why are you getting rid of stuff?"

"Scott. Because…I mean…what's the point?"

She knew then, that he was thinking about suicide.

"You want to know why I'm helping this not-boyfriend who betrayed me?"

"Because it's your job."

"No. Because I think he has changed. I have faith that all things are possible."

He snorted. "*All* things?"

"Yes."

He pulled on his jacket. She had to stop him.

"I need your help," she blurted out.

He paused. "What kind of help?"

"This not-boyfriend is trying to put on a fundraiser for the farm. You know the farm—I've told you all about the horses there."

Boot smiled. "You love those horses."

"Well, the farm is in trouble financially, and we are trying to raise money to save it. He has been looking for someone to play some music. You know, like a mini concert. We can't pay much. But would you… would you be willing to come and play for us? Only for about a half hour. Just something for the people to listen to while they are eating their dinner."

She saw him hesitate. Then, "No. I've given that up. I'm going to give my guitar to my friend at school."

"Please? Just this one concert. It would really help, and I'm afraid if we don't raise enough money, we'll lose the horses."

Boot studied her for a long moment, and she felt her heart hammering in her chest. She had just crossed a line. Inviting a client to participate with her outside of the session, especially a minor...

"It'll only be for a half hour," she said. "I can pick you up and drop you off. That is, if you don't have your car by then."

She saw Boot struggling with something internally. He was wavering. She held her breath and found herself praying silently. *Please God.*

Finally, Boot shrugged. "I guess."

Rachel felt a profound sense of relief. "Great!" she said. "We need your help to decide where to pitch the tent. The event is in two weeks. Can you come out tomorrow and help us set it up? I'll pick you up after I'm finished with work."

He hesitated again. Then he pulled out his phone. "Give me your cell number. I'll contact you and let you know where."

She knew what he knew, that his parents would never approve. She didn't mention this, and neither did he.

"Okay. Done."

And she gave him her number.

Rachel was stressed the rest of the day, and it was a relief to pull into the parking lot of Three Hearts Ranch. She didn't see Chris' car.

Faith greeted her with a whinny when she entered the barn. She fed her a few carrots. Dixie was back today, and their session was successful and fun. Then she brushed Faith, and took her for a walk.

When she got back to the barn, she put Faith back in her stall. Kim was there. She had just finished hanging a sign on Faith's door. Her name was printed on computer paper.

Faith.

Rachel would never get used it.

"Let's go get something to drink," Kim said. They went to the break room and got some cold teas out of the fridge. Rachel chose decaf, as usual. Then, they went out and sat on the little bench by the barn door, which overlooked the pastures. The evening was pleasant, and everyone else had left.

"Chris isn't coming tonight?" Rachel said.

Kim shook her head. "He called earlier. The hardware store got a big delivery today, and he needed to stay late and help stack things."

"Oh." She took a sip of her tea. They hadn't talked about last night's incident.

"How is he?"

Kim smiled. "He's fine. He's a tough dude."

"What happened? I mean, I know he had a flashback, but...how often does that happen?"

Kim took a sip of her tea, and ran her hand through her hair. "He gave me permission to share some of his background with you. More than what you know."

"Oh."

"He was in a field hospital for several days after the accident, before he was flown to a hospital in Germany. He had a closed head injury, ruptured ear drums, and was burned on over 30% of his body, mostly his torso."

Rachel set her tea down on the bench beside her.

"Before that, he was on the front lines. He was bombed, shot at, and attacked regularly. When a person lives under those circumstances for a period of time, their nervous system on high alert for so long, well, you know what it does to the system."

"It's hard to come down."

"He was in the hospital for six months. When he returned state-side and started coming off the painkillers, he couldn't relax. He turned to booze until he finally realized he was going to kill himself if he didn't shape up. So he went to AA, got into therapy. He's trying. But as you know, nothing is helping. So he's here as a last-ditch effort to slow the anxiety that is eating away at his life and keeping him from getting a full-time job."

Rachel gazed out across the fields and tried to reconcile the man Chris was now with the arrogant boy she knew in high school. She thought about his golden skin and the six-pack she had admired then, and wondered about scarring now on his perfect body from the burns. She thought about his intense fear last night, brought on by a simple truck backfiring. She remembered his reaction when he first saw Faith brought to the farm.

"Rachel." Kim waited until she turned to look at her. "Chris needs you. You have the perfect mix of therapy knowledge and horse knowledge to help him. We are his last chance."

"That's a heavy burden, Kim."

"I know." Kim sighed and turned back to the fields. She took another drink of her tea. "I know."

"I...I'm not sure if I can help him."

"Whatever the two of you have in the past, you need to get over it. That was more than ten years ago. Focus on the man he is today."

Rachel knew that Kim was right. She had to let it go. But she didn't know how.

"How's your knee?'

Rachel glanced down at her legs. She had a big bandage on underneath her jeans so the scab didn't rub. "It's okay."

"You realize he thought he was saving your life?"

"A truck backfired."

"But, in his mind, there was danger, and the first thing he did was pull you to the ground. He laid on top of you, covering you, protecting you. He was saving your life."

Rachel thought about that. She had landed face down, skinning her knee and banging her chin. She had managed to turn her head so she could breath, as his weight pressed her into the ground. Then, from under him, she had seen Faith rearing up over them. For a scary moment, she had been afraid that the lead rope was wrapped around her wrist, but she felt it pull free and slide out from between them.

Faith, her eyes wild with fear, came down, planting her forelegs close to Rachel's face, before she turned and ran. It was then that Rachel knew she had to get out from under Chris' crushing weight. She had started calling his name, trying to figure out what had just happened.

"Faith ran at first," Rachel said, remembering.

"Yes. Then she stopped a few yards away and stood watching. I ran to you. My gosh, I thought you were both dead—and after you got up, I was so relieved."

Rachel remembered that she was convincing Kim that she was okay, when they saw the horse slowly approach Chris. She had come to him, touched him with her soft muzzle, and comforted him.

"Faith helped him."

"She did," Kim said. "I think with you and Faith in his corner, Chris has a chance at leading a normal life."

Rachel smiled and picked up her tea. "He offered to go to that awful baby shower with me," she said, swinging her legs on the bench.

"Your sister's couple's shower?"

"That's the one."

"That man is braver than I thought," Kim said, and they laughed.

"Speaking of brave, I think I need to tell you what I've done," Rachel said. And she told Kim about Boot.

Chapter Twenty

Chris was grateful that he had to put in a long day at work, and wasn't able to go out to the farm. After last night, he wasn't sure he could face Rachel. He had acted like an idiot, tackling her to the ground over a stupid loud noise. What had he been thinking?

Kim had called to check on him this morning. He had assured her he was okay, and that he would be at the farm Tuesday morning to help with chores, if she still wanted him around. The parts he had ordered from the hardware store were in so he could get started on the bathroom sink.

She had laughed. *"If* I still want you around? Heck yeah!"

He was relieved to hear that, because he hadn't been sure. He was a liability.

"How are your sessions going?" Kim had asked next.

He had paused for a moment, then said simply, "Okay."

"I don't know what went down between you and Rachel back in high school, but she's the best therapist I know," Kim had said. "She can help you if you let her."

He wanted to shout that it wasn't him, but Rachel, who was the problem. Only now, after his incident, he wasn't so sure. Kim told him it would help Rachel if she knew more about Chris' background. After a few minutes, he had agreed to let Kim share some of what she knew.

Now he was having second thoughts. He wasn't sure Rachel was his ally in this. She had come around quite a bit lately, but she still hadn't forgiven him for what he had done. And now, after he had hurt her...

Her knee had been scraped and bleeding, and he was sure he had hurt her ribs, too, from his weight when he knocked her to the ground. *He* had been in such a moment of panic that all he could think of was protecting her.

But from what? A backfiring truck?

He felt like a fool.

"The new paint samples are in," Mr. B said. Chris shook the thoughts from his head.

"Okay," he answered. "I'll get them set up on that new display."

"Great."

He went to work, glad to bury his thoughts, even if it was by organizing paint colors according to shade.

The next day, after a restless night of sleep, Chris packed his tools into the tiny trunk of his car and drove over to Three Hearts Ranch. He worked on the sink for a while, then he realized a patch wouldn't fix the crack. The sink needed to be replaced. Still fueled by several cups of coffee, he headed over to the house to talk with Kim about the fundraiser before he went home. What he didn't expect to see was Rachel sitting at the table.

"Hello," Rachel said. "I need a favor."

"From me?" He glanced at Kim.

"Yes. I found us a musician for the fundraiser."

"I wasn't aware we were looking for one. I thought I'd DJ it."

"We are. And now we have one. Remember the kid I was telling you about?"

Chris nodded. "The boy I told you to bring to the farm for therapy?" He couldn't help the smile that spread across his face.

"Don't get all cocky, but yes, he's the one." Rachel said, smiling herself. "I talked him into being our musician. He plays guitar."

"Cool. What does he play?"

Kim smiled and then hid her face behind her hand.

"I'm not sure. Some kind of grunge stuff but also some folk stuff."

"You're not *sure?* What does it sound like?"

"I've never actually heard him play."

Chris' smile disappeared. "Hmm."

"Yeah."

"We're going on faith," Kim said.

"Seems there's a lot of that going around these days," Chris said and pulled out a chair. He sat. "Let's figure this out, then."

They decided that Rachel would pick Boot up after work that evening and bring him by the ranch. She was meeting him at a coffee shop and was very sketchy on the details of his parents or his background. Kim kept quiet.

"Okay," Chris said. They settled on 6 p.m.

"Meanwhile, I have to get back to work," Rachel said.

Chris got up and walked with her out to her car.

"Hey, I'm really sorry about last night," he said. "It seems I'm always apologizing to you. It's just that… well, I'm a mess." Words his previous therapist had told him to never use.

"So am I," Rachel said. "A mess that is. And sorry. I shouldn't have gotten so angry with you."

He nodded, hesitating.

"What is it?" Rachel said.

"Kim said she told you a little bit about me."

Rachel nodded.

"And I have no right to ask this, but, I'm just wondering why you're so angry? At me. At the world. At this couple's shower."

He could see that she was thinking, and he prayed silently that he hadn't frightened her away again.

"This makes me sound weak, but my sessions on Angel would go a whole lot better if I didn't feel your seething anger leaking out toward me," Chris added quietly. "You can see that I don't handle stress so well."

Rachel took in a long breath and let it out.

"You don't even like Faith's name," he said.

Her eyes filled with tears.

"This kid I'm bringing over tonight? Boot? I think he's contemplating suicide."

"Oh, wow," Chris said quietly. He had no idea it was so bad.

"I had this teenage girl a few years ago, a client. Her parents asked me to help her. I tried. I really did."

She paused and wiped her eyes with the back of her hand.

"She was depressed. I should have caught it in time. But I didn't."

"She…" Chris wasn't sure he should say it. "She committed suicide?"

Rachel let out an involuntary sob. "Yes." She turned to face the car and wiped at her eyes. "And I should have known it was coming. It was my fault."

"And her parents blamed you."

Rachel shook her head. "I don't know. I've never really spoken to them. They tried to contact me a few times. Then they sent me a letter, and I couldn't read it. I threw it in a box and have never opened it. I can't imagine they could have anything nice to say, and they must hate me so much. I should probably read that letter, to get what I deserve." She laughed, but there was no humor in it.

"Rachel," Chris said. He stepped closer to her. He longed to take her in his arms, to comfort her. "You don't deserve anything bad. You tried. I *know* you. I know what your heart was like back in high school, and I see how you are now, with the kids and the horses. I know you tried, just because of the person you are."

She turned back to face him. Her eyes were red.

"And I think Boot is headed in the same direction," she said. "I need to help him before he kills himself."

"Have you told his parents?"

She shook her head. "They wouldn't believe me. I'll tell my supervisor when I'm sure. But right now, it's just speculation. Just a gut feeling."

He was quiet, taking in what she said. "So, you're going to bring him here."

"I think the farm might be good for him. The horses, the open air. If only we can get him out here, I think it might heal him. Anyway, I've bought him more time. At least until after the concert."

Chris nodded. "I'll help in any way I can."

Chapter Twenty-One

Rachel pulled up to the address that Boot had texted her. It was some sort of club. There wasn't much to do for teenagers in St. Ives, so the restaurant owner next door had opened up this "teen spot" where kids came for dancing, karaoke, and open mic nights. It was a great place for them to stay safe while still feeling like they were having a party. It's where Boot had apparently been playing his music on and off.

The walls were solid and the windows painted black, but she saw him through the single glass door that led into the building. Someone had painted "OPEN MIC NIGHT TONIGHT: 7 p.m." in bright fluorescent pink lettering on the glass."

As soon as he saw her, he came out, carrying his guitar case in one hand. He was back to wearing his customary black jeans, black t-shirt, and he had on dark sunglasses. She smiled at his choice in clothing. Maybe Boot was back.

He put the guitar in the back seat and climbed in beside her.

"Hello," she said.

"Hi."

He glanced around, like he was worried. She didn't ask if his parents knew he was doing this, and he didn't say.

"The farm is about a fifteen minute drive," she said.

Boot nodded. He seemed nervous.

"We just want you to help us pick a spot for the entertainment tent and play us a few songs, so we can figure out how to advertise."

Again, just a nod. She glanced over at him a few times. He was tapping his fingers on his leg, to some rhythm in his head.

"You okay?"

"Yeah, I'm fine. This isn't going to turn into some sort of therapy session, is it?"

Rachel laughed. "No. I promise."

They drove on in silence. Boot leaned forward and played with the radio until he found an oldies station. A Pink Floyd song was playing. When Rachel pulled into the parking lot of the farm, she saw Chris' car.

"What do the three hearts stand for?" Boot asked.

"The owner, Kim, lost both her young daughter and her husband," Rachel said. "Two of the hearts is for them. The third is hers."

"Wow. Tragic."

"Yeah."

"How old was her daughter?"

"Ten. Brain cancer."

She parked the car and they got out. She saw Chris and Kim standing across the parking lot near the front of the barn. Their backs were toward them, and they were pointing into the yard.

When she closed the car door, they turned.

"Hey!" Chris waved. "We were thinking of setting everything up on this side of the barn, behind the house. The ground is flattest here."

They walked over.

"Is that the non-boyfriend?" Boot asked, his voice low.

"Yes," Rachel said, biting back a smile.

"Do you want me to shake him up a little bit?"

"Not a good idea. He has PTSD."

She saw Boot crack a smile.

They were standing under the cool shade of a big oak tree, which felt good because the evening was still warm. Rachel made introductions. Boot shook hands with Chris and Kim. He removed his sunglasses, and Rachel felt somewhat relieved to see the black eyeliner was back. She quickly looked at both Chris and Kim and neither seemed put off by his all-black clothing. He was a tall kid, probably close to six-feet, so his appearance could be intimidating at first.

"Where do you think we should put the tent?" Chris asked Boot.

Boot scanned the area. "Let's put the tent there, where it's the most open. People can come in here," he pointed, "and get their pizza and drinks, and then go sit down over there." He pointed again. "I'll be on the far side of the tent, because see that little hill? It'll act as a good backdrop, acoustically. And that's not too far away from the house, so we should be able to run an electrical cord out to the speakers."

Chris glanced at Rachel and raised an eyebrow. She smiled, proud of Boot. She loved how quickly his mind worked.

"I like it," Kim said. "Sounds good. I've ordered the tent already. It has sides in case it rains, but let's pray that it doesn't."

"That would be bad for the guitar," said Boot. "It doesn't like humidity. But I can make it work."

"Can you play us something?" Kim asked.

Boot looked around and spotted a picnic table. He went over, set his guitar case on it, and opened it. He pulled out a battered acoustic guitar. Rachel had been expecting some sort of amped-up electric instrument.

He sat down on the top of the table, his feet on the seat, and propped the guitar on his knee. He began to tune it. She noticed that his fingers were trembling a little.

The three of them stood there, watching. Rachel suddenly felt awkward. Music was so intimate, and watching this kid here, in his element, trusting them, was more than she could have hoped for. She felt the protective need to take the attention off of him for a moment.

"So," she said while he was tuning, "how much pizza do you have coming?'"

Chris turned to her. "Enough for about a hundred people."

"Wow."

"He's very confident," Kim said.

"Have faith, people," Chris said.

"I'm ready," Boot said. "What do you want to hear?"

"Just whatever you want to play," Rachel said. "Like I said, we'll have families here, and some older folks. Can you play something that would appeal to a lot of people?"

Boot thought for a moment, then started playing. The melody drifted across the lawn in the still evening air, filling the large space they were standing in. It was familiar to Rachel, and she was trying to place the tune when Boot began to sing.

"I see trees of green..."

He was singing "What a Wonderful World." Rachel wasn't sure what she was expecting, but this positive, uplifting song by Louis Armstrong was certainly not it. Coming from a black-clad, punk teen who was desperately searching for love and acceptance from his family, it seemed a paradox.

As he continued, she paid attention to his voice. It was smooth and completely in tune, and again, so contrasting to what he portrayed on the outside that she could hardly believe it was him. She felt a lump forming in her throat.

The three of them stood there, transfixed, until he finished. She glanced at Kim, and saw her quickly brush at the corner of her eye. Kim never cried. At least in front of people. She glanced at Chris. His jaw was tight, and he was swallowing, hard.

She was suddenly, incredibly glad she had brought Boot here to the farm.

Boot rested the guitar on his knee. "That's not one of my better ones, but it...you know...seemed appropriate for this setting, with the grass and all."

Rachel laughed. "You have *better* songs? That was one of the most beautiful things I've ever heard."

Boot rolled his eyes, but she could tell he was pleased.

208

He picked things up a bit with a rock tune that Rachel couldn't name, then ended with Bon Jovi's "Keep the Faith." Rachel knew the song was for her.

"Everybody keep the faith," he said as he strummed the last note.

This certainly didn't seem like a kid who was thinking of suicide.

Rachel was laughing. She hadn't been this happy in a long time. Suddenly, she felt like it was all going to come together.

"I think we're going to be able to save this farm after all," she said. "Wow. Boot. I had no idea. I mean, I knew you could play, but you should go on *America's Got Talent* or something!"

He smiled, putting his guitar away.

"Speaking of Faith," Kim said, "Rachel wants to show you our horses." Kim glanced at Rachel, who nodded. "And then I think Chris needs you to help him carry in a sink."

"The crack was too bad," Chris explained to Rachel. "We had to order a new one."

Kim reached out to shake Boot's hand. "Welcome to the team," she said. He hesitated, then put his hand in hers and shook it. Kim headed into the house, and Rachel led the two of them to the barn.

Faith whinnied as soon as she saw them.

"This is Faith," Chris said. As they approached her stall, he pulled out his baggie of sugar cubes. Boot stood back a little ways, as if unsure whether this large animal was dangerous. She often saw that kind of reaction from people who weren't familiar with horses. Chris placed a sugar cube on the flat of his palm. Faith gently gobbled it up.

"Want to try?" Chris said.

"Why is she so skinny?" Boot asked.

"She was a rescue horse from the humane society," Rachel said. "Her owner hadn't fed her in weeks, and her hooves were so grown out she could barely stand."

"That's awful," Boot said. He took a tentative step closer.

"She's gentle," Rachel said.

"She's big."

"She's about fifteen hands tall, which is average in horse size," Rachel said. "A hand is four inches. Back in the day, people measured horses by their palm width."

"Interesting."

Boot walked up to the stall door. As he approached, Faith's eye got wide, and she stepped back, watching him warily.

"She's afraid of me."

"She has to learn to trust people again, after what was done to her," Chris explained. "Just move slowly."

Boot stopped and put his hand out. "Come here, girl," he said.

Faith stretched her nose out until she could almost touch Boot's hand, and then sniffed. She snorted and backed up. Boot jumped.

"She's just unsure," Chris said. He opened the stall door and went in to stand next to Faith. He put a calming hand on her neck. "It's okay, girl. He's a friend."

Chris reached out and handed Boot a sugar cube. Then he explained how to safely feed her.

"I'm not sure about this," Boot said. "Her teeth are awfully big."

"She's watching you," Rachel said quietly from behind him.

Boot opened his palm and held his hand out. Faith sniffed the air, then turned to Chris and bumped him with her nose, as if asking *him* for a sugar cube instead.

"It's okay," Chris said again.

"This is good for her," Rachel said. "She needs to learn to trust others besides us."

Boot held still, and slowly Faith took a step forward. Chris moved with her, his hand still on her neck.

She took another step, within reach of the sugar cube, but watched Boot carefully for a moment. Then she very gently reached with her upper lip, and pulled the sugar cube into her mouth. She chewed, watching him. He withdrew his hand.

"Try again." Chris handed him another. Faith perked her ears when she heard the bag.

Again, Boot reached his hand out. Faith took it more quickly this time. With the third sugar cube, he was close enough to pet her. He put his hand on her neck.

"It's so soft," he said, stroking her. Faith nuzzled him, smelling his hair with her muzzle. Boot laughed.

They fed her until the sugar cubes were gone.

"Is all that sugar good for her?" Boot asked.

"Not really," Rachel said. "But a few won't hurt. Right now, she needs the calories. She needs the treats to build her trust back up. We want her to look at the presence of people as something to enjoy, not something to be afraid of."

Chris put the empty baggie into his pocket and looked at his watch. "Rachel tells me you've got to be back by 8 p.m."

"Yes."

"Before you leave, can you help me carry the sink into the bathroom?"

"Sure."

Rachel stayed with Faith and watched as Chris walked with Boot up the aisleway and toward his car, talking about whatever men talk about when they're about to do a work project together. She saw Boot nodding and Chris gesturing with his hands.

She turned to the horse.

"I think we just might be on to something here," she said.

She petted Faith, then looked down at the plaque tacked on Faith's stall door. Kim had printed a new one off of the computer and put it in a plastic sleeve. The horse's name was at the top in bold lettering, followed by a Bible verse.

Faith

"Now faith is confidence in what we hope for and assurance about what we do not see."
Hebrews 11:1

One of the same verses her grandmother had underlined in her Bible. Rachel ran her fingers over the name and felt a flicker of hope deep in her heart.

Chapter Twenty-Two

Chris finished up the work in the bathroom on Wednesday afternoon. He was pleased to see the sink was working. It was, after all, the first one he had ever installed.

His phone buzzed on the counter where it sat. It was a text from Kim asking him to stop by the house when he was finished. He pulled his work gloves off and wiped the sweat from his brow with a paper towel. Then he headed over to the house, stopping on the way to put his tools in the trunk of his car.

"Hello!" he hollered through the screen door.

"Come in!" Kim called.

He pushed it open, cringing at the squeak. He'd have to oil it for her.

"It's hot out there," Kim said, in way of greeting, and handed him a glass of iced tea, the condensation dripping from its sides.

"Thanks."

She motioned for him to sit down, and she too, took a seat at the little kitchen table.

"The banker comes here the day after the fundraiser," said Kim. "If I don't have at least a month's mortgage to give him, he's going to foreclose on us. I need to be able to show that we're doing good and that there's hope for this place."

Chris felt his stomach tighten at the news. "So it's really that bad," he said.

"It is," Kim said quietly.

They sat there for a moment in silence. Chris had everything lined up for the event, and he was sure it was going to go well.

"I've been praying," he said finally.

"We need it."

"With God, all things are possible."

Kim sighed. "Yes. It's my heart's desire that this farm continues to be a place where people can come for healing. I can't imagine, with me feeling so strongly about it, that God would let me lose it."

"Faith can move mountains," Chris said. "Just believe."

"I had the faith that my daughter would heal," Kim said quietly.

Chris didn't know what to say to that. God certainly didn't always answer prayers the way we expected Him to. "He hasn't taken away my PTSD, as you have seen first-hand."

Kim raised an eyebrow. "But we continue to have faith. We get up every day, move forward, do our best, and pray. We do this because we believe that God has a greater purpose than what we can see right now."

Chris nodded. "Sometimes the picture is bigger than just us."

"Sometimes it is."

Chris took a sip of his tea. He had a feeling Kim wanted to say something else, so he waited quietly. He was right.

"Rachel needs to forgive you," Kim said after a while.

He looked at her, surprised.

"I don't know all of the details of what happened between the two of you back in high school. I don't need to know. But you did something that upset her, and I do know that having you here is causing her a great deal of stress. She's struggling right now between wanting to help you and wanting to run. Your presence is stirring up a lot of bad memories."

Chris felt the butterflies creeping up in his stomach. Where was Kim headed with this? He kept his eyes on the table in front of him as the shame crept up on him again. What did Kim know about the guy he used to be? Or maybe the man he was now was too much for her as well? After his panic attack the other day, when he threw Rachel to the ground, he wouldn't blame Kim if she got rid of him.

But what about Faith? He couldn't live without that horse. Suddenly, he realized that he needed that horse in order to make it. He needed this farm. Since he had started doing the outdoor work for Kim, he had begun to sleep well. The nightmares had stopped.

But he was a liability. A danger. Kim couldn't have a man who went into a blind panic hang around horses or clients.

And hurting Rachel.

Slowly, he raised his eye to meet hers. "You want me to leave?"

Kim snorted, startling him. "Heck no, I don't want you to leave!" she said. "You're the best worker I've had around here in a long time. Since you've come, the flower beds look better, the sink is working, you've fixed the wheelbarrow, changed the oil in the tractor..." She was counting things off on her fingers. "I don't want you to leave."

"Then...what are you saying?"

"I believe you are penitent for whatever it is you did to her. I think she knows that too. But she needs help forgiving you." Kim set her glass down and leaned forward, looking at Chris across the table. "Rachel doesn't know Jesus. She grew up knowing a little bit about church and God, but she doesn't understand what it means to have complete and total forgiveness, and to be able to forgive, because we are forgiven. She has been hurt, a *lot*, and she needs some hope."

Chris ran his finger down the moisture on his glass, watching the droplets fall onto the table. They were creating a little puddle. It was warm in the kitchen.

"I've tried to talk to her. She isn't interested in hearing about God," Chris said. "And I don't think I'm the person to tell her."

"I disagree."

He looked at Kim again. Her eyes were sincere. She smiled, and sat back in her chair. "You're a man of great faith, Chris. Use that faith to change things. Move some mountains."

He leaned back too. Maybe God had brought him to Three Hearts Ranch for a reason.

"Maybe God didn't bring you here just to heal *you*," Kim said. "Maybe God has an even bigger plan."

Before he left, Kim had asked him if he could rearrange her basement and move the paperwork downstairs so the banker would see an organized house when he came. He promised to come back tomorrow afternoon and tackle the job. But now it was time for his session on Angel.

Rachel was waiting in the barn with Angel in the cross ties.

"Hey," she said. "Kim had you cornered in the kitchen?"

"Yeah, sorry I'm late."

He grabbed a brush and started on the left side of Angel's neck. Rachel took the other side. It surprised him how natural brushing the horse felt now, after only a few weeks. He tried to concentrate on the strokes. Brush, rub. Brush rub. But his mind kept going to Rachel and how he would tell her about Jesus.

Please God, give me the words, he prayed silently.

He helped Rachel put the saddle on, and today she showed him how to tighten the girth.

"You want to be able to get your hand under it," she said. "But it shouldn't be so loose it moves. Like this." She had him put his hand under the saddle to feel. "And it's also nice if you take their front feet like this," she said, picking up Angel's left front foot, "and stretch it to smooth the hair." She pulled the leg forward, and he could see the skin of the girth area sliding forward as well, laying the hair in place.

"Huh," he said.

In the arena, he climbed on easily. She instructed him to close his eyes, and they went through the motions to help him relax. Soon, as he concentrated on the animal under him, his mind started to slow down. He felt his muscles relaxing from the hard labor of the day, and his anxiety over talking with Rachel easing off.

He had been really embarrassed to face her again, after knocking her to the ground. But she didn't seem to think anything of it. She had never mentioned it. And then they got busy with Boot, and now it seemed like it was weeks ago, instead of just on Sunday.

Boot. He really liked that kid. On first impression, he felt that Boot was pretty cool and wondered what the problem was with his parents. He did look a bit rough on the outside, but he was nothing like that on the inside. If only people took time to figure that out.

His session was over before he knew it; Rachel was asking him to dismount. His muscles felt like jelly, they were so relaxed. He sighed, not wanting to get off the horse, but he did.

"I know. Back to the real world," Rachel said.

"Yeah."

"The real world is tough."

"Sometimes."

They led Angel inside and untacked her. Rachel let him lead Angel back to her stall. The barn was empty now, the others having gone home. His session was always the last of the day.

When he got back to the tack room area, Rachel was gone. He walked over to Faith's stall and found her there, petting Faith over the stall door.

"Thanks for the session," he said.

Rachel scratched Faith under the chin, which the horse loved. She responded by stretching out her neck and curling her upper lip in pleasure.

"Thanks for asking Boot to help you with the sink yesterday," Rachel said. "He needs to feel like he's capable of doing things."

"He's not the only one," Chris said.

Rachel turned to him.

"Is the horse therapy helping?"

"It is. I sleep like a baby now."

She watched him intently for a moment, as if she wanted to say something. Her blue eyes were as beautiful as he remembered them, and he would never get tired of looking into them. It surprised him how his body reacted, how he suddenly wanted to pull her into a kiss.

"Chris?" she said, hesitantly.

"Yes?"

"Why did you leave me?"

Her words cut into him. They were the words he had been hearing in his head for years, words he had repeated over and over to himself. Why had he left her? *Why?*

"Because I was a coward," he said. "And I was selfish. And stupid. And eighteen. And I have regretted it for most of my adult life."

She broke her gaze and turned back to Faith.

"It hurt."

"I know."

He wanted to tell her that he had loved her then. And that now…now what? Now that he was seeing her again, all of those feelings had resurfaced. The love, the desire, but also the shame. The guilt. He needed her forgiveness.

"I need for you to forgive me," he said. "I know I don't deserve it. But I need it."

He spoke plainly, humbly. As he said the words, as he offered her the gift of forgiving him, he felt the remorse that had been hanging over him like a weight for so long. "Please," he said, and heard his voice crack.

She looked at him again, met his eyes, and he let the tears fall unashamedly down his cheeks.

"I'm so sorry," he said.

He saw her resolve waver.

"I've tried," she said. "I've tried since you got here. I keep telling myself to forgive you, that we are past that now. But then…" She swallowed. Tears formed in her own eyes. "How?"

Chris put his hand on the stall door to steady himself. His heart was pounding. "I was always a disappointment to myself," he said. "*Always.* In school, I was good at football, yeah, but my grades sucked. In college, I lost everything I was given. In the army, I was the only survivor of that attack. There should have been *something* I could have done. When I returned home, I strung a bunch of women along and drowned myself in alcohol. I was a wreck. No matter where I went, or what I did, I was a disaster. I hated myself."

"You did?" Rachel said. "You were always so confident in high school."

Chris shook his head. "It was all an act. And my act fell apart. I was left realizing that I couldn't go it alone."

"So what then?"

"A friend told me about Jesus. About how he died for us while we were still sinners. Not *after* we asked forgiveness. Not *after* we did a lot of good works or earned our way into his graces. But he died for us *while* we were a mess. Like I was a mess. So I prayed a prayer and told Jesus that I knew that I needed him, that I had sinned, that things like forgiveness and letting go of anger were hard for me. And I turned my life over to him. And now I'm free."

Rachel had tears running openly down her cheeks now.

"It can't be that simple."

"It is. It's a gift. Scripture says *'For by grace we are saved through faith. It is a gift of God. Not of works.'"*

"All I need is faith?" Rachel asked.

"That's all," Chris said, wiping at his eyes. "Would you like to pray that prayer with me now?"

Rachel nodded.

Chris took her hands in his, and together, they prayed.

Chapter Twenty-Three

Rachel sat in bed that night, her grandmother's Bible propped on her knees. She leaned back against her pillows and ran her hand over the worn leather binding. Chris had suggested she start by reading the book of John, to learn more about Jesus.

But first, she leafed through the Bible again, reading the verses her grandmother had underlined about faith. The corners were bent, dogeared, and worn with wear. She wondered how often her grandma had turned to these verses.

Rachel felt lighter now, as if a heavy burden had been lifted. She wondered what this new feeling was, and if it would give her the strength to face other fears.

She thought again of Faith, the teenager. And then Faith, the horse. Both had needed her help. She had failed the one, but she was helping the other one heal. Or was she? What if Kim lost the farm? What would happen to Faith then? Rachel lived in an apartment. There was no way she could afford to take her and board her someplace. The cost of boarding a horse was expensive, more than a car payment every month. And what would happen to Angel and the others?

Maybe now, if she prayed hard enough, God would give her her heart's desires.

But no, that's not how God worked. He hadn't taken away Chris' PTSD. But then again, if He had, Chris would never have come to Three Hearts, she would have never known about Jesus, and she may never have invited Boot to help out. There would have been no fundraiser and no hope of saving the farm.

Faith.

She had to have faith that God was in charge of all of this and that He had a better plan than she did.

Thank you, she prayed. Then she opened her Bible to John and began to read.

Rachel sat in her office, waiting for her next client. She was early, and this particular client was always late. She looked over her notes one more time, then allowed her mind to wander to Chris.

He was a changed man. There was no trace of the arrogant, self-centered boy that she had known in high school. He said it had all been an act.

She thought back to what she knew about him then. He had never taken her to his home, or taken any girl that she knew of. All she knew about his parents was that he didn't want her to meet them. His dad had always been in the stands during football games, shouting, waving his fist. She remembered he got angry if a play went wrong, but wasn't that a typical parent? She hadn't paid much attention, because she usually sat in the student section with her friends.

She remembered Dillon, his younger brother. Quieter. Almost shy. He had a hard time following in the shadow of his big brother, the school's super star. Dillon played on the JV football team, she remembered that.

Had Chris' parents been hard on him?

She knew all about that. Her parents expected her to be perfect. How much of that had she brought on herself? Her need to make all As. To look good. To never get in trouble. Had that been her own perfectionism, or her parents pushing her too hard? It was hard to say what troubles she brought on herself, and which ones were imposed upon her.

She knew that she had brought Chris' upon her. She had wanted him. She had wanted him to want her. She would have done nearly anything to win his approval and have him ask her out on a date. Had she been that desperately in love with someone that she was willing to lose so much of herself for him?

And now, here he was. This same guy. But not the same. Willing to go to a couple's baby shower with her.

And he had seen her at her worst. Torn jeans, hair pulled up in a pony tail under a baseball cap. No makeup.

She had tried too hard in high school to impress him. And now that he had been the last person she wanted around, he wouldn't leave.

But she wasn't sure she wanted him to.

He had given her his phone number last night after they prayed, and told her she could call him if she had any questions or just wanted to talk.

She picked up her phone and texted him.

Are you still on for the baby shower this Sunday?

It was easier to ask in a text than in person. He had probably only said he'd go because he was trying to be nice. Being around her family had to be the last thing he wanted.

She remembered the tears in his eyes last night. How his voice had cracked when he asked her to forgive him.

That was real. He was hurting deeply. She had been so wrapped up in how *she* felt, that she had not taken the time to really consider how he felt.

She remembered how he had taken her down in the field after the truck backfired. He had been terrified. She thought about how his hands shook sometimes, and how he would often stop what he was doing and take slow deep breaths.

Most people were afraid when they got on a horse for the first time. In her anger, she had just thrown him up on Angel, not considering how he might have been afraid, too.

He was a man with anxiety, and she had put him in situations that caused more anxiety. Her constantly cold attitude around him couldn't have been helping. And yet he hung in there. Why?

She thought about how gentle he was with Faith and how he had won the mare's trust. He loved that mare. Rachel had been around people and horses long enough that she could tell when a bond had formed. She wasn't sure what the two of them would do without each other, if they were separated. He would never be able to keep the mare if Kim lost the farm. He barely worked part time, and he too lived in an apartment.

Her phone pinged.

Yes! Looking forward to it!

There was a smiley and a thumbs-up emoji. She sent him a smiley face back.

Then she heard the bell on the front door ring. Her client was here.

After work, Rachel headed over to the coffee shop where she planned to meet Boot. Boot was waiting outside for her, leaning up against the door with his guitar. He had said Tuesday and Thursday evenings were best for him. He didn't say why, and she didn't ask.

"Hey," he said, climbing into the passenger side of the car. He was wearing his usual punk look. "Dad isn't giving me my car back."

"Because?"

He pointed at the mascara.

Rachel nodded. "No worries. I can drive you. It's practically on my way to the farm."

Boot turned on the radio and searched for stations. She wanted to ask him how his day went, how his life was going, to check in. But she also didn't want to scare him away. She had promised him this wasn't going to be a therapy session. But when did therapy end and become just a friend showing interest? She wasn't sure where the line was, so she just kept quiet.

He found a song he liked and cranked it up. It wasn't a band she was familiar with, and the music was too hard for her. She told herself she could endure it for the car ride to the farm.

Chris and Kim were waiting in the barn when they got there.

"Hey," Chris said, giving Boot a fist bump.

"Julia is here early," Kim said.

"Oh!" Rachel said. Julia was the teenager who had refused to get on Angel last weekend but instead had ended up hugging her.

"She's in the observation room."

"I have to work tonight," Rachel explained to Boot. "Kim wants to go over your set list. Did you bring it?"

Boot patted his back pocket.

"Good. Chris and Kim also want to ask for your help with some of the planning."

Once she was sure everyone was settled, she went to find Julia.

The girl was sitting in the observation room, twisting her fingers together. She looked up when Rachel entered the room.

"I want to try to ride tonight," she said, looking eager.

"I think that's a great idea," Rachel said. "Angel loves being ridden!"

The session went well, and Rachel was floating on air when she walked inside the tiny kitchen to find Chris and Kim listening to Boot rattle off ideas for the fundraiser. He wanted to print off photos of each horse, along with a bio, and post it on their stalls.

Then people could walk through the barn ahead of the auction to see which horses they wanted to bid on.

"I have all of the volunteers on board that night," Kim said to Rachel, as Rachel pulled out a seat to join them. "We'll put them in the barns to watch people with the horses. The schooling horses are all on the east side of the arena, so I plan to section off the west side, where Faith and my own horses are kept. We want to keep people out of there."

The plans sounded fantastic.

"Can we go see Faith?" Boot said.

Rachel looked at her watch. "Sure. We have about five more minutes before we need to leave, if I am going to get you back on time."

They walked quickly across the parking lot and into the barn. Faith whinnied, her ears pricked forward. Chris pulled out his baggie of treats and shook it.

"You have her so spoiled!" Rachel said.

They fed her, and Rachel stood back, watching as Boot rubbed her forehead.

"Can I ride her some day?" he asked.

"She's too weak right now," Rachel said. "Maybe someday. But I have other horses you can ride. Angel is my personal favorite. But you'd probably like Tommy too. He's pretty cool. Anyway, Faith…"

Rachel looked at Faith, who now had her forehead against Chris' arm and her eye closed. "I think Faith is Chris' horse. He saved her. He's healing her."

Boot watched them for a moment. "Dude, that's definitely your horse," he said.

That pleased Chris, and Rachel saw him smile. That gorgeous smile.

"We have to go," she said.

Boot nodded. "I'll go grab my guitar out of the house," he said. "I'll meet you at the car. Can I have your keys?"

Rachel tossed the keys to him, and he sprinted off.

"*My* horse, huh?" Chris said, rubbing Faith on the neck.

"Yes. She has totally adopted you."

"I like that."

He gave the horse a final rub. "Mind if I walk out to the car with you? I need to get going myself."

As they walked, Chris said, "I saw you with Julia. Rachel, you are *so* amazing with kids. With her, with Boot, you have this gift."

"You're not so bad yourself. Boot really seems to like you. I haven't seen him open up like that...ever."

"I love kids. One of my favorite things is going over to Dillon's house and hanging with his three. They're a bit noisy, so I can't do it often. But I'm hoping that as soon as I get my nerves calmed down, I can do more with them. I think I want a few of my own some day."

"Kids?"

"Yeah."

"I never thought I'd hear the captain of Winchester High School's football team say he wants kids. There are diapers to change, you know. And crying."

"And cuddles and unconditional love. At least until they are teenagers."

Rachel laughed. They were at the car, and there was one punk teen waiting for her in the car, the music blaring. It was going to be a long ride home.

Chapter Twenty-Four

On Friday, Chris was sitting out behind the hardware store, unwrapping his sandwich. He was thrilled. Last night, Rachel had called Faith "his" horse! He knew that, legally, the mare didn't belong to him, but he felt a bond with her.

That made him all the more determined to save the farm.

The meeting with Boot and Kim had gone well. They had everything lined up and a lot of people had RSVP'd. Kim said she had heard from clients that she hadn't seen in years. He had faith that this was going to turn out well.

Rachel had left her baseball cap in the barn, and he had seen it this morning when he had run out to the farm to drop off some lumber. He put it in his car so it didn't get lost. But the truth was, he wanted an excuse to text her. He looked at his phone, hoping she'd be on a lunch break at work. He took a deep breath and called her. She answered on the third ring.

"Hello?"

"Hey. It's me. I'm sorry if I'm bothering you. Are you with a client?"

"No. I'm on lunch break."

"I just wanted to tell you that you left your baseball cap in the barn. Near Faith's stall."

"Oh, thanks."

"I put it in my car. Just so it wouldn't get lost." He realized as soon as he said it how stupid that sounded. She'd see right through his flimsy excuse.

"Thanks!" But she sounded cheerful.

There was a brief silence. He didn't want to hang up. He tried to think of something else to say.

"What should I wear to this shower on Sunday?"

"It's casual," Rachel said. "Maybe some khakis if you have them. I'm wearing a summer dress. Nothing fancy."

"Okay."

"Are you *sure* you want to go?" Rachel said.

Did she want him to back out? Did she regret that she had agreed he could come?

"Yes. It'll be fun. Or…interesting."

"Interesting is a more descriptive word," Rachel said. "I'll have to work a little bit. I won't be able to sit with you the entire time. I have to make punch and stuff."

"No worries," Chris said, although sitting in a room with her parents was already a bit scary. "Will your dad be there? Or just your mom?"

"Dad too. It's a couple's shower."

"Yeah. Right."

There was another awkward pause.

"Do you think they'll remember me?" he asked.

He heard Rachel laugh. "They've never forgotten you."

"Of course they haven't."

After he hung up, he went over the conversation in his head, and decided he sounded stupid. He took several deep breaths to steady his nerves.

Relax, Chris! She's just a woman you are volunteering with. That's it.

But she was his therapist too. This was just…he didn't know. Weird?

He thought of her sweet face and blue eyes. She smelled so good. He was still in love with her, and because he didn't know how she felt about him, he wasn't sure at all that his feelings were appropriate. He'd just play it cool and let her make the first move. If she ever did. And if she didn't…

Well, he'd think about that later.

He called Dillon.

"What's up?"

"Hey bro. On your lunch hour?" Chris could hear the clank of bottles in the background and the noise of the machines.

"Yeah, I have a few minutes. You okay?"

His family always asked him that now when he called. Maybe he should call more often so they didn't always think it was an emergency. He couldn't blame them. For a while after the army, his calls had been either because he was so drunk he needed a ride, or because he had lost a job, been evicted, and needed a place to stay. "Just overnight. Please," he'd say.

"I'm great," Chris said. It was true. "I just wanted to talk to you about Rachel."

He heard Dillon let out a sigh.

"Dude, you have to let this one go. You messed with her big time in high school."

"I've changed."

"This is true."

"She invited me to a baby shower for her sister on Sunday. Remember her sister, April?"

"I do. But wait—Rachel *invited* you somewhere?"

"Yeah."

Dillon whistled. It hurt Chris' ear. "Bro, that's um, great. I mean, it is. But won't her parents be there?"

"Yes. I've thought about that. I can hopefully have the chance to apologize to them."

"Chris, listen to me. I may be your younger brother, but I know a thing or two about life and that is NOT a good idea. You seem to be going around wearing rose-colored glasses these days. Nobody forgives that easily. You wrecked their daughter's graduation. You *wrecked* her graduation. Her mother does not have a photo of Rachel waking across that stage and getting her diploma and that is not something that Claire Walker is going to forgive. That's not something the mother of my *own* children would forgive! And didn't Rachel end up at some rinky-dink college because of that?"

Chris sighed. He was regretting that he called Dillon.

"I know. You're right." It was easier to side with his brother than argue the point. He asked about the kids, then hung up the phone. Dillon was right. What was he thinking, showing up in enemy territory? He'd just cause tension, and this was supposed to be a fun event. Maybe he'd call Rachel and tell her he couldn't go.

But he wanted to see her. This was his chance to support her. He *did* remember how strict and perfectionistic her parents were. And she was clearly dreading this event. Wouldn't his presence be a support to her? Or would it cause more problems?

He didn't know. He felt his stomach quivering and knew the anxiety was returning.

Make a decision and stick to it, Chris. That was the voice of one of his therapist talking. Anxiety was caused in large part because of indecision.

He decided to stick with his earlier choice, and to go to the shower. It was easier than calling Rachel and letting her down.

He was an army vet. He could survive one baby shower.

And one fundraiser.

But he didn't like crowds. He sighed.

I'm okay, he said to himself. Then he sat back in the kitchen chair and tried to picture himself on Angel.

One. Two. Three. Four.

Her hoofbeats soothing him. The rock and sway of her body under him. The quiet sounds of the farm.

Faith came to mind. Beautiful Faith. He wished he was at the farm now, so he could put his arms around her big, horsey neck.

Rachel.

She came unbidden back into his mind. She was so good at what she did. And she was so beautiful. He wished he could put his arms around her, too.

Oh Chris, you are a mess.

He gave up on trying to relax, and went into the living room to watch TV. There was a home remodeling show on. He'd concentrate on that, and forget about everything else for a while.

Chapter Twenty-Five

Rachel sat in the observation room at the farm, rifling through the her clients' paperwork. Kim was sitting across from her, at the breakroom table. They were alone, taking a break in between clients. Somewhere out in the barn, Jennifer was saddling up a horse for her next session, and the other volunteers were busy doing chores.

Rachel glanced at Chris' file. "I asked him to go to April's shower with me on Sunday."

Kim looked up from her own paperwork. "The couple's shower?"

Rachel nodded. "Am I breaking some sort of client/therapist rule by hanging out with him?"

Kim snorted. "What rules? You're not even officially on board. Right now, I just have the clients sign a waiver, saying that you are licensed but not liable. You know that."

"I know. I was just checking."

"I suppose we need to be semi-professional about it. Is it going to hinder his therapy?"

"No. I don't know."

"Then probably not."

Rachel nodded, then went back to her file. Julia's file was in front of her. She made a few notes.

"Besides, you're breaking bigger rules than that."

Rachel glanced up across the table. She knew Kim was talking about Boot.

"Is that going to get you in trouble?" Rachel asked.

"Is what?" Kim shrugged. "I have no idea what you're talking about. Isn't he just a friend you invited out to the farm?"

Kim bent down to look at her papers. Rachel smiled and returned to her own work.

That night, Rachel sat on her bed and read the rest of the book of John. She closed the Bible and sat it on her nightstand.

Her dress for the baby shower tomorrow was ironed and hanging on the back of her bedroom door. She had chosen one of her favorite light blue dresses that brought out the color in her eyes. She had already carefully painted her nails that evening, telling herself that she just wanted to look nice for the shower tomorrow. But she was really trying to look nice for Chris.

She remembered how many times she had chosen her clothes, or applied her makeup in high school, to impress him. She didn't want to go there again.

But she couldn't go to the shower looking like a slob.

Besides, she and Chris could never be an item. Despite what Kim said about her being a therapist not mattering, there were other reasons.

For starters, he wanted kids. He had said so. That was something she could never give him.

He could never love me. Not once he finds out.

She had been down that road before. She could never be with a man who wanted kids. Never again.

She couldn't pursue any kind of relationship with him, even if he wanted to.

But he was so good with the horses, and so good with Boot.

Let it go, Rachel.

She'd have to discourage any moves he made toward her.

She turned off her bedside lamp and slid down underneath the covers. The apartment was cool from the air conditioner. It *would* be nice to have a warm body beside her. Was she destined to live by herself forever?

Where did that thought come from? She needed to think about something else. She used one of the techniques that she gave to her clients when they needed to calm their minds before bed. She pictured a white clay jar with a lid. Mentally, she started putting her thoughts in the jar. Thoughts about Chris. About not being able to have kids. About seeing Faith's parents at the store and how she had run from them.

She pictured Boot's face. What was going to happen to her career if someone found out she was working with him outside of client hours?

That was another scary thought. *Geez, Rachel.* She closed the jar lid tight in her mind's eye.

She had to get some sleep because tomorrow was the baby shower.

Instead, she sat up and turned on the light.

What had she been thinking, inviting Chris? Her family hated him. This was supposed to be April's day, and she was bringing someone who would become the talk of the shower. Or maybe not. Maybe they wouldn't even recognize him.

Ha. She knew they would. Wasn't that part of why she was bringing him?

Was she causing trouble or did she really just need him there as a buffer? This shower bothered her for so many reasons. Her sister's pregnancy had come so easily. It had never been said, but Rachel suspected the baby hadn't been planned. At least not yet. They had been married less than a year when April got pregnant. Rachel was excited about becoming an aunt, but at the same time, April talked about the baby nonstop now, and it hurt to see her sister getting something she had longed for.

And would never have.

She needed Chris there, as someone on her side when fingers started pointing at her. And they would. Her mom would have at least a dozen critical things to say. Rachel would make the punch wrong, or she'd have made the little diaper pins incorrectly. Her dress wouldn't be good enough. Had she considered a different hair style? (Or *any* hairstyle at all?)

Her parents had stopped saying the hurtful things they used to say, but she knew they still thought them. When she found out Rachel was infertile, her mom told her she should have had a baby earlier. Tried earlier. "Remember the miscarriages?" she had said to her mom.

"That's what happens when you work so hard."

Rachel had been new at her job. She was only working forty hours a week, nothing extravagant. Her mom had blamed her. It was always her fault. Always.

Then, when her ex had left her for another woman... She remembered that conversation like it was yesterday.

"Well, honey," her mom had said, her tone sweet with underlying currents of disappointment. "You didn't give him the attention he needed. You let that girl's death bring you down. It's a terrible loss, but you need to leave work at work. That is your job. *This* is your life."

Her mom had always referred to Faith as "that girl" and said Faith's suicide was "part of the job description." She said Rachel should have known going in that psychologists had to deal with this stuff. That it was no reason to let her marriage fall apart.

Rachel reached over and turned out the light. Yes, she definitely needed Chris there tomorrow to run interference. Rachel growled in frustration and slid down into bed again. She let her mind drift from Faith the teenager to Faith the horse. Funny how Kim had given the horse the same name, without even knowing.

Maybe this was God's way of letting Rachel finally heal Faith. Maybe, just maybe, if they could get the money for the farm, she wouldn't lose this one as well.

Chapter Twenty-Six

Chris was nervous. He looked in the mirror and straightened the collar on his shirt yet again. He was wearing a light blue polo and khaki pants. He had chosen the clothes carefully. While this wasn't a date, it wouldn't hurt to look good.

And it *felt* like a date.

Also, he'd have to see her parents. He knew this was going to be difficult for her, but did she realize how difficult it was going to be for *him?* The last time he had seen them was back in high school when he had been the cause of their daughter not walking at graduation.

If they were angry at Rachel, he could only imagine how angry they were with *him.*

Why on earth had he agreed to go?

"Because you owe her, Chris," he said aloud to himself.

Maybe he'd be able to make up for what he had done in high school by supporting her today. He still couldn't understand why she was so upset about the baby shower. Or why she had cried over the picture of the crib set.

He took a long, deep breath to steady himself, grabbed his keys, and left his apartment. He was picking her up, and they were driving together. They'd get there early so she had time to make the punch, but she was insistent that he go with her. She said she wasn't going early to help decorate.

"I need you there for interference," she said when he asked her for the address earlier in the week. "I just don't want to be alone with them at *this* particular event. It's just too…."

But she didn't finish her sentence. And he didn't ask.

He sighed. The shower had her tied in knots for some reason. He vaguely remembered her younger sister, April, but not too well.

Her apartment complex was on the edge of town. He texted when he arrived, and she came out wearing a light blue dress and white sandals. She had curled her hair, and it hug in loose waves against her shoulders. She looked stunning.

"Hi!" she said, breathless as she climbed in his car.

"I could have come up to get you like a proper gentleman," he said.

"No. My apartment is a mess."

He waited for her to buckle her seatbelt. Her dress showed her shoulders, and he noticed she had a light spattering of freckles across them. She had put on a subtle shade of pink lipstick, and her cheeks were rosy.

"You look great," he said.

She turned to him, and her eyes looked bluer than ever.

"Thanks," she said. "You clean up pretty well yourself."

Chris smiled and put the car in gear. "Hopefully I look and smell better than I do at the farm."

Rachel laughed. "There's nothing wrong with a little hay in your hair."

The banquet hall was about a ten-minute drive. The traffic was heavy for a Sunday because St. Ives was a popular tourist town.

"Thanks for coming," Rachel said. "I have no idea how my parents are going to react. I told them I was bringing a date, but that's all I said."

A date. She had called this a date!

"I can only imagine they won't be too thrilled to see me," Chris said.

Rachel glanced over at him. "Are you going to be okay? I mean, it's not too late to back out."

"By okay do you mean am I going to tackle you to the ground again?"

"No. I just mean…there's a lot to be anxious about. Heck, I'm anxious and I don't have PTSD."

"You're getting all therapist-y on me," Chris said glancing over at her. "I'll be fine. And I'm not backing out and leaving you to the wolves. Not again."

Out of the corner of his eye, he saw her look at him. "Thanks," she said softly.

The banquet hall was part of a seafood restaurant that was known for their maple plank salmon. He had eaten here once, but hadn't gone back because it was pricey. He felt his mouth watering at the memory, though.

They had planned to arrive right as the baby shower began, so there would already be other people there. The plan had worked. As the hostess led them back to the banquet room, Chris could see that there were already several couples here, probably about half of the eighty that were expected.

"Mom isn't going to be happy with our timing," Rachel whispered. "But I *did* tell her I'd be late."

"She'll probably blame that on me, since I drove," Chris whispered back. So they were already starting off on the wrong foot.

"No. She'll blame me. She always does."

"Rachel!" He heard Mrs. Walker's voice and saw her hurrying toward them. She had a basket in one hand and a string of safety pins in another. "I'm so glad you're here. You can give these out as the guests come in." She turned to Chris. "And you *did* bring your boy—" She stopped short. Her eyes narrowed as she took him in. Chris didn't think he looked much different than he had in high school, only older. And hopefully wiser.

"Chris?" She looked shocked.

He nodded and offered her his hand to shake. "Mrs. Walker. It's so nice to see you."

She refused his hand and turned back to Rachel. "*Really?* This is your sister's big day and you decide to bring *him* here? You're not actually *dating* him, are you? The man who wrecked your life?" Her voice was a whisper, but he could hear the acid dripping in her tone.

"Mom," Rachel said, "be nice. He has changed. He's working at the farm, and I needed a date. It'll be fine."

Mrs. Walker scowled at Chris, then turned to Rachel. "Get him seated. Maybe somewhere in the back. Then hand those out. I have your dad handling the punch since you're late." Mrs. Walker frowned at Chris one last time then hustled off.

Rachel gave Chris an apologetic look, then led him to a seat near the front of the room. "I'm supposed to sit here," she said. "And you are my guest."

"Maybe I should sit back there," Chris said, pointing to a table in the far back corner.

"No. I need you with me."

He sat and introduced himself to another couple sitting at the table. The man worked with April's husband and had been best man at their wedding. Chris looked around the room. He was grateful that he didn't know that many people. It had been twelve years since he left high school, and ten for April.

A waiter filled his water glass, and he took a sip. April and her husband were sitting up front at a long table, like he had seen at weddings. There was a buffet table set up front as well, off to the side, and filled with an assortment of desserts. On the other side of the room was a table overflowing with gifts.

"Fish or chicken?" the waitress at his table asked, handing him a paper menu. He scanned it. The fish choice was the maple plank salmon, in a lunch portion, with garlic mashed potatoes. He'd get that.

His phone vibrated. It was a text from Rachel.

Order me the salmon.

He glanced up at her. She was near the door, handing out those tiny little diapers. He nodded at her, and she smiled.

He sat alone for about fifteen minutes before Rachel joined him.

"Shouldn't you be up at the front table?" he asked. She shook her head. "No."

Their salmon was delicious. Rachel kept up a steady stream of conversation and seemed overly engaged in everything he had to say. They talked about the farm, about work, and about the weather. Then she turned to the other couple and started asking them questions about what they did. From what he remembered of Rachel, she was an introvert. She was trying to avoid having to talk to her parents or her sister, that much was clear.

"Game time," Rachel whispered, and stood up so she could pass out the materials. First, he had to write a guess of the baby's name on a slip of paper, which Rachel collected.

"Do you know?" he whispered when she came to his table.

"That's cheating!" she said, and smiled. "But no. They've kept it private. I'll hear it along with everybody else."

He put down Lillian. It turned out to be Chelsea. The prize was a gift card to a coffee shop.

As Rachel was handing out Bingo sheets, Mr. Walker came over. He pulled out Rachel's chair and sat down next to Chris.

Oh no, Chris thought. *Here we go.*

He had put his glass of beer down on the table, and Chris watched the moisture create a ring on the linen table cloth.

"Sorry I only have the one," Mr. Walker said, nodding towards the glass. "I seem to recall how much you like alcohol."

Chris took in a long, slow breath and let it out before he responded. "I've quit drinking."

Mr. Walker's eyes flickered to Chris' water glass, then to Chris. "You have no right to be here."

"Look, I know I messed up…"

"Is that what you call it?"

"I owe you an apology," Chris said. He glanced around the room. Rachel was over on the other side, her back towards him, handing out Bingo sheets.

"You need to leave," Mr. Walker said. "Why don't the two of us walk to the door together?"

"Sir, Rachel invited me here. I can't just leave without telling her."

"Why not? That's what you did last time."

Chris suddenly felt a warm hand on his shoulder. He jumped, then saw it was Rachel.

"Dad, I need to sit down," Rachel said. "Can you move back to your seat? The Bingo is about to start."

There was a stony silence as Mr. Walker held Rachel's eyes. Finally, he gave a little grunt and stood up. "We'll finish this later," he said to Chris.

Rachel sat down, putting a pen and notebook on the table in front of her, and looked over at Chris.

"You okay?" she whispered.

"Peachy."

Rachel's mom stood up and explained the game. He had to fill out each box with a baby gift and when April and her husband opened it he was supposed to mark it off. If he filed in a straight line, they yelled "Baby Bingo!" and won a prize.

"Give me some hints," Chris said. Rachel's dad had retreated up front, and was nursing his beer.

"Well, we know there's a crib set," she said. She uncapped her pen. ""I have to write down who gives them what, so they can send out thank you cards."

The shower seemed to go on forever. The couple had a lot of gifts to open up. Chris watched Rachel's face carefully, trying to make out why she hated being here so much. There was more to the story than just her uncomfortable relationship with her parents, although that in itself was enough. At least for him. She kept her jaw set firmly, and didn't smile and ooh at the little pink dresses or blankets like the other women did. She was all-business, which wasn't like her. He remembered how emotional she was with her teens and the horses.

When April opened the crib set that he knew Rachel and her mom had bought, he saw Rachel swallow hard a few times.

Afterwards, as the guests started to leave, Rachel stood. "I need to help her get these packages into the car."

"I can help," Chris said.

He was given some of the heavier stuff and carried it out back to where April and her husband had parked their vehicle, a new minivan. They had fully bought into parenthood already.

He set the highchair in the trunk and pushed it deeper into the van.

"Thanks," April said.

"Sure."

Ms. Walker came out, carrying a gift bag filled with new baby clothes. She handed him the bag to put in the van, which he did.

"Why are you here?" she said.

He turned to look at her. She had her arms crossed in front of her. "I'm helping." He nodded toward the highchair and then lifted a heavy box with a glider-rocker in it. He pushed it to the front of the van next to the highchair.

"You know what I mean. You need to stay away from Rachel. You ruined her life once."

He turned to look at her again.

"Yes, why *are* you here?" April asked.

Chris looked around. Rachel was nowhere in sight. He took a slow, deep breath. "I owe your family an apology," he said.

"You owe us more than that," Mrs. Walker said. "You destroyed her life."

"I am sorry," Chris said slowly. He wanted to add that they, too, had destroyed her life, because whatever mental manipulation was going on was clearly making her miserable. But he held his tongue. "I was young and stupid and selfish. But I've changed. And I'm here to make amends."

"She's been through a lot," April said. "She doesn't need another heartbreak, and from what I remember from you, that's what you're best at."

"She is fragile," Mrs. Walker said. "If you mess with her, you're going to be messing with me."

Chris raised an eyebrow, uncertain of what to say next. He didn't exactly see Rachel as fragile. Not the way she handled her tough client cases and the horses. She was strong to do what she did. She had to be.

"I'll do whatever she needs for me to do," he said.

Just then, Rachel came out of the hall, carrying a laundry basket filled with baby clothes. She shoved it in the van and looked from Chris to her mother and April. "What's up?"

Chris shook his head. "Nothing. We were just catching up."

Rachel rubbed her hands together. "That's about it," she said. "Chris and I need to be going. I have a thing to do this evening."

"Does it involve a horse?" Ms. Walker said.

Rachel only smiled.

Mrs. Walker shook her head. "You need to outgrow that hobby."

"Hey, Rach," April grabbed her arm. "Do you want to come over and help me and Mom set up the nursery Tuesday after work? I'd like to do it tomorrow, but I have a doctor's appointment."

Rachel looked like a deer caught in headlights.

"It'll be fun," April said. "We can hang up the cute little onesies." She reached in and grabbed a small, pink dress. "I bought some tiny little hangers. And you can help me set up the crib and put up that cute little comforter you bought."

Rachel glanced at Chris. "We have a thing…"

"Always a thing," Mrs. Walker said.

Chris knew that Rachel had planned to pick up Boot after work. They were going to finalize plans for the event.

"I mean, I'd love to, but—"

"Come on, Rach! I have to be more important than some horses," April said. "Just this once! This is your niece we're talking about! I want you to be part of her life. I know how much you love kids, and this may be your only chance to—"

Mrs. Walker's elbow landed in April's side, shutting her up.

"Not here, April," she said.

"My only chance to what?" Rachel said, quietly and evenly. Her tone was icy.

"To, you know," April said, her eyes sliding to Chris, then back to Rachel. "Play with a baby. I mean, you're almost thirty."

"April." Mrs. Walker's voice held a warning.

Chris saw Rachel turn a deep shade of red.

"Rachel and I really need to go," Chris said, protectively taking Rachel's elbow. "And we have an important business meeting on Tuesday. Maybe you can get together another day."

He pulled Rachel toward him and steered her back through the door, through the restaurant, and out to the car. They got inside, shut the doors, and stared driving before either of them spoke.

"Thank you," Rachel said. She had put on her dark sunglasses but grabbed a tissue from her purse, dabbing at her eyes.

"Do you mind telling me what that was about?"

Rachel shook her head. "No. I can't." She looked over at him, but he couldn't see her eyes through the dark glasses.

"They hated me, but I get the feeling they aren't too happy with you either," he said.

"They think I've screwed up my life," Rachel said.

"And now that you showed up with me…" Chris sighed. "I can only imagine."

"They're right. I did screw up my life. One of my clients killed herself. My husband left me for another woman. And, at the age of twenty-nine, I live in a tiny apartment and play with horses."

"I wouldn't call what you're doing with the horses play," he said.

Rachel sniffed.

"You're helping *me*," Chris continued. "A few weeks ago I would have never been able to sit in a crowded room so far away from the door. And then, I was attacked in the parking lot by your family. But look at me. I'm fine. I'm just glad your dad didn't show up out back."

"He saw a man he knows from work. They started talking."

Chris put on his turn signal and turned right, heading back to her apartment.

"Can we go to the farm?" Rachel said.

"In these clothes?"

Rachel nodded. "Yeah. They'll wash."

The farm sounded like a great idea to Chris. Right now, he wanted nothing more than to see Faith and feel her warm skin under his hands, her soft muzzle taking sugar cubes out of his palm. He knew Rachel needed the therapy that the horses offered too. He had no idea what was going through her mind, but she was deeply hurting.

He turned left instead of right and headed toward Three Hearts Ranch. He finally understood how equine-assisted therapy worked. He got it, one-hundred percent. And that's where he'd take Rachel.

Chapter Twenty-Seven

Rachel spent the next hour with Chris, brushing Faith. By the time they were finished, they were both covered in a fine layer of golden palomino hair. Rachel had traded her sandals for the extra pair of riding boots she kept at the farm.

"Cute," Chris had said when she slipped them on with her dress.

They hadn't talked about anything serious, just the horses and the upcoming fundraiser. She was grateful that Chris didn't ask about the altercation back at the restaurant.

It was just like April to use the baby against her to get her way. Their mom had always done that, using things against her to force Rachel to perform a certain way. And now April did it. The apple didn't fall far from the tree. And for some reason it hurt more when it came from April.

April had always been a little jealous of the things Rachel had, which Rachel never understood because her life was certainly not one to be envious of. Not now. Not even in high school.

But April had always felt that she was in Rachel's shadow. She had never quite gotten the good grades that Rachel did or been as popular. She was pretty, but she envied Rachel's blonde hair. April had tried bleaching it, but the color didn't suit her darker complexion. She envied Rachel her husband, until he left her. Once Rachel's life fell apart, after the graduation incident, April had latched onto her failures. It was subtle, often disguised as "caring," but April often reminded her big sister how far she had fallen.

But using the baby against her was just plain mean. She knew Rachel wanted children, and had lost some. And could never have any of her own.

Rachel supposed April truly wanted her to come and decorate the nursery. But she couldn't go. Not with her mom there too.

She and April occasionally did "sister" things together and most of the time it was okay. But as soon as Rachel said she had other plans, April became defensive, thinking she was less important on Rachel's list of "things to do." They had had an argument last Christmas about that very thing. April always felt "last" on Rachel's list. So did her mom.

Maybe if they were *nicer*, Rachel would want to spend more time with them.

Decorating the baby's nursery would be fun under different circumstances. Rachel had made it eleven weeks before her final miscarriage, and she and her then-husband had started looking at nursery décor. She had settled on a baby farm animal pattern, mostly because it had horses in it, but also because she loved the outdoor feel that came with the colors.

Then, they had lost the baby, and she had filed
away the samples and magazine photos for future
use. Until she found out she couldn't have kids.

Faith turned and nuzzled her. "I'm out of treats,"
Rachel said, rubbing the mare's nose. "I should get
home anyway. I have to work in the morning."

Chris nodded and put his brush back in the brush
box.

They drove home together, neither saying much of
anything. Finally, Chris said, "The food was good."

"Yeah. I love their salmon. That's one of the
reasons they picked that place."

He pulled into her apartment complex and found
a parking spot in front of her building.

He shut off the car.

Rachel turned to Chris. The last rays of the evening
sun slanted through the car window, highlighting the
gold in his hair. She wanted to reach over and run
her hand through it. He met her gaze, his eyes soft
and sincere.

"Are you okay?" he asked gently.

"Yeah," she said. "I am. Thank you for being
there."

"I'm glad I could be."

"And thank you for not asking about it."

Chris nodded. "I understand the need to not talk
about certain things."

He did. His silent strength had carried her through
the rest of the evening when she had just wanted to
run home and hide under the covers.

He looked good in the polo. His arms were
muscled from hard work and probably from lifting
weights. His chest was broad and strong under the

shirt. She felt a stirring inside her, and she longed to lean into him and let him put his arms around her. It had been a long time since anyone had held her.

She remembered that one kiss so long ago and wondered what he tasted like now. But she could never know.

"You want me to walk you up?" Chris asked.

She did. She wanted him to walk her up and stay for a while. But she shook her head.

"No. I'll be fine." She had to stop this before it started. She quickly opened the car door.

"I've gotta go. Early morning."

"Sure," Chris said. "I'll see you tomorrow night? For my session?"

She nodded and then fled upstairs to her apartment.

Chapter Twenty-Eight

Chris stood in front of the barn at Three Hearts Ranch and watched Rachel drive up the long, winding drive. He could see Boot in the passenger side of her car.

He had only seen Rachel for a short while yesterday, for his riding session. It went well. She was pleasant but stand-offish. The way she had been looking at him in the car when he dropped her off at her apartment on Sunday made him believe she wanted more from their relationship. But then, she had grown cold and fled.

He couldn't quite figure her out.

"That's one cool kid," Kim said. She had just come from the barn, and the front of her shirt and jeans were a bit wet. She saw him looking at her. "I had an accident with the hose."

"I need to tape it," Chris said. "I'll get some waterproof tape from the hardware store in the morning."

"You're a saint."

"Mr. B's a saint. I tell him what it's for, and he just gives me stuff. Or heavily discounts it."

Rachel parked the car, and she and the kid climbed out. Boot had his guitar with him and also a grocery bag of stuff.

"I brought some posters," Boot said. "I made them on my computer last night. You don't have to use them."

He handed the bag to Kim. She reached in and pulled out a manila envelope. Inside were posters printed on white paper titled, "Adopt me!" Each one had a photo of one of the farm's therapy horses, and underneath, a description of each.

"Wow!" Kim said. "How on earth did you come up with these photos?"

"I took them on my phone when I was here last week. Then Rachel—um, Ms. Walker—told me about the horses. I tried to put their special characteristics on their adoption papers, like how Tudor's favorite treat is baby carrots and how he loves to be scratched under the chin, like a cat."

"And he sleeps in the patch of daisies in the pasture, like Ferdinand the Bull," added Rachel.

"Boot, these are really cool!" Kim said leafing through them.

"Rachel says you have plastic sleeves I can put them in to keep them dry."

"Yeah, which we definitely need," Kim said, pointing to her wet front. She laughed. "This is awesome. I'll get them up tomorrow."

Boot didn't say anything, but he looked pleased. In just the short time that Rachel had been bringing him to the farm, he had bloomed. His eyes were brighter, and he laughed more often. And he was really excited about the fundraiser. Boot was a good planner; a smart kid with a lot of ideas. Chis was glad he was part of their team.

"Rachel says I can ride Angel tonight if we finish on time," Boot said. He looked quickly at Rachel, then at the ground as if embarrassed by his enthusiasm.

"Of course!" Kim said. "I think that's a great idea!" But she shot a look at Rachel.

"Really?" Boot turned and grinned at Chris. "I'm gonna need a cowboy hat!"

Chris laughed. "A hat? Good idea. I'm still working on the boots! All I have are these work boots. They serve the purpose, but they're not nearly as cool as a proper pair of western boots."

The four of them got to work. With the fundraiser on Saturday, they had to make sure all the plans were in place tonight. Chris was going to finish up the final details tomorrow, but they still had a lot to get done tonight. And right now the weather looked like it was going to hold up. Sunny and in the seventies for Saturday. Perfect!

Chris hadn't felt this good about things in a long time. He was in charge of something important, and it was all coming together.

Chris, Rachel, and Boot worked on clearing out the area for the tent. A volunteer had mowed it recently, and they ran a string around it, marking off where the tent should go. Chris and Boot hauled a large wooden platform that Chris had built into the space. It was just a few wooden pallets with beams on top, but it made a pretty cool stage where Boot could sit with his guitar.

"You want to play a few songs and give it a try?" Chris asked.

"Sure thing." Boot ran up to the house to fetch his guitar. He had left it in the kitchen, out of the heat, while they worked.

"It's looking good," Rachel said, coming over to stand next to Chris.

"Yeah. It's pretty exciting. Kim says we're expecting over a hundred people."

Boot returned with his guitar and a kitchen chair. He sat down and tuned it, then played a few songs, mostly classic rock.

Rachel grinned. "He's a boy of many talents."

Kim joined the two of them just as he finished.

"Can I ride Angel now?" Boot asked. Chris saw that his eyes were shining. This sulky, serious teenager was as excited as a young kid about riding a horse.

"Sure!" Rachel said.

"Hold on a minute," Kim said, "two things." She looked at Rachel. "He needs a side-walker. He's a minor and we need to keep him safe."

"What's a side-walker?" Boot asked.

"It's someone who walks alongside the horse, with his hand on or near the rider. That way, if the rider is about to fall off, he can grab him. It's a safety measure."

"I'm not about to fall off of a horse," Boot said, looking offended.

"That's the rule. Otherwise, you don't ride." Kim looked at Rachel. "We don't have any paperwork signed."

"Got it," Rachel said. "A side-walker. Chris, that is going to have to be you. All of the volunteers have gone home."

"I can do that."

"What's the second thing?" Boot asked. "You said two things."

Kim looked him square in the eye. "You have to do exactly as Rachel says. Exactly."

Boot nodded. "Of course."

With that settled, Boot and Rachel trotted off to the barn. Chris was left holding the guitar. He handed it to Kim.

"Can you put it in the kitchen until we're finished? It's too hot in the car."

She nodded. "I wouldn't normally allow this," Kim said, looking at Rachel and Boot, who were about to disappear inside the barn. "But I think he needs a little horse therapy. It'll do him good."

"Why wouldn't you allow it?"

"We don't have any paperwork signed, clearing us of liability."

"Oh."

"But Angel is a good horse. He'll be fine. It's his parents I'm worried about."

"Maybe this isn't a good idea."

"I don't think his parents know he's here," Kim said. It was the first time he had heard either her or Rachel voice the thing they all suspected.

"I think you're right."

"Let's hope I'm not. But I think saving this kid is more important than following rules. Let's just pray it doesn't backfire on us."

"And if it does," Chris said, "well, when I was in Afghanistan, you had to do whatever you could to save the man who was down. No matter the consequences."

Kim nodded. "That's what I try to do here. Save the ones I can."

Chris stood beside Angel, on her right side, and put his hand on Boot's knee.

"Dude. This is not cool."

"You heard Rachel. I have to have my hand on you to steady you."

"It's too weird."

"It's Kim's rule. Side-walkers must have their hands on the rider," Rachel said. But she glanced up at the house. "I know it's weird. Chris, just walk beside him. Unless you see Kim."

"Ms. Walker, I had no idea you were such a rule breaker," Boot teased.

"Yeah, well, it's going to get me in trouble one of these days," she said. "Don't use me as an example of good behavior."

Boot laughed. "Now what?"

"Hang on."

Rachel started leading Angel, and Chris walked beside them, ready to catch Boot if something went wrong. But the kid was nearly as big as he was. Angel plodded along, her slow, steady gait rocking Boot in the saddle.

"Lay the reins on the horse's neck," Rachel said.

Boot did, totally trusting her.

"Now close your eyes."

It was interesting, watching this from the ground. Chris glanced up at the kid as they walked around the arena and watched his features soften as Rachel guided him into a state of relaxation with the horse. He saw Boot's shoulders relax first and then his face.

"Now put your hands on her neck. Feel the warmth of her skin?" Rachel said. "Can you feel the muscles of the horse under your palms?"

Boot nodded. After a few minutes, he said, "It's like music. Her gait is four beats. I can feel a rhythm."

Chris glanced over at Rachel, who smiled. "Exactly," she said. "Try to get lost in the rhythm."

"Is that my goal?" Boot said.

"Right now, yes," Rachel said. "Your goal is to concentrate on the horse so that everything else fades away. This gives your body and mind a chance to relax, to recharge. You'll probably write better songs after this session."

Boot was quiet, concentrating. The still sounds of the farm surrounded them. A few birds chirped in the yard, and a warm breeze rustled the leaves of the nearby maple trees. It was another perfect evening, neither hot nor cold.

"This is awesome," Boot said quietly. "I think I finally understand this horse therapy you talked to me about all the time. How come you didn't do this with me earlier?"

Rachel was about to answer when they saw a car turn into the driveway, heading toward the barn, kicking up a trail of dust. When it reached the arena, the driver stopped and jumped out. Chris could see right away that it was a man and he was angry.

"Oh no." Boot had opened his eyes at the sound. Rachel stopped the horse.

"It's his father," Rachel said. Chris heard the fear in her voice.

"What is going on here?" the man shouted, storming over to the arena. "Scott, get off that horse this minute!" The man's face was beet red, and he was pointing frantically at the ground. "*This minute!*"

Boot glanced at Rachel, and she nodded. She briefly told him how to dismount, and he quickly climbed off.

"Dad."

The man came to the arena and ducked between the rails. He stormed over to them, the tails of his suitcoat flapping behind him. Chris noticed his shiny black dress shoes were now coated in dust.

"What's going on here?" he demanded.

"Mr. Tellian," Rachel said. "I can explain. Scott was just helping us prepare for an upcoming fundraiser."

"This doesn't look like preparing for a fundraiser," he said. "You have my son on a *horse!* Without my permission! He could have been killed."

"Dad, Angel would never hurt me," Boot said.

"And *you.*" Mr. Tellian said. A wave of protectiveness swept across Chris as Boot's dad pointed at Rachel. "I fired you. What on earth are you doing still working with my kid?"

"Dad, it isn't like that," Boot said. "They needed a musician for their fundraiser."

"I know all about it," Mr. Tellian said. "I came home today to find you gone. I was home early the other day and you weren't home either. So I wondered, where can my son be? I opened the computer and saw this on the screen!" He pulled out one of the flyers for the fundraiser and waved it in Boot's face.

"I never gave you permission to do this! You are supposed to be grounded!"

"Dad, I—"

"Come on!" Mr. Tellian grabbed Boot's arm roughly and pulled him toward the car. The movement startled Angel, and her head shot up. Rachel put a comforting hand on the horse's neck.

"Mr. Tellian," Chris said. He ducked under the fence rail and stepped toward them. "We really need your son. The event is on Saturday and he's a fantastic guitarist. He's a hard worker and I think that this—"

Mr. Tellian stopped and spun around. "Who are *you?* You have no right to tell me what to do with my son. I'm trying to discourage this guitar playing. It's a waste of time."

Chris stopped short of Mr. Tellian. He didn't want to make things worse. He knew he could look intimidating when he needed to.

The other man looked him over, then turned away. "Come on," he said to Boot and pulled his son under the top fence post. Boot scrambled to keep up.

"I don't ever want him back here again, do you understand?" Mr. Tellian said, casting a look in Rachel's direction before he climbed into the car.

"Ms. Walker!" Boot stopped and turned to look at her, his eyes pleading.

"Boot, you should go," Rachel said. She nodded. "It's the best thing to do right now."

Boot climbed into the car. His dad turned around and left in a cloud of dust.

When the dust cleared, Chris saw Kim standing just outside the door of her house, holding Boot's guitar case. She walked across the driveway to them.

"His parent?" she asked.

"Yeah," Chris said.

Rachel came over with Angel.

"I'm sorry. This is all my fault," she said.

Kim shook her head. "That man's a jerk and clearly has anger issues. Rachel, why don't you go put Angel away? Then I guess we have to figure out what to do about music on Saturday."

Chris was angry. He had a death grip on the steering wheel as he drove home. They had decided he would act as DJ while people ate. But they hadn't had the heart to plan any further. They were all upset about the scene with Boot.

Chris took several deep breaths. Years of therapy had taught him to breath in, hold it, count, and breath out. He tried this several times.

"Please God, be with that kid," Chris prayed.

He had come to really like Boot over the time they worked together. He was a good kid. With some hard work to do and the realization that he was part of a team, that he was needed, he had started to heal.

Just like Chris.

The kid deserved more. If he kept living like he was now, with his parents so against him being who he was, he'd be hard-pressed to do well in college. Or in life.

Chris pulled off to the side of the road to think.

"Give me wisdom," he prayed to God.

It was almost dark now, nearly 9 p.m., but he figured Mr. Tellian would still be awake.

He brought out his phone and Googled "Tellian, St. Ives." Scott Tellian, Sr., Boot's dad, was the first result. His name was associated with Tellian Industries, a company that manufactured commercial and residential paint. Chris recognized one of the brands as a paint they sold in the hardware store.

He scrolled down and found the listing for the man in the white pages. He was rewarded with his address.

It was about ten minutes away. He drove straight there and parked across the street. He felt out of place in the big, fancy neighborhood in his small, rusted car.

Mr. Tellian lived in a giant two-story house. Immaculate landscaping with rounded shrubs and a layered rock berm wrapped around the big front porch. The front windows were lit, and he could see a television screen glowing on the far wall. Before he lost his nerve, he took a deep breath, then got out of the car.

He knocked loudly. Someone muted the television. The door opened.

Mr. Tellian stood there, his shirt undone and tie hanging loose around his neck. He had a newspaper in his hand.

"What do you want?" he said, his eyes flashing.

"I came to apologize," Chris said. "We never should have taken Scott to the farm without your permission. He just asked to come, and, well, I had no idea you didn't know about it."

Which was true. Chris had never asked.

"I should sue you all," Mr. Tellian grumbled.

"But I wanted to tell you what an awesome kid you have. He's smart, polite, and very creative. And talented. I can only imagine how blessed you must feel to hear him play in your home all the time! He is going to draw the crowds in tomorrow when he performs with us, if you'll let him."

"Talented? He wastes his time with that thing."

"Mr. Tellian," Chris said, "the farm is about to go under. It helps a lot of people. Kids, teenagers, adults. It has helped me a great deal. I am a veteran with PTSD, and I can honestly say, it has saved my life."

Mr. Tellian still looked angry. Usually, when Chris told people he was a veteran, he at least got a "thank you for your service" out of them.

"So?"

"So we need him tomorrow. Please let him play his guitar for our crowd. Then, if you want, he never has to set foot on the property again. Please, sir."

He added "sir" for effect.

Mr. Tellian folded his newspaper and threw it on the chair behind him. He crossed his arms.

"I think you people are all crazy. I don't see how a horse can heal anybody. And furthermore, I don't appreciate you inviting my son to play cowboys when he needs to be studying calculus. Do you know he has a C in that class right now? That's why he's grounded.

"I pulled him from Rachel Walker's care. She was doing a terrible job with him, putting the wrong things into his head. I haven't seen a change in him since he stared therapy *months* ago. If anything, he's worse."

"He's depressed," Chris said.

"Don't tell me what my son is. He just needs to suck it up and face reality. He needs to get good grades and get into a good college, where he might have some hope of getting a good job. You people have crossed a line. Rachel Walker has crossed a line. She should have her license revoked. Good night."

Mr. Tellian started to shut the door, but Chris planted his boot in between the door and the frame.

"My dad was hard on me," he said. "Nothing I did made him happy. I walked a fine line all the time, caught between wanting to please my dad and wanting to be the authentic me. You need to love Scott for the boy he is, Mr. Tellian. And he's wonderful. But he can be even more wonderful if he has your love. All kids crave that. All he wants is for you to love him for who he is."

"For who he is? A freak?"

It was then that Chris saw Boot come down the stairs.

"Is that what you think I am, Dad?"

Mr. Tellian turned. "You're supposed to be in your room."

There was a brief silence. Then Boot turned and ran back up the stairs. They heard a door slam.

"You've done enough damage here, Mr...?"

"Chris. My name is Chris."

"Good night."

Chris removed his foot and Mr. Tellian shut the door firmly in Chris' face.

Chapter Twenty-Nine

Rachel woke to rain on Friday morning. The weather fit her mood. She'd had trouble falling asleep last night, after the incident with Boot and his dad. She had lain awake, trying to figure out what she could do. There was nothing. Boot was someone else' kid, and like she had done with numerous kids before, she had to let it go.

But she wasn't sure she could.

She took a long, hot shower, then ambled into the kitchen in her bathrobe and sliced a banana into her cereal. Her first client wasn't until 11 a.m., so she had a while before she went in to work.

Maybe she should call Boot's dad and apologize. She had his number from the paperwork he and his wife had filled out.

She wanted to call Boot. She had almost texted him last night to check on him, but she was afraid his parents had taken his phone, and the last thing they needed to see was a text from Boot's former therapist, who had broken more than a few rules.

She was in enough trouble with them as it was.

She wondered briefly if Greta had heard about this, then dismissed the thought because it was too upsetting. She needed a job. If she got fired over this, who would hire her? What had she been thinking?

She stirred her cereal, watching the bananas mix. What were they going to do about the fundraiser now that they had no entertainment? Last night, she, Kim, and Chris had decided that Chris would put together a playlist on his phone and play it over the speakers. But they had advertised "live music."

Would people leave? Surely not. They were there for the horses.

Maybe she'd call Chris. But he was at work this morning.

Finally, deciding there was literally nothing she could do, she finished up her cereal and went to get dressed for work.

She arrived at 10:30, a half hour before her first client, so she could catch up on some paperwork. It was pouring outside, and she shook her umbrella off in the clinic's outer hallway, then peeled her rain coat off before she went inside.

"Good morning," she said to the receptionist. She was on the phone, so gave Rachel a nod.

Rachel walked back to her office and hung up her coat behind the door to dry. There was a knock on her door.

She looked up. Greta was standing in the doorway.

"Come in. I have a few minutes before my next client arrives."

Greta came in and shut the door. She continued standing just inside the doorway, a sad look on her face.

Uh-oh.

"Rachel, I got a call from Scott Tellian's dad first thing this morning."

Rachel felt a wave of panic. She swallowed. "You did?"

"I think you know what it's about."

Rachel dropped the paperwork on her desk. She felt her breakfast turning to acid in her stomach.

"Do you want to defend yourself?" Greta asked, gently.

"Yes," Rachel said. Her knees suddenly felt weak. She pulled out her chair and sat at her desk. "We're doing a fundraiser out at the farm and needed a musician. I knew he played, so I asked him. He agreed. I had no idea his parents didn't know."

Greta's eyes narrowed. "Did you ask them?"

Rachel dropped her eyes. "No."

"Don't ask, don't tell?" Greta said.

Rachel looked back up. Greta wasn't just a boss. She was a friend, someone who had walked with Rachel through Faith's death, her divorce, and the grief of her miscarriages.

"He wasn't ready to quit therapy," she said. "He was going to kill himself."

Greta's eyes widened a bit. "He was? You know you're supposed to report that."

"Well," Rachel said. "He never actually said he was. I just saw the signs."

"What signs?"

"He suddenly went from sullen to cheery, like he had made a decision. He started giving his stuff away."

"What did he give away?"

"He was going to give his guitar to his buddy at school," Rachel said.

"*Going* to?"

She knew she was losing this argument.

"He apologized to me for wasting my time. He gave me an album."

"That's not a lot to go on."

"Darn it, Greta!" Rachel smacked her hand down on her desk and stood. "I went with my gut, okay? I felt something was wrong so I did what I thought was best. After what happened with…" she let her voice trail off. She shouldn't have gone there.

"After what happened with Faith?" There was compassion in Greta's eyes now. Or pity. "Rachel, is it possible that you are still measuring your clients by that one experience? It was a terrible experience, but you can't let it color everything you do or see."

"I don't."

Great raised an eyebrow to show that she thought otherwise.

"Greta…"

"At any rate," Greta said. "You broke some serious rules. You crossed some lines. I have looked the other way for the past few years when things have gone wrong: when you missed appointments, when you lost paperwork, when you were an emotional mess and I thought you should go home. I continued to let you work through all of this. I fought for you. But Rachel, you've gone too far this time."

A cold, icy fear grabbed hold of Rachel.

"I have to let you go."

Rachel sat back down. She looked at the papers in front of her, then glanced up at the clock. Her 11 a.m. would be here soon.

"I canceled your appointment."

"What?"

"Your 11 a.m. She's not coming. I told her you were ill."

She glanced down at the notes again. The words swam.

"Rachel, I'm firing you."

She looked back up at Greta. "Please. I won't do it again."

"You need to leave."

Rachel wondered what would happen with her afternoon client. The little boy was terrified of everything and school was a nightmare for him. He needed help with his anxiety. They were doing so well together.

She thought about the girl with the eating disorder. What would happen to her?

But that was part of being a therapist, wasn't it? You helped them the best you could when they came to you, but when they left, you had to let them move on. Sometimes, *most* of the time, you never got to know the end of the story.

She thought of Boot, and how his eyes had lit up around the horses, of his amazing ability to play the guitar. Suddenly, she wasn't a bit sorry for what she had done. Maybe Boot had gotten in trouble. Maybe she had been fired, but she, Chris, and Kim had given him something he longed for—acceptance and unconditional love. Maybe it was just for a few hours over a few weeks. But that might be all it took to give him some hope.

She stood.

"Fine," she said. "You don't have to fire me, because I quit."

She reached for an empty paper box and packed her things: a mug, a framed photo of her riding Angel, and a small toy horse that a client had once given her. That's it. That's all she had here to mark her five years of work. That and her books.

She plucked the few off of the shelf that were hers and added them to the box. Then she marched over to the door and grabbed her still-dripping coat off the hook on the back of the door.

"I'm sorry," Greta said. "I'll call to check on you."

Rachel met her eyes, but said nothing. What was there to say?

"Your heart isn't here at the clinic anymore," Greta said softly. "I think you know that."

Rachel looked at her friend. Greta had given her plenty of chances. She couldn't be angry with her boss. "I know," she said. "I'm sorry."

Gretta smiled. "No, *I'm* sorry. I hate to lose you. But I think it's time for you to move on. It *has* been, for a while."

Rachel managed to give her a little smile. "Thank you, Greta. Thank you for everything." Then she left the clinic without looking back.

Rachel's heart was pounding as she drove away from her job. Fired! She couldn't believe it. Reality was starting to set in. How would she pay her rent? Where would she work? And if she had to move…

If she had to move, to leave in search of work, she'd have to leave the horses. St. Ives was a small tourist town. There wasn't much work here.

She pounded her fists on her steering wheel.

She thought about going to the barn, but she wasn't ready to face Kim.

She passed the hardware store and thought about stopping in to see Chris. She suddenly realized she wanted to tell someone, to complain about her life and have someone put their arms around her and tell her they understood. She had done so much alone for so long. Greta has been there, yes, but as a counselor. Not someone who came over for tea, or brought a meal, or sat with her and ate chocolate-chocolate chip ice cream and watched sappy movies.

She had no one.

And she certainly couldn't call her mother or sister. She suddenly realized how truly alone she was.

She turned the car around and pulled into the parking lot. She sat there, looking out her windshield, trying to spot Chris inside. She wanted him. She wanted him to hold her and to tell her that everything was going to be okay.

Then she thought about her promise not to lead him on. What was she to him? He loved kids, and she couldn't give him any.

She felt hot tears running down her cheeks. *Rachel, get a grip. You've been through worse.*

She backed the car up, turned around, and drove home.

She felt a little better after a warm bowl of soup. She had changed into a pair of soft jeans and a long-sleeved t-shirt. The weather was a little cooler today. The rain still beat on the windows, pouring down from the heavens. It was like the sky was sad along with her.

Was her mother right? Did she mess up everything she ever did? Everything good that touched her life?

She crumbled some crackers into a second bowl of soup and knew she needed to change her thinking around. That's what she would tell her clients. Think about the good things.

What good things did she have?

She thought about the horses. But what if they didn't make money during the fundraiser? Kim needed a lot to keep the place going.

It had all started when Faith died. Rachel had been hanging in there pretty well until then. She had worked her way through the miscarriages; she was working on her marriage.

She had first sensed trouble two years in. Her husband had started wanting less sex. At first, it was because they needed a break from the pregnancies, which were inevitably followed by loss. Then it was because he was "tired." Finally, when they decided to try again, it became more of a chore, tracking ovulation and fertility. He had switched to wearing boxers and she had taken up meditation, trying to "relax" her way into becoming pregnant. When none of that worked, they started visiting doctors.

She could have probably brought him around. In time, she could have made him see that in-vitro would still give him his own child and let her carry one. They could have used someone else's egg.

April had actually offered. She had completely forgotten the marvelous gift her sister had suggested. Because that same week, Faith had committed suicide.

And Rachel's world had changed. She had beat herself up, wondering how she could have missed the signs, torn because after one year counseling this girl, she had grown to love her. She had broken the rules of therapy by growing attached to one of her clients.

And then she had lost her.

Small, tiny Faith. She always sat on the chair across from Rachel, her feet curled up under her, her big blue eyes watching the world carefully, as if it was about to pounce on her. Afraid to make friends for fear of rejection. Afraid to speak up in class for fear of being wrong. Afraid to upset anybody, ever.

Sweet Faith.

Rachel suddenly remembered the letter her parents had mailed to her. They had called the office several times, leaving messages, but Rachel never returned them. She had taken a leave of absence; she stayed home, curled up in a little ball in her bed. When she returned to work after six months, she saw old, unopened emails, but she deleted them.

Whatever they had to say, she didn't want to hear it. She knew she had screwed up. She didn't need for them to tell her.

But they had mailed a letter. She had stored it away in a box someplace. She remembered now. It was in the box where she kept her tax receipts.

She went into the spare bedroom and opened the closet door. It wasn't hard to find, only about halfway down the pile of paperwork. It was a long white envelope, one of the business-sized ones. It felt thick.

She needed to know what they said. At this point, she couldn't hurt more than she was already hurting.

Before she could change her mind, she sat back and ripped it open. The paper was thick stationary, with roses on it. She unfolded the two sheets and something slid out and landed on her lap. Something shiny.

She picked it up. It was a gold chain, and on it was a pendant with the word "Faith" in script.

No, not a word. A name.

A sob escaped her.

This had been Faith's pendant. The girl had worn it every day. Every time Rachel saw her, she had it on. Her parents had given it to her.

She picked it up, wondering what it was doing here, why she had it.

She unfolded the letter. It was written in longhand, in a beautiful, careful handwriting. Faith's mother.

Dear Rachel,

Pain has a way of changing us, of reaching down inside and pulling out the very best and very worst of who we are. Pain is a thief, that steals and destroys, and yet it can also be a tool for growing us in ways we never thought possible.

Faith's dad and I have walked through that pain, and it is still a daily visitor, four months after our daughter's death. It reaches its cold hand out to grip us at unexpected times, when we think we are safe. Washing the dishes. Mowing the lawn.

In the little ordinary things of life. When you think your mind is occupied by something else, pain comes to pull you back down to those dark places.

But that's not where we should stay. That's not where Faith would want us to stay.

It's a terrible thing to lose a child. We gave Faith this necklace when she turned thirteen. She had struggled with depression for a long time. Nothing we could do seemed to change that. No amount of love could help her see the bright side when she was having one of her "blue" days.

But God is bigger than our problems, and we promised her that He would never let her go. No matter what was going on in her life, no matter how dark the days seemed, God would always be her guiding light.

Her name came about after four miscarriages. We never thought we'd be able to conceive. Then, when Faith was born, she had a congenital heart defect and had to have surgery. We were afraid we were going to lose this tiny baby that we were finally given. But she survived.

Through all of those years, we held on to the one thing —the only thing—that we knew was firm. Our faith.

We're giving you Faith's pendant to remind you that whenever the world feels like too much, hold on to your faith. When our daughter had her good days, she lit up the world. She was creative, and funny, and very sensitive. I'm sure you remember how she so quickly sensed when others were hurting and how much she loved animals. She nurtured those around her. And she was always finding the little things in life that many of us take for granted. She told me that chocolate chips were shaped like tear drops, that leaves curl up in the fall, like tiny hands trying to hold on to the branches.

Her sensitivity was a gift, but it also made the world a difficult place for her to live.

Rachel, we don't blame you for her death. She was her own unique person, and this world was too much for her with all of its pain and hurt. She couldn't quite see past that. You know, as well, that depression is a medical condition. Her brain just didn't make enough of the good stuff.

Faith loved you. She talked about you a lot. She liked to share with us the stories that you told about college and about how you love music. She even listened to some Bon Jovi.

I guess I wrote this letter to tell you to go out there and live. That's what Faith would have wanted.

Love,
Jill and Michael Reiner

When Rachel finished reading the letter, she had tears streaming down her cheeks. A great weight had been lifted from her.

"Thank you," she whispered. "Thank you." She curled up on the floor, there by her closet, clutching the small pendant, and cried for a very long time.

Chapter Thirty

Chris was at the farm bright and early on Saturday morning. There was a lot to do before people started arriving for the fundraiser at noon.

He had been up late, creating a playlist of songs to use during the "live music" hour. He was torn about what had happened yesterday. He wasn't sure if going over to Boot's house had been wise. Nothing had changed, and it had taken him some time to settle his nerves down afterwards.

He was supposed to be avoiding stressful situations.

The sun was already warm, and it was going to be a hot day. But it would also dry off the grass from the soaking it had taken in yesterday's rain.

They kept the stage up. There would be no Boot performing, but Chris didn't really want to set the speakers up on the grass. He had already built it anyway. It would be a good place for Kim to give her announcements and for the auction.

Rachel showed up around 9 a.m. She was smiling and radiant. The light blue t-shirts that he had printed with the farm's name on them matched her eyes.

"You look good," Chris said.

"I feel good."

She was wearing a gold necklace with a pendant that said, "Faith."

"We need some of that today," Chris said, pointing at it.

"We already have it."

Her joyous mood was contagious. He started setting up the chairs with a renewed energy.

At 10 a.m., a taxi pulled into the driveway. Chris stood up from the popcorn machine that he was trying to get to work, and wiped the sweat from his forehead.

"Who's that?" he asked Kim. She shrugged and wiped her hands on a towel.

Rachel was filling up balloons with the helium tank that the florist shop had loaned them. She stopped and held her hand up to her eyes, squinting in the sunlight. The three of them watched as the backdoor opened, and a black-clad figure stepped out.

"It's Boot!" Rachel said. She tied off the balloon she was holding and ran toward the driveway. Chris saw her envelop the boy in a hug.

"I'm sure that hug goes against some clinic rules," Chris said, laughing.

Kim nodded. "Something has changed. Not sure what."

"I noticed. She's unusually happy today."

They walked over to greet the kid.

"What's up?" Chis said, high-fiving the boy.

"You guys still have my guitar."

"It's in the kitchen."

"So I had to come and get it. And I figured, while I was here, I might as well play."

He grinned.

"Awesome!" Chris said. "Because my playlist sucks."

Kim was frowning. "Does your dad know you're here?"

Boot glanced at Rachel, as if for permission, then shook his head. "Nope."

Kim put her hands on her hips.

Chris said, "Does it matter at this point? If this doesn't work out, you lose the farm anyway, right?"

He saw a smile tugging at the corner of Kim's mouth. Finally, she gave into it. "What the heck. Go tune that thing."

"All right!" He gave Rachel and Chris a high-five and ran off to the kitchen to get his guitar. His smile said it all.

"This is probably the end of life as I know it," Kim said.

"Kim," Rachel said. She waited until Kim looked at her, then she pointed to her necklace. "Have faith."

There was a larger turnout than they expected. Chris was glad he had ordered extra pizza, because it was going fast. The crowd gathered at the table under the tent, eating their pizza as Boot tuned his guitar. Then he started to play.

At most events Chris had been to—graduations, wedding receptions, summer employee parties at the bottle factory—people talked while the band performed. The music was more of a background to their visiting and eating. But this was different.

Just a few measures into Boot's first song, the crowd had quieted. His voice was clear, filling the tent and carrying over the lawn where extra chairs had been placed. Boot had been right about this being the best place acoustically.

He played for a half hour, then took a few requests. His repertoire amazed Chris. He had a lot of songs memorized.

"A lot of different genres," Rachel said.

Chris nodded. Boot had stuck to mostly folk and light rock, but he covered a few different generations of music.

"Look," Rachel said.

Chris looked in the direction she indicated. There was a pretty girl, about sixteen years-old, watching Boot closely.

"That's Julia," Rachel said, smiling. "I think he's caught her eye."

"Well, I need to wrap this up so we can have the auction," Boot said. "But before I go, I want to play you one last song. It's one I wrote myself."

He started off slowly, quietly, the acoustic strings leading into the melody. It was a song about faith, and how all things were possible.

"Did he write that just for today?" Chris said.

Rachel shrugged. "I wouldn't put it past him."

The song grew in intensity as he continued, and grew louder as he gained confidence in his own work. By the time he was finished, Chris felt inspired. It was the perfect song to lead into the auction.

As the last note died away, the crowd was silent. Then, from the back of the tent, one man stood up and began to applaud. Chris turned to see who it was.

It was Boot's dad.

The rest of the crowd followed, many offering a standing ovation. Chris looked back at Boot, and his eyes were on his father. Chris saw tears forming in the boys eyes and watched as he fought the emotion.

Then, Mr. Tellian did an amazing thing. He walked through the crowd, squeezing in between chairs as he made his way carefully up to the stage. Boot sat on his stool, watching his father, unsure. Mr. Tellian said something to Boot, which Chris couldn't hear over the clapping, then Boot stood. His dad wrapped his arms around his son and held on to him tightly. As they embraced, Boot's face was buried in his father's chest, his fists clenched against his back, as if he was afraid to let him go.

When they finally parted, both of them were wiping their eyes.

Chris turned to Rachel, who had her hand to her mouth.

"Sometimes, it all actually works out after all," he said.

She nodded and reached for a napkin so she could wipe the tears from her eyes.

The auction was going well. The crowd was fired up from the music, and many of them had visited the horses before the concert, rekindling old relationships with their favorite therapy horse. Children begged their parents to bid on their favorites. Chris was kept busy handing out "adoption papers" as people "bought" shares in the horses. He had run an extension cord out to the lawn, with Kim's printer, and was using his laptop to print out individual papers with people's names on them.

It was really busy. There was a long line of people waiting for him. The kids were loud. The microphone kept squealing as Kim auctioned off the horses. He should probably go and try to adjust it, but he was so busy here…

He glanced up and saw Mr. Tellian sit down at a table and eat a slice of pizza with his son. A volunteer rushed past them to the sound system and toyed with the sound until the mic stopped giving feedback.

Chris printed off more papers. Handed them to more people. He wondered where Rachel was, then remembered she was giving tours of the barn.

Chris saw Mr. Tellian get up. He gave Boot an affectionate squeeze on the shoulder and headed over to the table where Chris was working.

"I owe you an apology," Mr. Tellian said, coming around behind the table. He offered his hand.

Chris took it and shook hands with the man.

"No worries," he said. Chris nodded in the direction of Boot. "You did good."

"I learned a few things yesterday," he said. "You were right. You both were."

Someone in the line cleared their throat.

"You're busy now and I need to get to work," Mr. Tellian said. "We can talk later. Where's Ms. Walker?"

"She's inside the barn," Chris said.

Mr. Tellian gave a brief nod and headed back. As Chris typed in the next name, he glanced back over toward the tent. Boot was still smiling.

His dad had showed up. And applauded.

It was a start.

"Mister? Can I have mine printed in purple?" A small girl piped up.

"Of course!" Chris said. He changed the font color.

He was feeling a little nauseous. Maybe it was the sun. Or the pizza. He had eaten it pretty quickly.

He pulled his baseball cap a little lower over his eyes and took a sip of water. When he set it down, someone bumped the table and it spilled, running down the uneven slant toward the papers he had just printed off. He quickly grabbed them.

Somewhere, he heard a balloon pop. He jumped. A volunteer came up with a handful of napkins and helped him mop up the water.

He took a deep breath.

I'm okay.

"It's too hot out there for those balloons," he heard someone say. "They should be moved under the tent."

The mic squealed again.

"Since she had her name in purple, can I have my name in pink?" The little girl must be a sister. She was only about five.

"Sure," Chris said.

A wave of dizziness swept over him. He griped the table. The mic squealed again.

"Can someone fix that mic?" he said. He saw Boot heading over toward the sound system.

Someone grabbed a handful of balloons to move them under the tent.

"I changed my mind!" the little girl squealed. "I'd like mine in blue instead. Because that's the color of my horse's halter!"

The balloons must have been right behind him. A loud crack shattered the air, followed by several more.

Part of Chris' brain knew they were balloons, but the other part of his brain didn't care. He backed up, catching the printer cord on his foot, and pulling it off the table. It landed with a crash.

He put his hands to his head, as if to stop the sound. The ground was spinning.

Frantically, he looked around for Rachel. He thought he saw her blond ponytail, and he reached for the person's shoulder. She turned. It wasn't Rachel.

"Are you okay?" the stranger asked.

He wasn't. He stumbled ahead, and then ran toward the empty side of the barn, the part that was roped off with caution tape. He ducked under the tape, and ran blindly down the aisle, until he reached Faith's stall.

He leaned up against it, breathing, counting, trying to calm his racing heart. He thought he might throw up.

He turned around, folding his arms across the stall door. He put his head down in them, but couldn't still the panic in his heart. He heard the voices outside, and tried to concentrate on the quiet inside the barn. He breathed in the smells, the hay, the pine shavings, and Faith.

He felt the mare's warm breath on the back of his neck.

"Hey girl," he said. He raised his head and unlatched the stall door. Pulling it closed, he gasped in several more breaths, as if fighting for his life.

Faith moved close to him and pressed her shoulder up against his body, like he had seen Angel do so many times with Rachel. He wrapped his arms around her neck and pressed his face against her, hiding in her long, silky mane.

And he cried.

Chapter Thirty-One

Rachel was telling a young client, Samantha, about Tommy, their old but faithful Shetland pony. The posters Boot had made helped a lot, even though she knew each horse's personality by heart. Samantha was a client who started about three months ago as a physical therapy patient, but her therapist, Jennifer, was already talking to another family.

She was about to tell them that Tommy would love to have his ears rubbed when she saw Mr. Tellian coming down the aisle at a good clip.

"Rachel? Can we talk for a moment?"

"Sure," she said. Then, to Samantha's parents, "Excuse me."

She led him aside, into the tack room, where they could have some privacy. His face was serious, and he looked a little sad.

"I owe you an apology," he said. "I was wrong. And I think you may have saved my son's life."

Rachel looked down at his hands. He was holding a folded up piece of paper in them. Her heart sunk.

He offered it to her.

"Please read it."

She unfolded it, suddenly aware that her fingers were trembling. It was a letter, printed on computer paper.

Dear Ms. Walker,
I'm writing this so that you know none of this was your fault. You believed in me when nobody else did, and for that I will always be grateful.

Rachel looked up.

"I thought he wrote it on Thursday, after his mom and I pulled him from therapy. But it's dated two weeks ago."

She looked down and kept reading.

I'm sorry to do this to you, but I feel I have no choice left. I can't imagine not having my music as part of my life. I know you understand that.

If you are reading this letter, I will be gone. And these things will be done. I have given my guitar to my friend Ralph at school. You've heard me talk about him. And I am leaving you my record collection. You'll be happy to know there are some more Bon Jovi albums in there.

None of the rest of it matters. It's just stuff.

The letter wasn't finished. She stared at it for a moment, then closed her eyes, imagining what might have been.

"I found it on his computer. He was going to kill himself." Mr. Tellian choked on the words. "And it would have been my fault. If you hadn't..."

He took a deep breath and turned away from her, looking out the tack room.

Rachel looked up from the paper, and at the back of the man she had hated for so long.

"Hey," she said softly.

He turned back to face her. "But he didn't. And it's not too late. What you did today, you made a great start. You let him know that you love him."

Mr. Tellian nodded. "I guess."

Then, he looked at his watch. "I have a work meeting to get to."

"Okay."

Rachel watched as he turned, lifted his chin, and strode back down the barn aisle. He was a man who had trouble showing weakness or admitting failure. As the CEO of a large company, she knew he was used to being in control. This loss of control over this most important asset must have come as quite a blow. She hoped he had learned a lesson.

She carefully folded the paper and put it in her back pocket.

"Ms. Walker!" Samantha's voice piped up from Tommy's stall. "Come and show me how he likes to be petted!"

She started walking that way, when she felt her phone vibrate. She pulled it out of her pocket and saw that it was a text from Kim.

Go check on Chris. He headed in the direction of Faith's stall.

Rachel replied with a quick okay.

"I'm sorry!" she said. "I need to go check on a friend."

And then she ran.

She found Chris pressed against Faith's neck, his face buried in her mane. He was breathing heavily, and the mare had her body wrapped protectively around him, pressing her shoulder against his. Her head was turned, cradling his back, her muzzle against his side.

"Hey," she said quietly.

Chris jumped, then slowly removed his arms from the horse. He brushed roughly at his eyes with his hand before he turned to look at Rachel.

"I made a fool of myself out there," he said, trying for a laugh. It came out more like a sob.

"I missed it," she said. "I was sharing Tommy's many attributes with paying clients."

He smiled at that.

"I'm sorry. Is anybody handling the adoption papers? I was printing them out when...." he shrugged. "When *this* happened."

He held out his hand. It was shaking.

"I'm sure Kim has someone on it," she said. Chris had a light sweat on him, and he was shaking. He kept taking deep breaths, trying to calm himself. Faith held herself still and firm against him.

"Try breathing out longer than you breath in," she said. "In for four, out for six."

He did.

"In for four, out for eight," she said slowly. She kept her voice low, calm.

"What's wrong with me?" he said.

"It's a classic panic attack."

"I know. But what's *really* wrong? Why does this keep happening?"

Why did anything bad happen?

"In for four, out for eight," she said. "Too much stimulation, probably. There was a lot of noise, the heat, the emotional ups and down of the past twenty-four hours. Also, there's a lot at stake with this fundraiser."

"I know," he said. He ran his hand along Faith's neck. She responded by pushing her muzzle into his palm and then sniffing at his pockets.

"I don't have any sugar cubes today, girl," he said.

"Keep concentrating on your breathing," Rachel said.

His body was starting to calm. Whether it was from the controlled breathing, or the presence of the horse, she couldn't tell. Probably both. In her experience, behavioral psychology and equine-assisted therapy together worked miracles.

"I'm sorry," he said. "I keep messing up. I'm a liability."

"You're fine," Rachel said. She opened the stall door and let herself in. He was still trembling. She walked toward them and put her hand on Faith. The mare nuzzled Rachel, welcoming her.

"Come here," she said and put her arm out. Chris hesitated. She moved closer and pulled him into an embrace. "Today has been a lot for both of us."

He put his face against her shoulder, closing his eyes. She held him close, wrapping both of her arms around him. He smelled of aftershave and slightly of sweat, a manly mix that she found intoxicating. She closed her eyes, keeping her arms around him.

"Keep breathing," she said quietly.

He took long, slow breaths.

"Imagine yourself on Angel. Feel her rhythm. Take yourself back there, to that place of peace."

She felt his breath slowing, felt his body relaxing. When he was breathing normally again, she reluctantly stepped back. It had felt good to be so close to him.

"Better?" she asked.

He looked up at her. "Yeah. Thanks." He turned and busied himself with Faith's mane.

"Don't worry about what happened out there," Rachel said. "People have probably already forgotten about it."

"Everyone thinks I'm a freak," he said. "Look how many jobs I've lost because of this."

"Not everyone," Rachel said. "Do you realize how many people out there have special needs kids, or are here because they are struggling themselves? We have kids out there with autism. That's why Kim insisted we have that quiet play area in the front yard, so they could get away from the noise. And we have closed-head injuries, cerebral palsy, learning disorders, and of course, my clients who range from mildly anxious to suicidal. We're all a mess. And we're all okay with that."

Chris turned to her, a small grin on his face. "So, you're saying that I fit in?"

She smiled. "I'm saying that life isn't perfect; none of us are perfect. We go through life with the hand we've been dealt. We can't always control what happens to us, but we can control how we respond. You'll brush yourself off and get back to work, like you always do."

Chris nodded. "How'd you get to be so smart?"
"It's not brains. It's horse sense."

The event ran from noon until 4 p.m., but by the time they cleaned up, fed the horses, and put everything away, it was nearly eight.

"How much do you reckon we made?" Chris asked. They were sitting around Kim's kitchen table, just Chris, Rachel, Kim, and Boot. The volunteers had all left to go home. The farm was back to the peace and quiet that they all loved.

"I have no idea," Kim said. "I have to get through this stack of checks. The auction went really well. And then there's an additional box of donations that needs to be counted. And the credit card transactions. It's possible we came close."

"Close to saving the farm?" Boot asked.

Kim nodded. "But there's no way to tell before it's all counted."

"Well, let's get counting!" Chris said.

"I have to get this guy home," Rachel said, nodding toward Boot.

"I can stay!" he said.

"No, you can't. Your mom called and asked that I bring you home before 8:30. It's a really big deal that your dad is coming home for dinner tonight instead of leaving on his work trip. He postponed it until Monday because he wants to be with you. That's huge."

"I guess." Boot said reluctantly.

"Give him a chance," Rachel said.

She hadn't had time yet to talk to him about the note, and it had been weighing on her mind. "Let's go."

She stood, and he grabbed his guitar. "You guys count and let me know."

"I won't have a final count until tomorrow," Kim said. "I've got to wait for my other volunteers to give me the credit card charges and what's left after we pay the vendors."

"Call me as soon as you know."

She looked at Chris. He was sitting at the table, relaxed. He had fully recovered from his panic attack earlier in the day.

"Good night."

"Good night," he said. There was a tenderness about him when he looked at her. She liked it.

"He has a thing for you," Boot said when he shut the car door.

"Who? Chris?"

Boot nodded. "I don't get why you hate him. He's really cool."

"I don't hate him."

"I know. So what are you waiting for?"

"I'm not about to take love advice from a seventeen-year-old."

He laughed. It was a good sound to hear.

As she drove, she thought about the note Mr. Tellian had found and wondered if she should mention it now. By the time she got to his house, she had made a decision. She pulled over to the curb and stopped the car a few houses down from his. It was almost dark out now, and the street was quiet.

"Why are you stopping here?" Boot asked.

"I want to ask you something."

She reached into her back pocket and pulled out the note. She handed it to him. He unfolded it, and she saw a deep red color creep into his cheeks. Angrily, he crumpled it up and shoved it in his jeans pocket.

"Your dad found it on your computer."

"He had no right."

"Were you going to do it?"

His face was turned away from her, looking out the passenger window. She saw the tension in his shoulders. He was silent for a few moments, and she didn't think he was going to answer her, when he said quietly, "Yeah."

She closed her eyes briefly, feeing the weight of his words.

"Are you still?"

He wasn't moving, something unusual for him. His fingers weren't tapping to some song in his head, nor was he humming. He was just looking silently out the window. He suddenly seemed so young and vulnerable to her.

He turned then, and met her eyes.

"No."

She tried not to let the relief show on her face. She felt that dry prickle in her nose that came just before tears. She took a minute to compose herself before she spoke.

"I'm glad."

He smiled a little bit, and turned back to the window. "I feel better now. The horses have helped.

And this whole fundraiser made me realize that there's something bigger out there than me and my problems."

Wise words for a seventeen-year-old.

"But tomorrow or Monday, things are going to go back to normal," Rachel said. "We're going to come off of this high of a successful event, of the fun time we had together. Life will get real, and you'll have to work on your relationship with your parents. And figure out your music. And what it means in your future."

"I know."

"I need for you to promise me that if, no, *when*, those feelings start to return, that you'll tell me. Or tell somebody."

He looked at her again and nodded.

"Promise," she said. "I need to hear the words."

"I promise," he said. "Geez."

Rachel smiled and started the car back up. "And I would like for you to continue therapy someplace."

"Can't I stay with you as my therapist?"

Rachel pulled into his driveway. "I quit my job."

She glanced at him. His eyes narrowed. "You *quit?* Or you got fired? It was because of my dad, wasn't it?"

"Good night, Boot," she said. "I'll text you tomorrow to let you know how we made out financially."

He looked at her for a moment, then grabbed his guitar and climbed out.

"Boot?"

He leaned down to look in. "Yeah?"

"Remember your promise."

He nodded and closed the car door. She watched him walk up the drive and let himself inside. The house was brightly lit, and, through the window, she saw Boot's mom give him a stiff hug.

Chapter Thirty-Two

Chris was just leaving church when his phone rang. He pulled it out of his pocket. It was Mr. B from the hardware store. He hoped everything was okay.

"Can you come in for a few minutes?" he asked.

"Sure."

Because Mr. B was a Christian, the store was always closed on Sundays. Chris wondered what was up.

When he got there, the back door was unlocked. He let himself in and found Mr. B sitting at the counter, a coffee cup near him, and the Sunday paper spread out before him. He was working the crossword puzzle.

"I love these things," he said. "Do you know a four-letter word for quick?"

"Fast," Chris said.

"Of course."

He wrote the word in with his pencil.

"Have a seat."

Chris sat down at the stool next to Mr. B.

"What's a five-letter word for…"

Chris didn't want to do the crossword puzzle. He wanted to know why Mr. B had called him here.

"Mr. B, what's up?"

The old man laid his pencil down and took a sip of his coffee. Finally, he turned to Chris.

"I'd like to have more time to do crossword puzzles," he said. "And my daughter called. She's moving to Traverse City. Her husband got a job transfer. So I need more time to travel."

Chris wondered where this was going. Was Mr. B going to sell the business?

"And when I'm away, or at home, working these," he pointed to his crossword, "I need someone reliable to be here, running my business. You know, my dad started this place."

"I know." Mr. B had told him the story more than a few times. "So…you're letting me go?"

Mr. B laughed, and laid a wrinkled hand on Chris' shoulders. "No, son, just the opposite. I'm here to ask you if you'll come on full-time. I need a manager. There will be a pay raise, of course. And benefits."

Chris didn't know what to say. He loved working here.

"You mean…you want me to work full time?" he repeated.

Mr. B laughed again. "Yes. Why is that so hard to believe? You're good at what you do. You're a Christian, which goes a long way with me, and you're handy with tools. Do you accept? Or maybe you need some time to think it over."

"No!" Chris said. "I mean yes! No, I don't need any time to think it over. I accept! I'd love that! Thank you!"

Mr. B held out his hand and Chris grasped it firmly and they shook.

"Welcome aboard, son."

Chapter Thirty-Three

Rachel sat in the car, fingering the pendant around her neck. She was parked in front of a two-story bungalow.

They had moved since their daughter's death; the address was different than the one on the envelope. She'd had had to look it up on the internet.

She had waited until after noon, because she knew they went to church, or, at least they had back then.

Taking a shaky breath, she climbed out of the car and knocked on the door. Jill Reiner, Faith's mom, answered.

"Rachel," she said.

Up close, Faith's mom looked older than she had four years ago when Rachel last saw her. She had streaks of gray running through her shoulder-length hair, and creases around her eyes and mouth. Pain changed people.

"Hi," Rachel said quietly.

"You're wearing it," Jill said. She put her hand to her own neck.

"Yeah."

Rachel felt tears prick her eyes. "I just opened your letter. I had put it away. I couldn't bear to read it. I thought you must hate me."

"Hate you? No. You never got my calls or emails?"

Rachel shook her head. The tears escaped her eyes and she let them roll down her cheeks. "I'm so sorry," she said. Her voice cracked.

"Oh honey. We don't blame you. Come here."

Jill Reiner stepped out onto the porch and pulled Rachel into a hug. "It wasn't your fault," she said. "It wasn't your fault."

Rachel drove away two hours later, feeling light and free. Jill had invited her in for tea, and her husband had joined them. They told her about Faith's younger years and even pulled out a photo book. They shared stories of how people had come forward since the death, asking them for help with the grief of their own children's deaths. These parents had formed a support group of sorts, through their church, reaching out and ministering to parents who had lost children to suicide.

When Rachel got up to leave, she said, "I don't know how you do it."

"God doesn't promise us that life here will be easy," Jill said. "But what He does promise is that He will never leave us. You're not alone, Rachel. And neither are we."

Now, here she was, her heart filled with joy as she drove away from their home.

She was about to turn on the radio and search for a Christian radio station when her phone rang. It was Kim.

"I have the final tally," Kim said. "It's not good."

Chapter Thirty-Four

Chris was flying high on his way back home to his apartment. He couldn't wait to get inside. He was going to make himself a celebratory sandwich and call Rachel. He wanted to tell her the good news about his job.

But she called him first, just as he was unlocking his apartment door.

"We're $10K short," Rachel said. "That's a lot of money."

Her voice cracked. She sounded like she was about to cry.

"Are you sure?"

"Kim counted three times. So did her volunteers. We're short, and the bank guy comes tomorrow."

Chris let himself in the apartment and closed the door behind him. He felt the joy from his job offer draining from him. He thought about Faith and what this meant for her and the other horses.

"What now?

"I don't know."

"Is there any way…can Kim…"

"She's finished," Rachel said. "She's exhausted. It has been a long, tough decade for her. She's going to call around tomorrow and see if she can find homes for the horses."

Chris thought of Faith. She'd be standing in her stall now, waiting for her dinner. They had talked about letting her out tomorrow in the pasture for the first time. She was strong enough.

"Faith," he said.

"I know."

"There has to be a way."

"I can't afford anything right now," Rachel said. "I lost my job."

"You what?"

"My boss found out about Boot. Look, I'll tell you about it later. I promised Boot I'd call him when we got the total."

Chris sighed. "Good luck with that. I'll say a prayer."

"Yeah. I'm going to need it. He asked if I would continue to be his therapist. I thought maybe at the farm. But now…"

Chris wanted to say something encouraging about having faith, about how God would provide. But he suddenly felt very tired.

He thought of the horses and how much they had taught him over the past month. And he thought of Rachel.

She didn't treat him like someone who was weak. When she had found him in the stall with Faith, scared to death, she had put her arms around him. She hadn't thought less of him, or told him to get a grip. She had just held him.

Was she finally softening to him, or was that just the therapist side coming out in her? He had lost her so many years ago, but he finally had a chance to make that up. He was trying so hard to be the man, now, that she had needed him to be back then. He should have made his friends stop the car and gone back for her. When the school administrators asked for names, he should have refused. He would have lost his scholarship, but saved his integrity.

He should have taken the blame and protected her.

He had failed her then. And he had failed her again.

"I'm sorry," he said quietly.

"It's not your fault. You tried. We all did. And there was something else good that came out of it. Boot's dad is trying to turn over a new leaf. He came home early last night to have dinner with his son."

"That's great," Chris said. And he meant it. If nothing else good came of this, Boot's life was going to be better.

"But he won't be able to work with you now, though."

"I know," Rachel said. She told him about a letter Boot's dad had found.

"So, it's good you followed your instincts and brought him to the farm," Chris said. "You may have saved his life."

"It wasn't just me," Rachel said. "It was you, too. And Kim. You're so good with kids, Chris. You're a natural. A lot of people don't know how to act around kids, especially teenagers. And after just a few weeks together, heck, after just *one day*, that kid latched on to you as a role model."

Chris laughed. "Who would have thought that Chris Adler would be anybody's role model?"

"You're mine now, too," Rachel said softly.

Her words were warm and loaded with meaning.

"Rachel?"

"Chris, I never responded to you when you asked me if I could forgive you. I owe you an answer."

He felt his heart rate quicken.

"The answer is yes. Yes, I forgive you. I never should have held on to that anger for so long. It was foolish. And looking back, there is a lot of good that came out of me going to the college I did. I met my awful ex, yeah. But I also made good friends. And I got my degree, and started working for the clinic in St. Ives. If I had gone to the University of Michigan and gotten that big fancy degree, I would have probably found a job somewhere else. Not in this little town. I love St. Ives. I love Three Hearts Ranch, and I never would have met Kim or the horses or Boot. None of this would have ever happened."

"And I wouldn't have had you as my therapist on Angel," Chris said. "You've helped me more in a month than other therapists accomplished in years."

"It's more than me," she said. "It's the horses. And the quiet of the farm. The outdoor work. It's all a combination for success. It's feeling like you have control of something again, even if it's just a horse."

Chris nodded. He knew what she meant.

"I just wish Boot could experience that."

"Me too," Chris said.

"I need to go," Rachel said. "I need to call Boot. I'll see you tomorrow. Kim wants us back at the farm for a last hurrah. Noon. Can you make it?"

Chris had to work, but he was pretty sure Mr. B would let him off.

"I'll be there," he said.

Chapter Thirty-Five

Rachel drove slowly out to the farm. She wasn't in a hurry to get there, knowing that this was one of the last times she'd make the beautiful winding drive down the shore of Lake Michigan and turn inward across the dunes and fields of grass toward the farm.

Chris was there. He had just pulled up when she arrived.

"Hey," he said, getting out of his car.

"People! Come in!" Kim shouted.

There was another car in the driveway. Not unusual, since it was Monday, and Jennifer was there giving a client their physical therapy session.

The car looked like Boot's.

"Come in!" Kim shouted again from the back door.

Chris and Rachel walked slowly toward the kitchen and let themselves in. Boot was sitting down at the kitchen table.

"You got your car back?"

"Yep."

"Things are looking up for you."

"Yep," he said. Then he looked at Kim. He had been trying to suppress a grin, but he failed. "Tell them. Tell them now!" he said.

Kim broke into a smile. "Well, we got some news today," she said. "Oh heck, I'll just tell you! We can make it! We got a huge donation just a little while ago! We're staying in business!"

"What?" Rachel said, and turned to Chris. He smiled and high-fived her.

"You'll never guess who it's from," Boot said. "Tell them!"

Kim laughed. "I think they should sit down first."

Rachel and Chris both pulled chairs out and quickly sat. "Who?" Rachel asked.

"My dad!" Boot blurted.

Rachel looked at him, then at Kim.

"It's true. Mr. Tellian sent Boot over here with this." She waved a check. "He included a note." She unfolded it and read: "Please hire Ms. Walker as one of your therapists. This should cover her first year's salary, plus some extra for the farm expenses."

"No way!" Rachel grabbed the check, and then showed it to Chris. Chris whistled.

"Rachel," Kim said, looking at her across the kitchen table. "Would you do me the honor of coming here to work full time at Three Hearts Ranch?"

"Oh my gosh!" Rachel said. She jumped up, then sat back down, then got up again and ran around the table. Throwing her arms around Kim, she said, "Yes! Yes! Yes!"

They all laughed. Rachel stepped back, wiping her eyes. "Oh my gosh." She looked down at Boot.

"I told him you lost your job," Boot said. "And I told him the farm was going bankrupt. So, he got out his checkbook and started writing. He claims he did it for the tax deduction."

"Oh my gosh," Rachel said again. She felt like everything she had ever wanted was finally coming together. Well, almost everything. She glanced at Chris.

"Now you can be my therapist!" Boot said. His face grew serious. "I mean, it only makes sense. It would be a waste of time for me to start over with someone else. You know what I mean."

"I do," Rachel said. "I do!" He tried to pull away from her, but she managed to give him a quick hug first.

"Ewww," he said. "Stop! You're my *therapist*."

Rachel laughed. "This is one of the best days of my life!"

She and Chris left Kim and Boot inside making plans for the money his dad had donated. The two of them walked side by side, and Rachel could feel the heat of Chris' body beside her.

"Kim says we can turn Faith out into the pasture tonight if we want," she said. "I think we should give it a try."

"Sounds like a plan."

The mare greeted them with her usual, enthusiastic whinny. Rachel got Faith's lead rope and handed it to Chris.

"You can do it," he said. "I know how much this horse means to you."

Rachel shook her head. It was true that when he first got there, she was protective and even a little jealous about Faith. But she didn't feel that way now.

"She chose you," Rachel said. "I have the other twenty horses. You can have this one."

Chris smiled and clipped the lead rope onto Faith's halter. Then, they walked her out to the back pasture. The other horses were in their stalls for the night, so Faith would have the pasture to herself.

Chris slipped her halter off and turned her loose. She stood there, looking at the five acres of grassy pasture in front of her, unsure what to do.

"It's been a long time since she's been free," Rachel said.

Faith shook her head and took a tentative step. Then another.

"Go on, girl," Chris said.

She looked back at them, unsure. Then she took another step. She lowered her head and plucked a bite of the long, rich grass.

"Rachel," Chris said. He turned to look at her. "I need to say something, and I know you probably don't feel the same way. But I need to say it."

He took a deep breath, as if gathering his strength.

"I loved you back in high school. I was too proud and too scared to admit it, but I loved you. You were so much more than the other girls I dated, and I wanted you. I thought I wanted you because you were another trophy for me, but in reality, I was afraid of you. I was afraid you'd reject me. I was afraid of the feelings I had for you. I had never experienced anything like that before.

"When I saw you again a month ago…I guess, what I'm trying to say is, I still have those feelings. Only, they're different now. Purer. And I have tried so hard to change and to become a man that you can be proud of. One that can take care of you, and stand up for you, and never hurt you again the way I did once. What I'm trying to say is…"

Rachel shook her head. "Don't," she said.

She saw the hurt look in his eyes. "I'm sorry," he said. "I just had to let you know. I don't expect you to feel the same way. I have no right to expect that of you. Not after the way I treated you."

Rachel felt her heart melting. She wanted him so badly it hurt. "That's not it," she said. "There's another reason we can't be together."

She felt a lump forming in her throat, the shame creeping up her, turning her neck red, then her face. "It's…"

"What?" Chris looked at her. "You can tell me anything."

Rachel took his hands in hers. "I do feel the way you feel," she said. "I do. You *have* changed. You are a man that any woman would be proud to be with. But me…I'm not what you need."

"Why would you say that?"

"I see how you great you are with kids. I know you want your own. I can't have kids, Chris. That's why my husband left me. I'm barren. I've run out of eggs. I will never have kids, and I don't want this relationship to get going and then have to end. Because it will. Because you want kids."

But Chris was shaking his head. "Oh Rachel, that's not true at all." He reached up and put his hand on the side of her face. She pressed her cheek into its warmth. "I love you," he said quietly. "I love you and nothing will ever change that. You're the woman I've been thinking about all these years. And the woman I want now. There are other ways to have kids. There's in-vitro. There's adoption. There's foster care. If we ever get to that point, we can look into fostering kids and bringing them here to this farm to heal."

Rachel laughed then, a warm, bubbly laugh that came from deep within her. "That's something I've always wanted to do," she said.

"Then let's put it out there," he said. "Foster kids. We can have a huge gaggle of them. But we need to start at the beginning."

He raised his hand and pushed her hair back behind her ear. Then he caressed her cheek. "You looked incredible at the prom. I wanted to forget about the party afterwards, and just be there, with you. Just enjoy the night without worrying about what came next."

Rachel raised her eyebrows. "You did?"

He nodded. "I pretended I didn't because it scared me. I should have told you how I felt. I should have kissed you."

She felt her stomach flutter.

"May I kiss you now?"

Rachel nodded. Chris bent toward her, his hand still on her cheek. His lips were soft and moist and tasted like mint. She felt the warmth of his hand on her face, as it moved from her cheek to the back of her neck, drawing her in.

She put her arms around him, kissing him back. His strong body against hers felt like she had imagined it would, only better. She smelled his aftershave, and felt like she was rising up above a sea of darkness and into a shining new world. She fit here, in his arms, and was comforted in the truth of the man he was now, and in the God he loved. She, too, wanted more of this God that had changed his heart. And she wanted more of him.

Faith whinnied, the noise pulling them apart.

They turned to look at her, still holding each other. The mare tossed her head and took another step. Then, she gave a little hop, lifted her tail in a banner, and took off in a run. The breeze caught her cream-colored mane, blowing it out behind her as she galloped around the pasture, and the sun glinted off of her dappled coat.

"She's beautiful," Rachel said.

Chris turned back to her. "How did I do?"

"With the kiss?"

He nodded.

"It was pretty good," Rachel said, smiling. "But I think we should try again. Practice makes perfect."

Chris laughed, and bent toward her. As their lips met, there in the pasture among the rustle of the trees and the grass. In the background, Rachel could hear the drumbeat of Faith's hooves, pounding out the rhythm of her newfound wings.

The End

Read more books in the "Horses and Hearts Inspirational Romance" series. In *Saving Grace*, Hannah Whitney and her horse Amazing Grace are hoping to qualify for the Olympic competition in freestyle dressage. But when her world-class trainer quits just ten weeks before the event, Hannah's dad hires Chase Livingston to replace him. Chase is a man who just might turn Hannah's world upside down.

Turn the page to start reading...

healing faith

Saving Grace

Chapter One

Hannah Whitney rode the horse like she did everything else, as if her life depended on it. Leaning forward over the animal's neck, the black mane whipping in her face, the thunder of hooves under her, the muscles of the horse propelling her forward at a breakneck pace, twenty-three year old Hannah was running away from her life.

She wasn't supposed to gallop the horse. Grace was a very expensive pureblood Hanoverian, seventeen hands of warmblood sports horse, her equine ancestors carefully bred over the generations to produce perfection in and out of the show ring. Purchased for Hannah by her father, Grace was "the horse" that would take her to the Olympics. "Guaranteed" is what her breeder said. Hannah and Grace trained together every day, *every single day,* for the past four years and this was finally the year they would see if they qualified or not. Her qualifying show was in ten weeks.

But today she was running.

It wasn't her fault. Her dad had come out to the barn a few minutes ago, while they were training, and given her the bad news. *Really* bad news.

"Hans quit," he had said simply.

Marcus Whitney was a multi-million-dollar real estate investor whose properties spanned the United States. He stood there with his hands in the front pockets of his tailor-cut pants, the tails of his suit coat billowing in the breeze, and looking quite lost for a tycoon who could afford his own sports car collection.

"What?" Hannah had ridden Grace over to where he stood. The morning sun showed the creases around his eyes, more noticeable this past year, as was the graying in his black hair. For a moment, she felt a pang of sadness at this little bit of vulnerability, as if he had been unmasked.

"He quit," her dad said again. He looked up at her, then lifted a hand to shield his eyes from the morning sun. "He says he can't take it anymore. You're difficult. You're rude. You're too driven. Those were his exact words."

Hannah frowned and ran her finger under the chin strap on her riding helmet. She felt a growing panic in the pit of her stomach.

"But he *can't* quit! The trials are in ten weeks. I don't have a program for Grace choreographed out yet. He was supposed to help me with that. I told him he was moving too slowly, that Grace and I need more time—" She heard her voice rising. She did that when she was afraid. She had tried to break the habit, for her sake, for Hans, but she couldn't.

"Hans is old. Seventy-five. He has thought of retiring for years," said her dad. "Since his wife started showing signs of dementia, he thought now was a good time."

Hannah thought back to yesterday. Hans had gently suggested that there was more to life than winning, and she had yelled at him. She accused him of not knowing anything, of not understanding what it was like to be *her.* Winning *was* everything! What did she have left if she didn't win?

"He called me last night," her dad said. He was watching her, like he did his real estate investors, to see how she would react, to figure out which card to play next.

No. That wasn't it. He wasn't like that anymore. Her dad had changed not long ago. She still couldn't get used to this new, caring man he had become. He'd had some religious experience or something. It would all fall apart soon enough. She was sure of it. She only had to wait and her cold, business-first father would come back. *That* was a man she knew how to handle. This one threw her off her game.

"Last night?" Hannah said. "And you waited until *now* to tell me?"

Her anger flared again. It was fear, really. But she knew better than to show it.

Marcus Whitney shrugged. "I wanted you to get a good night's sleep."

A good night's sleep? She would never sleep again. Not now.

"Besides, I wanted to reach out to someone else. Another trainer for you. He responded to me first thing this morning. Just a few minutes ago, actually. He came in person."

"I don't *want* a new trainer," Hannah said. Hans had been the best that money could buy. An Olympic-caliber dressage trainer, he was a two-time gold medalist for Germany before he came to the US to teach. His students regularly won medals in international competition.

"I want Hans back," she said. "I'll just call him and apologize."

"Too late," her dad said. "I hired this one already."

"*What?* Without me meeting him first?" There was that shrill voice again. She took a deep breath.

"I had actually reached out to him a few months ago, just in case."

Things had been rough with Hans for a while now. She had never really liked the old man. He was grouchy, cold, and yelled a lot.

"I knew Hans would quit," Hannah said. "You just can't count on people."

"Not if you drive them away," her dad said quietly.

Hannah straightened in her saddle and switched the riding crop and reins to one hand so she could rub Grace on the neck. Grace was her best friend. A pretty bay mare, her dark brown coat had caught Hannah's eye the moment she saw her. She had four big, white socks running up her legs, ending just below the knee. Her mane and tale were black.

A white blaze ran down her face. White was unusual in Grace's breed, sometimes frowned upon. But Grace was so beautiful when she moved, so fluid, that the extra color made her exceptionally eye-catching.

"Who is he?" Hannah asked. "I should at least read up on him before I meet him."

"I told you, he's here *now*," her dad said.

"Now?" Hanna looked around, startled. "Where?"

"I asked him to wait up at the house."

"Dad, why on Earth…"

"Hannah, listen to me. You don't have much choice who we hire. You've run out of options. You've fired or lost the last four trainers. This is who is left. He's an Olympic winner himself."

"What's his name?"

Her dad hesitated. Then she saw him put on his game face. His jaw set, his chin raising a little as if daring her to defy what he was about to say. It was the same face he had used to tell her eight-year-old self that her mother had left them.

"Chase Livingston."

"*What?* No. No way." She shook her head. Grace snorted and stomped her foot, as if to agree. Hannah rubbed her neck. "You would let the world know that Chase Livingston is training Marcus Whitney's daughter? You really want *that* kind of publicity?"

Her dad's chin dropped a little. He ran his hand through his greying hair. "I just want you to be happy."

"Dad! No way! Are you trying to ruin my life?"

And that's when she ran. The problem is, there was only so far she could go on the farm.

Fieldstone Farm and Dressage Center was a one-hundred acre expanse of rolling green pastures lined in white fencing. The barn itself was a beautiful structure, a long stretch of white building with green shutters, and black peaked roofs topped by cupolas.

There was even a wrought-iron horse weather vane atop the largest cupola.

Hannah pulled Grace up to a stop, and jumped off. Both of them were panting. She had raced down the winding gravel path that led to the back of the property. There was a small pond here, surrounded by willow trees. It matched the pond up behind their large house. Only here, there was a white pagoda. She came here often for lunch. Or to hide.

She could barely see the house or barns from here, and it was the only place other than her bedroom that she could be truly alone.

She wrapped her arms around Grace's neck, and the mare bent her head down to nuzzle Hannah gently on the shoulder.

"Oh, Grace," she said. "I've messed up again. I'm so sorry."

Chase Livingston was six years older than her. He had won a gold medal in the Olympics in dressage when he was only eighteen, which put her at age twelve at the time. What had made him so famous was not only his age, but the fact that he had trained his own horse and choreographed the freestyle competition *himself*. She remembered it like it was yesterday. She had attended with her nanny, and together they had watched his horse dance to Queen's "Under Pressure." He didn't lose points in anything, and his horse, Debonair Man, had moved so gracefully that at times it looked like he was floating on air. They beat the Germans and Chase took home the gold.

She had never met Chase in person. He went on to win nearly every competition he entered, still with no trainer, which was unheard of. A prodigy, they called him. And then, four years later, at the next Olympic games, he had messed up. The mistake had cost him the medal, a lucrative sponsorship deal, and his career. He had gone into hiding from the harsh media and hadn't been seen since. There was no way she'd be paired up with him. The embarrassment would be too much.

Hannah heard a motor, and looked up. It was her dad in his bright yellow Jeep. There was a passenger beside him.

He slowed the vehicle down as he approached Hannah and stopped. He got out, looking once again spry and like the man-in-control she knew. Another man got out with him, who she guessed was Chase Livingston. He was broadly built, not the slender eighteen-year old she remembered from the Olympics. She put her hand up to block the sunlight. He had sunglasses on and a baseball cap.

The two men walked over to her.

"Hannah," her dad said, and nodded, "meet Chase Livingston."

For a moment her heart stuttered. He had once been her hero. She had clipped photos of him from the *Sports Illustrated* and *Dressage Monthly* magazines and hung them up in her room. She had made a scrapbook of articles about him. She had followed his career, wanting to be like him someday.

Until he'd embarrassed himself. In a fit of fury, that coincided with the day her nanny quit, she had burnt them all.

"Hello," she said quietly.

"Hi."

He reached out a hand for her to shake. She took it. His hands were warm. He had large muscles in his arms and a broad chest under a tight t-shirt. He removed his sunglasses, and looked at her with the same dark brown eyes that had stared out at her from her posters for years. She'd had a crush on him back them. Big time.

"It's really nice to meet you," he said. His voice was deep and warm. He stood about six-feet, just slightly taller than her dad. "So is this the horse we'll be working with?"

Hannah tore her eyes away from him, to look at Grace. "Yes. This is Amazing Grace." She ran her hand along the horse's neck, and was glad for her own sunglasses to hide behind. She glanced back at Chase, and felt her heart patter again.

"We can start this afternoon," he said. "Or even now. I need to get an idea of what type of music you like, and what moves your horse does best, and I can start putting something together for you right away."

"Okay," Hannah said. She glanced at her dad. She wanted to be mad, but she hadn't expected Chase to have this effect on her. She had abandoned him along with the rest of the world when he had failed at the last Olympic games. She had been angry at him, a complete stranger to her, for messing up. For not winning.

But now that he was *here* in the flesh, well, she hadn't expected him to be so… *handsome.*

But how *good* was he?

"Are you good at your job?" she said, trying to regain some of the momentum she felt she had lost. She had to come across as strong. Always. First impressions were important. She couldn't let him think she was weak.

"I am," he said. He met her eyes.

Marcus Whitney cleared his throat. "Hannah, I need to get to work," he said. "I'll drive Chase back to the barn. Why don't you meet us there and give him a tour? Then the two of you can decide when you want to begin."

"Sure," Hannah said. She nodded at Chase. "I'll see you in a few minutes."

"Want a leg up?" Chase asked.

She glanced at her dad, then back at Chase.

"That would be nice, thank you."

He moved over to Grace's side and cupped his hands, so she could put her foot in them. Then he gave her a boost up onto her horse. Once she was on, he took the stirrup and put it on her foot, his arm brushing her calf in the process. Her heart caught again.

What was *wrong* with her? She might have had a crush on him as a girl, but she was a grown woman now. And he was a grown man. This was ridiculous.

Remember how far he has fallen, Hannah, she reminded herself.

"You all set?"

From atop Grace, she looked down into his brown eyes. "Yes. Thank you," she said. He held her gaze for just a moment too long, then smiled. Gosh, he was gorgeous.

"Great. See you in a few minutes."

She watched as the two men walked back to the Jeep and climbed in. Then she nudged Grace with her legs, and her mare broke into a smooth canter.

She raced past the jeep and up the gravel trail, ahead of them, beating them to the barn.

This was certainly going to be interesting.

To continue reading *Saving Grace: A Horses and Hearts Inspirational Romance*, visit PamelaGossiaux.com..

Acknowledgments

Since I was eight years old, I have been surrounded by horses. There are so many people who helped to make that possible, and I owe them a lifetime of gratitude. To paraphrase Winston Churchill, "There is something about the outside of a horse, that is good for the inside of a girl." We horse-crazy girls (women) never seem to outgrow this passion. It overtakes us, and there is little we can do to fight it. It's an almost genetic longing, like it's in our blood, and we don't feel quite complete unless we can wrap our arms around a horse's neck. Thank you to everyone in my life who has helped keep me close to a horse:

My grandparents, who gave me my first pony. My parents, who supported me (and still do) in my crazy passion for horses. My husband for understanding, moving us to a horse farm, fixing fences, putting up hay, and helping in the overall hard, sweaty, and yes, expensive, life of horse ownership. You are my hero! And to my boys, who follow me to horse shows, volunteer at horse events, and even clean out stalls. I know sometimes you're only pretending to be enthusiastic, but I appreciate it!

I also want to thank the owner Kathy, and the tireless volunteers and horses of Michigan Abilities Center, an equine-assisted therapy center. I spent a few years there as both a volunteer and a rider. Much of the material in this book comes directly from my experiences there, working with both clients and horses. I tried to make the details in this book as authentic as possible. They were great teachers. All mistakes or inconsistencies are mine.

Writing, like horses, takes a lot of work and is difficult to do on your own. Like the people who help me stay in horses, I have a whole stable of folks who carry me on my writing journey as well. My family, of course, and my writing friends:

Rachel, my friend, editor, and assistant. Thank you for keeping me on track, helping me get the word out about my books, and making sure my words make sense (and are spelled correctly!) You are a blessing in so many ways. I thank God for sending you into my life!

My critique group: XP2+A. Xanthe, Pam, Anna: You women are incredible writers, dear friends, and exceptional critique partners. I couldn't do this without you. Not only do you read my early drafts, but you pepper our meetings with much-needed nerd-girl discussion and fun facts. Sometimes, there are even snacks.

My beta readers. What would I do without you? Anna and Sheila, you have been especially helpful throughout the evolution this book, reading some very rough drafts. Thank you for your words of wisdom, your Godly insight, and for pointing out those little things, like when my leading man's eye color changes halfway through the book. LOL!

My readers: You are the people I write for! Thank you, thank you, thank you for reading my books! I hope that my stories can transport you to another world for a little while, where love is sweet, faith is present, and all things are possible. I also hope that you loved the horses in this book, and that my writing gave you the opportunity to feel like you were there in the barn, giving one of them a sweet rub on their soft, velvety muzzle.

And finally, to Jesus, my Lord and Savior. I humbly write because of you. To God be the Glory. Always.

Other Books by Pamela Gossiaux

A sweet romantic comedy!

Meet Amy Summers, a big-hearted heroine whose simple life gets turned upside down when she finds a winning lottery ticket worth millions…but should she cash it?

Amy Summers has it all: the world's best job, an awesome boyfriend, and a happily-ever-after in sight. Then, in one very bad day that involves burnt toast and a police arrest, she loses everything – except for a winning lottery ticket her ex left behind.

Afraid to cash it, she decides to give up men and become a Bohemian novelist. She takes her laptop to Starbucks and literally bumps into caffeine-free, easy-going Josh Gray, a life coach and very handsome man. (Not that she's noticing.) When he offers to help Amy get back on her feet, she decides to hire him.

Her heart is telling her that he's the man for her, but Josh is big on honesty and Amy has a huge secret that could push him away if he ever finds out.

"Richly meaningful while wildly entertaining, GOOD ENOUGH is a major new book by an exceptionally talented author."
– Grady Harp, Amazon Hall of Fame Top 100 Reviewer

"This story is such a fun read, it is impossible once you have opened it not to be thoroughly captivated by Amy's escapades."
– Susan Keefe, *Midwest Book Review*

"GOOD ENOUGH touches a nerve every woman faces. Are we ever going to be good enough? Gossiaux has written a funny, revenge romance that will have you cheering on the heroine, Amy, until the very end."
—Diana Lesire Brandmeyer, author of CBA Best Seller *Mind of Her Own*

Available at PamelaGossiaux.com

About the Author

Pamela Gossiaux is the international bestselling author of the *Russo Romantic Mystery* series, the romantic comedy *Good Enough,* and the inspirational books *Why Is There a Lemon in My Fruit Salad?* and *A Kid at Heart.* She is also a keynote speaker, freelance writer, and teaches writing workshops. She lives and writes at her horse farm in Michigan, where she resides with her family and three cats. Visit her website at PamelaGossiaux.com. Follow her on Instagram, Facebook, Twitter, and BookBub.